Nea

on Nantucket

By

Peter Clayton

To Karen - a long time friend

Peter

Llumina Press

ISBN: 1-59526-004-8 PB

Library of Congress Control Number: 2005925542

Printed in the United States of America by Llumina Press

Nantucket's young astronomer finds herself in a life and death struggle to learn why she now has the gift of healing…and to discover what shocking treasure was brought to Nantucket on the whaler Columbine in 1732.

For Colleen who started me on the path.

For Annabelle and Joan and Geoff and Bruce and Joanne and all the rest who made me stay the course.

For Marshall Arisman and his wonderful art.

For Dee Ito's friendship.

For Nancy

Prologue

The giant wave rolled toward the twin-masted whaler, shoving her bow under great masses of swirling black water. The ship shuddered, tried to broach then rose clear. The smaller following waves continued to smash down on the forward deck, the water sweeping along until it spewed out the side ports. With each wave the captain wondered if his vessel would survive as, sluggishly, the bow would reappear before disappearing again beneath the moving mountains of water.

Lightning streaked the sky, throwing the masts into momentary relief, bare but for a small canvas for steerage. The two men lashed to the wheel struggled, fighting the crushing energy of the sea. Water cascaded down their faces, ran dripping down their necks and lingered, soaking them to the skin even through their oilcloth storm gear. Both shivered from the cold and the wet and their fear of the storm. Beside them the captain hung on to the railing, trying to keep his balance in the blackness of the storm. Then the darkness seemed to become less dense. Soon all three realized their vessel had been enveloped in a glowing light or fog. No matter how hard the wind blew the lightness continued to envelop the ship.

As the men twisted and turned at the wheel they continued to shiver in the cold and wet and now the new fear of being caught up in some force beyond the fierceness of the storm. No matter how deep the bow went beneath the weight of the waves the ship did not founder but rose quickly, throwing off masses of wind-swirled water in the process. It was unnatural, frightening, but they had no time to do more than heave at the wheel, trying to keep the compass needle on its bearing. The only light was the small lamp shining on the compass and the bolts of lightning that exploded above their heads.

The night passed. The wind began to abate, the giant waves gradually losing their power. The sky lightened to a dull gray with low, fast moving clouds. The whaler Columbine continued to lumber and toss but the worst of the weather was past. The glowing fog of the night before was gone. As the morning skies brightened, holes in the racing clouds let a weak sun peek through.

Captain Rodriguese slumped, aching, tired and cold. He scanned the rigging and deck and puzzled over their luck. It had been the most severe of storms but there was little damage. Two of the whale dories had broken loose at the height of the blow, smashing themselves against the gunwales. A spar was missing from the foremast. His master carpenter would have the dories rebuilt within a month. There would be little other work for him now that they were within hours of making their homeport of Nantucket. The mast would do until they were safely anchored.

Ordering more canvas aloft, the captain gave a new bearing to the man who had replaced the exhausted pair from the night before. He took one last look around, fighting tiredness, then turned to climb slowly down from the wheel deck to where the passenger cabin sat next to his own.

Without ceremony he pushed open the door and entered the small space. His two passengers looked up at him from where they sat around a small table. These mysterious strangers, big men with dark, swarthy complexions, had sought him out while he lay anchored in the harbor in Upper Canada. They talked a language he did not understand, but also spoke fluent, if somewhat stilted English.

When they boarded they carried only saddlebags and the old-looking box now sitting on the table in the small cabin. The scarred leather was bound with thin leather straps and closed by an intricate gold clasp. The leather was embossed with a series of unusual crosses, each with a semi-circle running through the upper three shafts. When one traveler was out of the cabin, the other was always there. Neither man was ever far from their strange, small package.

Their clothing, too, was foreign. They wore rough linen shirts with the same cross that embossed the leather of the box embroidered in red just above their hearts. Around their necks each wore the same cross, carved from some greenish stone and suspended from a golden chain, its links tiny crosses with the half-circle running through the upper three shafts.

Each man wore a second chain supporting a deep red stone that glittered from its setting of gold. Around the gem, complex figures were carved into the metal. In the center a figure with wings was etched into the stone. The whole pendant hung from a fine chain, the links of which, although unknown to the captain, had been carved from a single piece of solid gold. Both crosses and pendants had the look of some other civilization. Strangely, whenever either of the men approached the leather box the red stone seemed to glow with its own internal light.

During the voyage the captain had tried to soften the men with wine but neither drank more than a cup and that only with his meal. They were never loose in their conversation. By their bearing they smacked of fighting men, hard men from some army but from where he couldn't say. They had offered gold to be transported to the Island of Nantucket; good business for him as it was his destination anyway, having been away for over three years. He winced at the thought. Three years since he had set eyes on his wife and children.

The two strangers greeted him with smiles.

"Captain, what news?"

It was the dark haired one who asked. The other, the one with the scar that ran a ragged course from eye to chin, rarely said anything but the scar made him appear to smile, deceptively. His belt held a large knife in a leather sheath. Both the knife and sheath looked well used.

"Good news, my friends. We're only hours from making port on the Island of Nantucket. You and your box will be safely delivered as promised."

The two exchanged looks and the dark one took a leather pouch from his coat and threw it on the table.

"Here, Captain, share this with your crew. They are decent men and blessed good sailors. God has brought us all safely through the danger. It was to be expected, even at the height of that storm. We are all better protected than you might imagine."

With that he turned back to his friend, addressed him in the strange language they shared, then turned back to the Captain.

"There is a certain priest on your island, Captain. I believe his name is Mordicai Starbroke. We will need to meet with him when we go ashore."

The captain took this news with a frown then shrugged at the speaker.

"That won't be difficult, Sir. Mordicai's not hard to miss. His family has a common failing. They're short, I mean really short."

With that he smiled, but grimly. Mordicai was not a man to treat lightly, short or not. His hold on the Nantucket was absolute, unusual for such a Quaker group. Short he might be, but he was an absolute despot, controlling the island with his strange obsession for unwavering faith and adherence to God. He'd never seen the like of it on the mainland or elsewhere his ship had sailed except, perhaps, in the Far East. But then everything on Nantucket was more than a little different.

Whaling brought in great wealth for the island. They would be adding to it with this voyage and for all on board the Columbine. They had been more than lucky to find many of the big sea beasts in the last three years. The hold below was jammed with barrels of whale oil and cash would flow for all once they made port.

The year was 1732.

Chapter One

There was little wind and the sun beat down on the sweaty teams as the game was drawing to its close. One more batter. Three more strikes and West End Motors would advance to the finals. Maybe.

"Hey, the loser's up next. Can't hit a barn door."

"In your dreams, Shirley."

Cyndy smiled, white teeth flashing from a sun-brown face. Dark auburn hair edged the batter's hat as she turned, boyishly slim in her uniform, and walked with easy strides to the plate. It was an important at-bat. Peter's Deli was in deep trouble if she couldn't score two more runs. Marylou had made it to first on an error. Now it was up to Cyndy to make or break the game.

Reaching home plate, she waited a moment before taking her stance, then with a deep breath swung the bat twice in a flat arc over the plate.

"No batta, no batta."

The old litany came chanted at her over the excited crowd noises. Cyndy loved the noise and the fun and thrill of baseball, even at this level. If they won this one then they'd be in line to repeat last year's championship.

It was dry for this time of the year and a faint haze of dust hung in the air. A shadow swept past and she glanced up to see a Nantucket osprey gliding overhead, a flash of silver showing the fish just taken from the water. Swallowing to quiet her nerves, she returned her attention to the game, carefully watching the lanky redhead swing her arm, then hearing the smack as the ball hit the catcher's mitt.

"Strike one."

The muffled voice of the umpire sounded behind her. The infield chanted louder and the crowd noises increased. Cyndy tapped the end of her bat onto the plate then took her stance once more. The hometown crowd was distracting her, which was probably not what they intended. The pitcher was into motion again; she tensed, focusing only on the ball and shutting out the noise of the crowd and the other players. Again the long arm swung around and the ball began its arc toward her. Cyndy, now watching it almost in slow motion, began her cut and felt the bat vibrate in her hands.

Whack! The ball had met the club exactly in the sweet spot. In one smooth motion Cyndy let the club slide through her hands as she took off running then just jogging as the ball cleared the back fence.

Now the noise was fierce but she was laughing and shouting herself. That hit had just won the game. As she crossed the home plate behind Marylou she ran into the arms of her teammates as each and all tried to give a pat, a hug to whatever part of her they could find.

Somewhat damaged by the enthusiasm, she shook off the well-wishers and walked to the bench where she stowed her gear in her game bag and turned to leave.

"Hang on just a darned moment."

Shirley, her best friend on the team, had grabbed her by the arm and stopped her as she headed to her truck.

"You and George coming to the party tonight?"

Shirley gave great parties and had been planning a victory bash to follow today's game.

"Well, I'll come. You know that. Can't vouch for George though. He's busy rebuilding that bike of his and I know this is one night he's set aside just for that."

"Oh, get George up off his ass and tell him he has to come. The gang'll be wondering about you two if George keeps hiding out in the garage and never takes you anywhere."

Cyndy glanced down for a moment to hide her eyes from Shirley's inquiring glance.

"I'll talk to him, Shirl. Can't promise though."

With that Cyndy turned, opened the door of her flashy red Ford pickup and slung her bag onto the passenger seat as she climbed in. Within minutes she was on the road, headed back towards her house.

The sun was slanting but still warm in the late afternoon. Cyndy drove with one hand on the wheel and barely one eye on the road. In her mind she reviewed the last play of the ball game. It was a soft, lazy summer day. She had played her regular spot as shortstop. The team was doing just great. Indeed, it looked like it might be a repeat of last year when they had swept the league and won the championship. Great team, great bunch of ladies.

Mind you, playing softball on this little island wasn't quite the challenge it might be on the mainland, but then what was. Nothing on Nantucket was like the mainland. Even as a child she had known that to be born on island made her unique. Nantucketers were special; visitors to the island, those off-islanders who drove or biked or walked off the steamer in the busy summer months, were tolerated but rarely accepted.

She smiled at the memories. There were day visitors, summer visitors and islanders. To be an islander you had to have been born here. Mind, summer visitors were tolerated a bit more than most, as they were the ones who had property on Nantucket and the ones who employed the local labor, bought building supplies and food and paid taxes. Yeah, they were tolerated better, but not many were all that much liked.

The shiny red truck sped along the road and the summer afternoon, a shimmer of heat rising in the distance. Cyndy continued to relax after the stress of the game, getting comfortable, just thinking about her life and the strangeness of Nantucket.

Oh it was funny, but once she had seen an obituary in the Inquirer and Mirror for a dear old woman who had died at the ripe age of 98 years. She had arrived on Nantucket when only two months old. The paper had reported her death and that she was, "one of the most popular off-islanders". Seemed 97 years and 10 months of living on Nantucket didn't make you a Nantucketer if you weren't born on the island. And that was that.

Cyndy stretched her back and shoulders.

"Damn, that hit felt good."

She hummed to herself and felt again the bat vibrate in her hand as ball and bat connected for the home run. Even as the images of the game flashed in her mind, another flash caught her inattentive eye. A large truck came suddenly, frighteningly, into her field of vision. Then noise, screaming metal, sudden forces and thrusts, pain, and finally just blackness.

It was the scream of an ambulance that woke her. She felt disoriented, wondering where she was. At least she could still remember the speed of light and her name, Cyndy Vorester.

Everything felt soft. She was looking up at the sky, which had a scattering of puffy, cumulus clouds set in an impossible color of blue. The sun beamed strongly and the warmth felt comforting. She felt like she was floating, weightless without a worry in the world.

The siren was louder now. She could hear the roar of the engine then the slithering sound of tires biting and holding on gravel. The noise made her curious. The siren had such an urgent sound. Carefully she looked around but could see only the wonderful sky. Then she thought, I wonder how I look down? Even as the thought came to her she rolled over, noticing as she did so that she was somehow suspended some distance above the ground.

That was odd. Well everything was odd. She wondered why she felt so unconcerned then looked around to see where the siren noise had come from. Just then the siren cut out. Now she could see the ambulance where it had pulled to a stop beside a car with flashing blue lights.

Surprised but still not frightened, she watched the action below as two paramedics opened doors at the back of the ambulance. It had parked with its lights still flashing. The other car, its lights pulsing blue, was a Sheriff's department vehicle.

It was so unreal, as if she were watching a movie or something. And why was she up in the air looking down? Her thought seemed to echo in her mind as she continued to look around. No question about it, she was several feet above the ground and the action. And what was everyone doing anyway?

She thought she heard words and realized it just her own thoughts again.

She mused a moment feeling extremely lazy and comfortable as she watched the ambulance crew wheel their gurney to where a body lay half in and half out of a badly smashed red pickup truck. Strange, but that truck looked very familiar. Two concerned-looking deputies were already stooped over the body in the truck. She recognized them; they were friends of Shirley's. She'd met them a time or two at parties.

"Damn but that looks just like my truck. Jesus, it is my truck. What's going on?"

As she focused on the activity she could see the face of the accident victim. Shock caught at her. "My face? My truck? That's me!"

She was confused yet strangely unworried just curious. Cyndy thought for a moment. For someone who's apparently just had one hell of an accident, I really feel good. I don't know what's happening here. I wonder if it means I'm dead or something. Still feeling unconcerned Cyndy looked around. The road and the crossing were familiar. She drove here at least once a week during the baseball season. It was the most direct route to and from the ballpark.

"Is she still alive?"

"Yeah, but just barely. Christ, be careful."

The voices came from below her. Cyndy returned her gaze to the scene below. The larger of the two paramedics was working over her body as the two deputies stood helplessly by. He looked over at his buddy.

"It's OK. I've got her neck stabilized. Now easy...on to the board."

The voices kept her attention on the scene below her level of vision while she continued to somehow float above all the activity.

Still fascinated and curious but feeling an unusual sense of ease, Cyndy watched the body, now carefully stabilized with a neck brace, as it was strapped in place on a board. Now what, Cyndy wondered to herself. What should she do, what could she do? She watched the body, her body, as it was slid carefully into the ambulance, secured and the doors closed.

Then dust swirled under the wheels and the ambulance began to drive off, lights flashing, siren screaming. The two sheriff's deputies, Fred and Mac, got back into their patrol car. The blue lights stopped their strobing as the car started up and drove off, following the ambulance. Cyndy felt more than a little lost. It was then she noticed a swirl of brightness out of the corner of her eye.

She turned to get a better look then wondered how she had managed to turn. As she looked at the brightness it continued to swirl strangely and look more and more like the opening of some sort of tunnel. The light became brighter and brighter and it seemed to be pulling her towards it. Even as she drifted she felt a renewed sense of warmth and peace and love and didn't resist but continued to float until she was swept up into a brilliant white tunnel. All the while it was like lying back in a warm bath and letting the soothing warmth suffuse her body.

Well, it was something like that, except now she was conscious of rising up until she was in a space of pure whiteness and coming closer and closer to a misty brightness that had appeared.

"This is crazy, but it sure doesn't feel bad."

She wondered for a moment if her words were being spoken or were they just thoughts?

She didn't resist but let herself be pulled closer and closer to the glowing, misty light as, more and more she felt peace and love surrounding her. Then a new sensation swept over her as she felt a presence, heard a voice speaking to her. She listened carefully. What was it saying? Something about, welcome Cyndy? She felt the wonderful sensation of total love flowing around her.

"Who are you? You seem to know who I am?"

"Yes, Cyndy, we know who you are. Don't be frightened. You are safe and loved."

The voice was deep and mellow and made her feel like she was just a kid again and her dad was picking her up after a fall or something.

Cyndy then felt even better, if possible, an overwhelming sense of love and comfort, a knowing that she could trust and love in return.

"I don't know why but I'm not frightened. I just feel so good. What's happening to me? Who are you? Where are you?"

"You have just had a serious accident while driving your truck, Cyndy. The trauma of the accident has caused your spirit to leave your body. However, I am sorry, but you cannot stay here, Cyndy. You must return. It's not nearly time for you to come home."

"Spirit left my body? What do you mean, my spirit left my body? Just what's going on here, anyway?"

There was no immediate answer.

"And how do I return anyway? How do I do that when the last time I saw my body it was in an ambulance and racing up the road?"

The voice continued although Cyndy still couldn't see anyone near her, just a misty glowing cloud.

"You must return to your body, Cyndy. You had a very bad accident and you came near to dying, but it isn't time for you to die, so now you must return. You have a manifest destiny waiting for you. You are very special to us. Your presence on earth is needed for many years."

"Who's talking? Why can't I see you?"

There was no answer. Cyndy looked around but all she could see was whiteness and the glowing mistiness beside her. Oh, this felt too good to leave. She hadn't felt this good since she had been a child and her mom used to hold her and rock her and sing songs to her. It hadn't been so comfortable for a long, long time, not since her mom had died. And certainly not since her grandmother had died and left her depressed and crying. Suddenly everything blurred and the light disappeared and she was lost in a world of darkness, then nothing.

Soft beeping and antiseptic smells were the first thing that her emerging consciousness detected, then a stir at her side.

"Cyndy!"

She tried to look around but nothing responded. Someone was speaking to her.

"Cyndy!"

Damn, there it was again.

"What? Who's that?"

Cyndy tried to speak the words in her mind but nothing came out.

"Cyndy, Cyndy can you hear me?"

At last she recognized the voice. It belonged to George, her husband. Cyndy lay still; it seemed impossible to move anyway. Pain began to push at her. Tubes apparently were in every orifice. Something terrible was stuck in her throat. Air pushed at her and made her lungs expand. Remembrance of the feelings of floating and comfort and love overwhelmed her. She'd never felt so depressed. Tears began to trickle down her cheeks.

"Nurse, over here. I think she's crying. She may be awake."

There was a whispery sound and another voice, a softer voice, spoke.

"Wonderful, I'll page the doctor. Keep an eye on her, George."

Chapter Two

Cyndy lay still and felt pain. It was there when she went to bed and it was still there when she woke. She had been home now for over a month but still couldn't get used to the need to move slowly, the never-ending pain stabbing across the back of her shoulders and up into her neck. Drugs had been prescribed to minimize the pain and encourage what sleep she could get. She hated the idea of taking drugs. Fortunately she had access to other medication, herbs from her own garden. They helped and felt less threatening than the doctor's prescriptions, but nothing made the pain really go away.

Each morning was a struggle just to get out of bed. Even the bedclothes hurt where they pressed against her. Her hard muscles had become flabby; her legs tired easily when she walked any distance. It was just too much.

"Damn it all, what did I do to deserve this, anyway?"

Her question didn't go unanswered. A scrabble of legs and then a large fuzzy head appeared, dark brown eyes watching her for a signal, a slight whimper of greeting escaping. Lady, her faithful and loving Lab had slept on the mat beside the bed, as she did most nights. Every morning Lady was the first to greet her. Cyndy forgot her troubles for a moment and reached out a hand to stroke Lady's head.

"Hi girl. You ready for another day?"

Lady bounced back and gave a small bark.

"All right all ready, don't push. I'm moving. I'm up."

With that Cyndy groaned and pushed herself upright in the bed. Morning sunshine streamed through the partially opened curtains stirred now and then by a soft breeze. She listened and heard a purple finch as it sang its territorial songs. Outside, the world seemed a beautiful place. Inside, she felt only despair.

Grunting, she gradually pulled herself out of the bed, finally standing, with difficulty, clinging to the bedpost. She took a deep breath as she readied herself for another day. It seemed the same every morning. The doctors had assured her that she was making an unusually swift recovery from her accident, but all she knew was that life had taken on a whole new dimension, and it was called pain and frustration.

Part of the frustration was trying to explain to her doctors about the amazing experience she had had, of floating above the accident scene, and of the tunnel and voices. They had smiled and looked across her at each other before looking back to tell her she had just experienced the results of concussion or something like that. No one would take her seriously, especially her husband. George had even told her to forget it; she was just imagining the whole thing.

Now she kept the experience to herself although she knew deep inside that it had been real. She had even gone so far as to ask the two deputies, Mac and Fred, who had first found her, to describe the scene and their description was just as she had remembered as she looked down after the accident. But it made her so angry. Why wouldn't George, especially George, take her seriously? Why did it seem to make him so uneasy?

Cyndy sighed and glanced around at the bedroom. It was her bedroom now but it had been her grandmother's until three years ago. When her beloved grandmother had died and the will read, Cyndy found she was the sole beneficiary. She had inherited the house, herb garden and all her grandmother's possessions. The conditions were absolute; it could not be a shared property. If she chose to legally share it with George, the will would be revoked and her estate would go instead to a charity, The Island Pet Rescue.

This had not gone down very well with George, who thought he should share everything Cyndy had, but Cyndy was thrilled. She liked having something of her very own.

Since she had returned to Nantucket with a Ph.D. in Astrophysics and had taken over the Maria Mitchell Observatory, she divided her time between creating new science and cultivating an old one.

The old one was a secret known only to her and a few close friends on whom she occasionally practiced. It was a secret science of herbs and plants and other natural aids to healing, something she had shared with her grandmother for many years. The herb garden had taken on greater importance when she rediscovered her grandmother's secret still room hidden in the cellar under the old stables at the back of the property. The herb still room and the carefully tilled garden gave her all the incentive she needed to keep up her grandmother's herbal practice.

When she was just a child Cyndy had first watched and then helped with her grandmother's herbs. The day after her grandmother's death, when she had found the hidden door and let herself into the still room, she had felt a sense of coming home. She found neatly filed, immaculate notes on how to make each kind of tincture and potion, what each was good for and in what quantities. Reading her grandmother's carefully scripted writing had brought on another bout of tears.

As a child, her grandmother had cautioned her to keep their secret, and it became their game. Even when she was a very small she had understood and she had kept their secret from family and friends alike. During those years she would help pick plants, grind powders and just watch as her grandmother's wise hands mixed, measured and portioned.

Those long-ago days spent with her grandmother in the special garden, that was when she had learned the names for the many strange and interesting plants and how to use them for healing. It had made her feel special to share her grandmother's secrets. And she did love her grandmother so. As she grew older, she couldn't continue to help as much, especially while she was off-island at the University. However, she had always made grandmother's house her first stop whenever she came home.

Cyndy was deep into this reverie when she sensed rather than felt some sort of motion in the room. She looked around to see if it was her dog, Lady, but her wise old friend had curled up again as she waited for Cyndy and was lying quietly on her mat. Nothing seemed out of the ordinary until she glanced over to where the antique, seven-spindle pine rocker sat in the corner of her bedroom. An elderly woman was sitting there watching her, bright blue eyes crinkling in the corners as if she was trying not to smile.

Cyndy gaped at this phantom figure and felt the room spin around her. Falling back, she finally ended up sitting on her bed. Then the shock lessened to be replaced with wonder. She felt the softness beneath her and was glad she was seated on the bed and had not fallen on the pine-board floor. Finally she was able to speak.

"Grandmother?"

Lady leapt to her feet and growled. Cyndy realized she could also smell the sweet apple scent her grandmother had always worn. The figure now did smile, her mouth edging up at the sides, her shocking blue eyes sparkling with energy. However she remained silent.

"Grandmother, is that really you?"

Lady came up to her and nuzzled her hand with a small whimper. Cyndy sat on the side of the bed and stared at the silent figure in the chair.

"I'm going crazy, I just know I am. First I think I'm floating out of my body and now this. Damn that concussion anyway."

"Relax my darlin', you are the sanest thing in this house, I declare. And Lady, come say hello little sweetheart."

The voice was low and hard to hear but the cadence and sound was just as it has always been. Cyndy, who had grown up spending so much time with her beloved grandmother, couldn't mistake the voice now. Lady, too, seemed to remember as she barked with excitement, her tail wagging her happiness as she ran to where the figure sat in the chair.

Ever since Cyndy could remember she had trailed after this lovely woman, being picked up and hugged when she was upset or crying, the gentle voice soothing her until she felt better again, receiving one of the sweet treats always to be found in grandmother's apron pockets.

It had been one of her worst days when she had made her usual call and found grandmother seemingly still asleep in her bed. It had taken many moments for Cyndy to realize that this sleep was one from which her grandmother would never waken. Her best friend and supporter had left her. Cyndy had cried much of that day and through the night.

Now what was this? Her grandmother, just sitting in the chair and grinning at her? Surely she was completely insane. When would the men in white coats show up to take her away?

"No, my darlin', you're not bonkers. The only bonkers person around here is that husband of yours, though Lady sometimes tries to compete. That George, he can't stand any ideas that conflict with his darn fundamentalist religion, that and the healing they do over at the church. Old Maaiken Starbroke has become stranger and stranger over the years. It's probably the close contact with the power. You'd do well to stay clear of him, Cyndy girl. He's strange enough under any circumstance but he's always resented anyone doing any healing outside of that church of his. I know he resented me and my little herb patch. Thinks he has the only right to do healin'. Well, I'd probably say damn if I didn't think it might upset God. Wouldn't want to upset God now would we?

She smiled an impish smile.

"That's why George won't listen to your story of floatin' around after the accident. For one thing it terrifies him. And for another, that just don't wash in his world. If any floatin' around is going on George thinks it should be at the church, not that they do any, of course. The only thing they know is that the power can heal. 'Course the power is much more than that but what do they know?"

Again she smiled, then laughed out loud. Cyndy heard other, more natural noises, of birds and a far-off lawn mower coming through the open window. Still her grandmother talked on.

"And there are other bothers he's havin' with you right now, like you not doin' every darn little thing he wants just when he wants it. The boy's a bit of bully, grew up that way, some do. Then there's you bein' so bright and all. That silly boy, no idea what a treasure he married."

Grandmother sniffed in indignation. Cyndy only heard half of what her grandmother was saying. The shock was still too great.

"I don't believe this. Grandmother, how can you be sitting here with me? You're...you're...."

"I think you're tryin' to say I'm dead. Go ahead dear, say it. Grandmother, you're dead. Can't hurt my feelin's. After all I am dead. At least in terms of this world, I'm dead. 'Course people don't really die, Cyndy. They just change a little bit and then go back home. That's what the spiritual world is all about, you know. It's really our home. This old, cold, difficult world is just a place for us to come and learn a lesson or two; that's all it is, sort of an Earth school."

This made her laugh again and become slightly transparent. Becoming more solid, grandmother leaned back and smiled again, dimples in her cheeks, a wisp of hair escaping from the bun at the back of her head.

"Now sit down, girl, and stop bein' so frightened of me. I've been given special leave to come back and help you understand just what's happened to you. You've got very special powers now, even if you don't know it yet."

"Special powers? What're you talking about, grandmother?"

"That bump you got has sort of changed you, darlin'. When you popped out of your body and had a brief visit with Jesus, well that just has to change a person. It's changed you, that's for sure."

"Changed me, changed me? What, how...Jesus?"

"Yes dear, Jesus. You weren't seein' all that good what with crashin' your car and jumpin' out of your body, but yes, you had a brief visit with Jesus. Very impressive, if I do say so. Most of us just see a friend or maybe an angel. But Jesus came to you, you lucky girl."

"Jesus...came to me?"

"Yes you lucky thing. Now, enough of that. I want you to get better just as fast as you can. You've got a new life to live and I want you to get on with it. Hear me, now?"

Cyndy watched while the figure in the chair seemed to grow faint. The pillow with its herringbone pattern started to show through.

"Grandmother, don't leave me." Cyndy started sobbing, the figure became quite solid again.

"Now hush up child. I can't just hang around here all day."

"But I don't want you to go." Cyndy's sobbing turned into serious crying. Just then the door opened and George stuck his head in.

"What's wrong, Cyndy? Why're you crying? Are you all right? Did I hear you talking to someone?"

George pushed the door fully open. Cyndy, still sobbing, looked frantically at the chair but it was empty. Grandmother was gone. There was, however, still a hint of apple scent hanging in the air.

Cyndy now cried harder than ever. George looked puzzled, stopped and stood just inside the doorframe.

"Why're you crying so, Cyndy? Everything's OK."

He moved slowly over to her and put his arm around her shoulders. She turned her head, then her body until she was pressed against his chest. Her mind still spun from the events of the last few moments. How could she explain any of this to George? He already thought she was crazy because she kept trying to tell him about floating out of her body. His first reaction had been to tell her it was just the result of bumping her head or some sort of dream. When she kept insisting he had become angry. She realized now the anger was at her going against church teachings. The church didn't believe in people floating out of their bodies, or indulging in healing folks outside of the church. If you didn't play with their rules then you weren't one of them. If you weren't one of them, life could be difficult on this strange little island in the Atlantic.

She pulled away from her husband and sat in the chair so recently occupied by her grandmother, but not until she carefully felt it with her hand. It was definitely empty now.

She sat quietly and watched her husband pacing around the bedroom. It was a strange kind of religion, this Fundamentalist Church her husband espoused. She knew all this although she hadn't grown up attending it. Her family had gone to the small Methodist Church when she was little, a church that had finally faded away from lack of attendance. George's church had triumphed over all challengers and had grown stronger with the isolation of Nantucket and the generations of clannish islanders who thought that they knew things that damned off-islanders would never know.

There was no denying it, the healings at the church were really phenomenal. People had started to come from all over the world to be healed here. Cyndy wondered about that. She'd tried to get George to tell her what was going on but his only response was he was bound by Church Law not to discuss anything that went on there. This worried

Cyndy, who thought they might even be like some of the cults she had read of. Maaiken and his parishioners believed that you were damned to hell if you broke any of the rules, and the committee that ran the church seemed to make rules to suit themselves.

Well, anyway, there was little she could entrust to George, as he was one of the committee. Indeed, George was president of the congregation and second only to the leader and Rector, harsh Maaiken Starbroke, that sour, wizened dwarf of a man who saw everything as a blasphemy. More like he was a blasphemy, she thought.

By this time she had stopped her crying, except for the odd sob, and had her composure back. Slowly, she raised her eyes to George, who looked as if he wished he were anywhere else, sniffled at him, pulled herself out of the chair and walked over to look out the window.

"The garden's needing some weeding. Think I'll just go get the hoe."

She walked past George who was scowling a bit and looking suspicious.

"What're you growing out there anyway, Cyndy? I never did know what your grandmother was up to when she was here. What's all that stuff you look after so carefully? I know some of it you use to spice up your cooking. And you made a poultice of some of it when I got that infection in my hand."

He walked to look out the window then turned to glare at her.

"You know how dangerous it is to be doing healing. You never listen to me. I had to be very careful not to let Maaiken know you were doing healing on me."

He calmed down a bit, and turned back to looking out the window.

"But what's all the rest for, anyway, Cyndy?"

George never called her Cyn. Too much like 'sin' she guessed. She turned to him at the door.

"Well, George dear, that's just grandmother's collection. She liked to collect plants just to see if she could identify them and make them grow in her garden and I like to keep it up. Helps me remember her."

Cyndy turned away from George without more of an answer. George left the room.

Slowly but with determination, Cyndy went through her morning routines, pulled on a light rose blouse and white shorts and let herself and Lady out into the garden. The air was fresh, just a hint of cooling from the morning fog, birds giving full throat to the glory of summer. Cyndy thought about her grandmother's brief appearance in her bedroom, sighed, picked up the hoe from where she had left it and began to work. Her sore shoulders ached with pain as she moved the earth around a row of odd-looking plants. Lady took care of other business.

Better George didn't know just what she was cultivating, these healing herbs and plants her grandmother found on their early morning walks, or collected from her many friends, each plant with its special properties. Cyndy had been an avid listener and student to her grandmother. But this was her secret and she knew it would be considered damning evidence of her knowing ungodly things if Maaiken ever found out. Her grandmother had always cautioned her not to speak of these things and, older and wiser, she wasn't about to break that vow now.

As she carefully weeded, digging out a bit of grass between the rows, Cyndy thought of her friend Shirley and suddenly it was as if she could see into Shirl's brain. Cyndy shook her head but the vision wouldn't leave her. She could feel the pain in Shirl's head and could see a nasty peach pit sort of thing that was growing where Cyndy knew nothing like that should ever grow.

As suddenly as it had appeared, the vision lifted and she was looking at her garden again. She thought of what she had seen. The brown peach pit, which was some kind of tumor. She was sure although she didn't know how she could know such a thing. And it could kill her friend if not treated properly. Again she wondered at this knowledge. She made a mental note to ask Shirley if she had headaches when she saw her that evening.

In the meantime, she weeded carefully around the St. John's Wort and moved onto the next row where the Echinacea grew and flowered. It would be time soon to take some these plants to her still room at the back of the garden and start to make distillations or just to dry for later use. She still had some of her grandmother's herbal preparations, but she replaced them as they were used up.

Although Cyndy never advertised her precious products, some of her friends relied on her for potions to help them feel better when they were sick or had monthly cramps or even, and this was one of the darkest secrets, when they didn't want to get pregnant. Needless to say Maaiken was dead set against birth control. If he ever found out what Cyndy was supplying to some of her best friends, she thought, he might just have her burned at the stake.

She giggled at the thought then turned serious. He might not burn her at a stake but she knew it would be very bad if the secret ever leaked out. She turned another row and stopped to rest her back.

Once she got going on her day, she began to feel better but working stooped over with the hoe for any length of time made that tender area along her back rebel. She wished she had some magic remedy for her own pain, but she knew that anything she could make that would stop this pain would be too strong to take regularly. She had no desire to become a drug addict.

As soon as the thought passed through her head she immediately saw a picture of a fungus in her mind. It was like one that her grandmother had pointed out to her years ago but was located too high for a little girl to reach. She knew that this wasn't for her own pain but something to help Shirley, to heal whatever was growing in her head.

Now it seemed imperative for her to go into the woods behind the house to see if she could find any of that fungus. As she turned she was sure she caught a glimpse of her grandmother standing at her shoulder. But when she looked, it was no more than a reflection from the sun off the windowpane in her bedroom where the curtain still fluttered in the breeze.

Cyndy looked around but she was alone in her garden, alone as one could be with the purple finches fluttering around the feeder and the black beetle strolling across the tip of her shoe and Lady sniffing around the gate at the back. Carefully brushing the beetle off, Cyndy walked towards the trees and gate at the back of the property. Lady looked up and waited for the gate to open. Together they entered the woods.

Chapter Three

The blunt-ended car ferry was docking amidst the usual bustle of people getting ready to disembark. Those with cars had already headed for the car deck. Foot passengers gathered on the top deck, waved at those below on the dock, then began to gather up their belongings and themselves and stagger unevenly, upset by the boat's continued pitching and rolling, to gather finally near the folding gate at the bow.

The ever-present beat of the engines increased. The deck vibrated more heavily as the propellers reversed, causing water to geyser between boat and dock. Deckhands shouted and threw ropes over bollards, leaning back as they pulled them tight, the heavy ropes creaking as they took the strain of the boat. Soon after, with a grinding and clanking, the forward gangway lowered, the folding gate clanged back and the way opened for the waiting foot passengers to begin walking off. From the lower deck, a line of cars and trucks spewed fumes that carried forward in the breeze as motors idled and drivers waited their turn to drive off the ferry and onto the island.

The foot passengers carried, pushed or pulled a variety of luggage. Some toted duffel bags, some pulled suitcases on wheels. One man, taller than the others by several inches and bigger in every way, had easily shouldered a backpack and begun to thread his way through the traffic. He rolled with the boat's motion though his fellow travelers took lurching steps along a deck still moving as the steamer swayed with the ocean swell. He walked like a man used to the sea.

Before long the big man was ahead of the line, off the ferry and striding purposefully up the dock and onto the cobbles of Main Street. His speed suggested both a sense of purpose and a previous knowledge of the geography of Nantucket. His clothes suggested nothing in particular, except for his watch cap, which hinted at a familiarity with the sea, but then so did most everything else on this island. The gun slung inside his jacket made no bulge. There was little anyone could have commented on except for his unusual size and exceptionally bright-red hair. For the moment that was mostly hidden by the watch cap.

As to the gun, well, it was a small gesture to an impressionable mind that had feasted on Dashiell Hammet, Sam Spade, Philip Marlow and Humphrey Bogart. With his unusual skills, a gun was unnecessary baggage, probably dangerous, too.

One man who had reason to notice all things was the Nantucket Sheriff, sitting parked where his car wouldn't impede traffic. On first meeting Sheriff Taylor Russell, with his beetle-browed face and small brown eyes, you wouldn't immediately sense that he bred Manx cats and showed at many State cat shows.

Small eyes or not, there was little that escaped his field of vision. His memory was a legend on this small chunk of wind-swept land. He read all the wanted posters and had been instrumental in recognizing and apprehending more than one would-be break & enter practitioner before the man in question had much more than got his feet down on dry land. The locals were appreciative of this particular talent.

Sheriff Russell had other talents that bred less appreciation among the locals, particularly when some drinking and shouting and a few punches became a spell of cell time in the lockup. Cell time wasn't so popular unless the miscreant was an off-islander. Then no islander was offended, only the off-islander. And who really cared about him or her?

The Sheriff's sharp gaze was first attracted by the size of the man with the backpack. It was hard not to take notice, if for no reason more than such a big man just attracted attention. Something about the man made him stop and think a moment. The encyclopedia that he called a mind kicked in and matched the watched man to previous meetings several years back. At that time the observed had been doing a stint with the Coast Guard and had been in uniform.

The Sheriff sucked a tooth, made a mental note and sat back to watch the remainder of foot traffic as it straggled up the street. One of the stragglers seemed somehow familiar. He took a closer look then opened the car door and stepped out into the path of a poorly dressed man with runny eyes and straggly beard.

"Hold on, Luke, you're not goin' anywhere."

The man named Luke turned as if to run but the heavy arm reached out and held him fast.

"Just get into the car Luke or do you want me to cuff you out here?"

The big man had seen this, he missed little, and just shook his head. His senses were more acute than most and he had felt the Sheriff's inquisitive gaze. When he had seen the Sheriff's car he'd remembered meeting its occupant during his first stay on this Island. He also remembered the man's fabled memory and figured he had been recognized, not that he had made any real effort to disguise himself. Still, he was disturbed. The probability was that the Sheriff would not be the only one on this island with reason to remember him. He just hoped it would not get in the way of his new investigation. His mission here would be simpler if no one remembered him. But he knew he stood out in a crowd, so there was little point to trying to disguise himself.

He shrugged, settling the backpack more comfortably on his broad shoulders, and tried to remember if his run-in with the Sheriff might have left any lingering questions or disclosed anything that might compromise him now. The Sheriff would be certain to remember his previous Coast Guard cover. He hoped that was all the man would remember.

The cover had been legit. He'd spent a full five years in the service just to give himself the time to fully complete his previous investigation. That time it was the smuggling of South American antique artifacts that were being routed by way of fishing boats that still called in at Nantucket. He had been able to find enough evidence to put a temporary stop to the trade. Sadly, he suspected it still went on, new players, new trade routes. Now he had a new assignment.

Unlike most, time had little meaning for him. Five years for an investigation was more than many would be prepared to put in, but for Johnathan it was just another small span of time.

Although there was no way to tell just to look at him, he'd been born in the late 1800's. Yet he looked to be no older than his mid-thirties. When he'd thought about it while crossing on the ferry, it had made him laugh out loud, causing his fellow travelers to look his way. He'd just grinned at them. He looked big but harmless, just an ordinary guy. Little did anyone here know, but his life had been far from ordinary ever since he met the Masters those many years ago.

Finally he took a turn onto Milk Street, looking for the house where he had reserved a room under the name of Johnathan Millar. It was the house where he had rented a room occasionally the last time he was here. Johnathan Millar was also the name he had used during his last posting to the island during the stint in the Coast Guard. Government records being what they were, it had been expeditious to keep to his birth name, his fictitious birth parents and schooling and other small ordinary facts of life rather than try to go another false route. It wasn't a bad name although he usually tried to use different names as he went from case to case.

To appear to be a regular citizen he had left only a small trail of confusion as he hacked his way through the computer files, more than enough to cover the fact that he'd really been born before the turn of the century. A small change in the computer files and his real parents became his great-grandparents, a genealogical tree invented to explain the missing generations. Johnathan Millar was not, however, the name given to him by the Masters. Theirs was a name he had answered to for the last ninety-five years but only when at home.

George opened the door from the kitchen and entered the big garage that butted up to the gabled, silver-gray house. The fluorescent buzzed, clicked and flickered a couple of times, then steadied to reveal a room filled with parts of a Harley Davidson motorcycle. George felt his spirit lift a little as he walked over to the old, oil-stained bench where pieces of motor were carefully laid out on a soft, oily cloth. This bike was an old friend and with it went a lot of history of racing on the bike circuit.

He picked up one of the spark plugs and examined it carefully. The tip was dark with unburned carbon. That might explain the lack of power he had been experiencing. Looked like the mixture had been too rich. He'd have to take another look at the carburetor.

George looked the part of a circuit bike rider, slim, well muscled, a lean, strong six-footer with black hair and deeply tanned face. During his bike glory days many women had responded to that face and figure. But that was the past. Now his life had gone through as many twists and turns as a bike track.

Leaning on the bench, he put the spark plug down and began to twist the large silver ring on his finger, a ring that supported a finely wrought cross etched into a deep green stone. As he looked at this symbol of his status as President of the Congregation of the Poor Soldiers of Christ Church, he thought again about his wife and frowned, feeling the usual sense of irritation that any contact with her, physical or mental seemed to bring on.

Damn if she didn't get him mad all the time. Why was that? He remembered how good it had been when they were first married. They'd both been athletic, sports enthusiasts, she with tennis, baseball, swimming and sharing with him his love of sailing, plus skiing and other winter sports. She had even enjoyed the big Harley as she sat post, arms circling his chest. That was after he'd dropped out of circuit riding and taken up electronic circuitry instead.

In the past his special pleasure had been motor bike racing, that and sailing competitively. He looked reminiscently at the pieces of his only remaining connection with bike racing, now a hobby, the stripped-down Harley. That brought on a feeling of sadness too, but he'd had to grow up and finally get to work at his chosen profession, computer engineering, work that, when taken seriously, left no time to indulge racing motor bikes.

As it happened, George was also a computer freak, a bit of a genius in his own right. He didn't look like a geek but his mind worked like one. In his new life he now ran a small but highly regarded computer business located off Commercial Street. There wasn't a lot of industry on Nantucket; most of the commercial focus was on tourism and its related infrastructure, that and what was left of a commercial fishery. George's was one of the few businesses that didn't depend on tourists or the sea. And he did well at it.

Yeah, he thought, things had been great with Cyndy when they were first married. Then, for some reason, their marriage had gradually lost its passion. It had all started long before her grandmother had died.

For some reason Cyndy'd become less than enchanted with his fishing buddies down at the Crawfish bar. And she seemed to resent his lack of interest in her own career.

Well, at least he still had the 40-foot sailboat in a slip at the Island Marina. The boat, the Harley, and his work of course, were now his only passions. Well, maybe there was one more. The thought pleased him and he chuckled softly.

It was only in the last three or four years that Cyndy'd become really difficult. Now she didn't do what he told her worth a damn. This old Harley responded better that she did. It was that old grandmother. Filling her so full of shit. Good thing she went when she did.

Bloody lucky Cyndy wasn't dead, too. That accident had been a doozy. As far as he could tell Cyndy was still a bit out of her head. Kept trying to tell him she'd been to Heaven or some such nonsense. Sometimes, when he was more than just a little pissed at her, he wondered if he should try to get her committed to some hospital. Maybe she was really out of her head. With her out of the house he wouldn't have to sneak around so. He grinned. Then maybe he could do what he liked with the house, too.

The elderly house was a damn sight better than where they had been living before, even with the money his business brought in. Better location, much more room and a view to die for. Only thing was that he had no control over what Cyndy did with the place. Now if Cyndy'd just plough that bloody garden under and let him build a pool. That'd be the ticket. But she'd been really pissed at him for suggesting such a thing.

What was it with that garden? He wondered if he should just go out one night and spray the whole area with weed killer. He smiled at himself and looked over to where the weed killer was stored up on the shelf. Cyndy wouldn't have chemicals like that around but he'd bought it and stored it one day after having a couple too many beers. He'd just put it up on the shelf when he got home and by the next day knew it would take more nerve than he had at the moment if he was ever going to do such violence to Cyndy's garden. But he smiled, you never knew when the moment might come and he'd maybe had another few too many.

He turned back to the bench, picked up a crescent wrench, and began to turn the bolts out of the cylinder head. Relaxing, he put disturbing thoughts of Cyndy out of his head and turned his mind back to solving a problem with a computer application he was writing.

If he could just get it right, but it was a tough one. When he did get it right, the banks here on Nantucket would pay him handsomely. It would give them a competitive edge with mainland banks for the first time.

Chapter Four

Cyndy walked along the path through the woods. These old trees were on the 50 acres of land her grandmother had owned and now belonged exclusively to her. She wondered idly why the will had been so explicit about that. Why did her grandmother make such an unusual will as to stipulate that the property was not to be considered as communal between her and George but had to be in her name alone?

Although she liked the arrangement the way it was, Cyndy had asked Sherry, her lawyer, just what would really happen if she tried to share ownership in any way. Would the will's stipulation stand up in court? Would the property be sold immediately and the money given to the charity that sponsored The Island Pet Rescue? Sherry had warned her that, in her opinion, was exactly what would happen. Cyndy had wondered about this for a while but then her grandmother had always been a little cool about her marriage to George. Hadn't exactly warned her off, but she sure hadn't been enthusiastic either.

Suddenly she saw it. A small, grainy, off-white fungus growing in the cleft of two large branches of an old beech tree. It was too far above the ground for her to reach. She looked at the tree, noticing some broken branches that would give leverage. If she was careful, she could climb high enough to reach up and pull off the fungus. At least it seemed that simple until her back screamed at her. After a struggle to get high enough, she reached her hand to the fungus and discovered that it was firmly attached. She was also aware that her upper back was now hurting so much she could scarcely hold on.

"Damn!"

Cyndy swore as she tugged and tugged at the obstinate growth. Then she heard a voice, her grandmother's voice. The shock, plus the streak of pain across her shoulders, caused her to let go and slide uncomfortably to the ground. She sat hugging herself, hardly able to breathe, until the pain subsided, then examined herself for damage. Again she heard the voice.

"Cyndy, you're not usin' your God given talents. Stop tryin' to use brute force and use your mind."

Cyndy carefully rotated her shoulders and looked around but couldn't see anything but the woods and the damned fungus, looking rather smug, she thought.

"What are you going on about, grandmother and where are you hiding?"

"Sorry darlin' but I can't put on a body just every time you get into trouble, now can I?"

"Grandmother, I don't know what the hell you can do and what you can't do."

Cyndy was getting a little upset at her grandmother's unpredictable comings and goings.

"Please, Cyndy, watch your mouth dear. You never were one to say things sweetly, but please keep hell out of this conversation. It's just not polite."

"Well, pardon my French, grandmother, but remember I got most of what I know from you, you know. And that includes my expletive vocabulary. You weren't exactly careful around an impressionable little girl."

"Oh, bring up my foibles if it makes you feel better, girl."

There was a little edge on grandmother's voice now and it made Cyndy smile. That was her grandmother all right, if she had ever doubted it before. Grandmother had been a feisty one. That was one memory she would never forget, especially when her grandmother found someone injuring an animal or bird or destroying growing things on her property. Yes, she had heard some very blue language from her dear, sweet old granny. Cyndy carefully worked her back muscles, tensing and releasing.

"All right grandmother, stow the lecture and tell me what you meant by using my mind."

Cyndy smiled into the green grass at her feet. She seemed to be getting accustomed to this shade of a grandmother. She looked around at the empty air.

"I thought I was using my mind."

"What I meant, Cyndy, is that you can do things with your mind that you never could do before, and it's time you started to do so."

"Well I'm sure I don't know what you're going on about, grandmother. As usual you don't make any sense."

Having said that, Cyndy thought she might have overstepped the mark just a bit. She was sure when she heard her grandmother take a deep breath even if no body was in sight.

"Sorry, grandmother, I didn't mean it. You always made sense."

For a moment the thought made Cyndy feel like crying. She was still grieving for her dear departed best friend. She let out a little sob and then straightened her blouse, which had caught a branch on the way down, popping open a few buttons and exposing the fact, to no one except her grandmother and a brown thrush nearby, that she wore no brassière. Apparently the thrush didn't care. The grandmother was another matter.

Finally finished re-buttoning, she sat under the tree admiring the pattern of sunlight dappling the ground around her and beginning to breathe more easily. Her back pain was now just a faint but lingering twinge. Then one streak of sunlight began to take on form. In a moment, with a pronounced popping sound, her grandmother stood before her once more.

"There Cyndy dear. Does this make it easier?"

Grandmother smiled.

"Sorry, though, you have to get your own bottom off the grass. This body isn't as solid as it looks. And don't you think you should be wearin' a brassière, young lady?"

Cyndy was rapidly getting used to the idea that her grandmother could come and go and wasn't as dead as the funeral three years ago had led her to believe. She just shook her head at the phantom.

"O. K. grandmother, enough with the magic show. What were you talking about when you said I should use my mind? I thought I was using my mind. I mean what am I doing talking to you and climbing trees and falling off if not using my mind?"

Cyndy glared at her grandmother with make-believe fury. The forest glade rang with laughter.

"I thought you were all broken up with grief about me. Is this the way you treat your dear old grandmother? I mean really."

Then she laughed again.

"O. K. my dear. Time I told you a little about what you've been through and how it's changed you. Seems when that truck pulled into your path, you chose to take this as sign that you had died and plopped out of your body. Well, then, just to complicate things, you took a detour to where we all go when we die. That's where you had a little talk to your teacher, indeed, a very well-known teacher."

"My teacher?"

"Yes, dear, your teacher. Seems you've been blessed with a teacher with whose wisdom few choose to disagree and I do mean Jesus."

"You said that before, about Jesus talking to me. You must be mistaken. I'm not even sure I even believe in Jesus, let alone believe that he took time out to talk to me. Jesus..."

Cyndy stuttered to a halt with an angry look on her face as she tried to stare down the old woman.

"Hush up, Cyndy. I know all about your poor understandin' of the spiritual. Probably my fault. I was so intent on teachin' you about healin' with plants that I think I forgot to give a proper spiritual upbringin'. And then, later, when you chose to hang around all those hormonal, physical types, it was really too late to do much about it. 'Course then I didn't know you were a chosen one."

"All right, grandmother, now explain please, a chosen one?"

"Yes, you lucky thing, you're a chosen one. You really ought to be just jumpin' up and down with joy."

"Sorry grandmother, but I hurt too much to jump up and down for anything, 'specially joy, since that damned accident."

At this point it occurred to Cyndy that it might be more dignified if she at least stood up and stopped sitting on the grass. Besides, she was afraid she might have green stains on her seat, not that getting up now was going to help that little problem. Groaning a bit, the pain just never seemed to go away from her shoulders, she pulled herself up using a low-hanging tree branch as a support.

"Oh you poor dear. Well we'll just have to see if somethin' can be done to heal that soft tissue damage to your back. In the meantime, your instincts were right on the money, honey. Your friend Shirley has a tumor growing in her brain. If somethin' isn't done soon it'll kill her."

Cyndy gasped.

"No that can't be. I thought maybe I made the whole thing up. Besides, how would I know a something like that?"

"More about that later, Cyndy darlin', but first just let it sink in, you're right about Shirley. And you're also right, that piece of fungus growing there on the tree will provide just the right medicine to help your friend stop that cancer from destroyin' her young life. Course you could do it another way but I want you to remember that there are natural substances all around us that can heal. Just because you have developed the power to heal by touchin' shouldn't stop you from usin' the natural growin' things."

"Heal by touching...?"

"Yes dear. You have the power in you to do healin' by touchin'. But you could get into serious trouble doin' that on this island. Usin' the fungus is one way people will accept your powers much more easily. Alternative healin' with plants and herbs is becomin' all the rage. You'll fit right in. Save the touchy stuff for later when you go out in the world as a healer."

Here her grandmother laughed.

"You don't even know what I'm talkin' about. Oh, well. You'll find out about these powers of yours. The lessons'll be comin' thick and fast. But we're goin' to have to be 'specially careful. Just don't let anyone on Nantucket know you're a healer. They might try to burn you at the stake or somethin', like the witches in Salem."

"You must be reading my mind, grandmother. I had the same thought not long ago. But, what did you say about using my mind to get this darned old fungus off the tree?"

"Thank you for remindin' me child. I think I would forget my head if I still had a head to forget."

This seemed hilarious for she had a great spasm of laughing. Finally getting control she continued.

"Your mind, oh yes, you've got a most unusual mind now. Ever since your little accident you've grown some awesome powers."

She paused and looked serious for a change.

"Don't panic or anythin' but just stand there and ask that fungus to come to you. It's easy even for a thick headed, obstinate young thing like you."

Now she laughed again, looking anything but serious.

"Go ahead, try it."

Cyndy didn't know what to think but she was used to doing what her grandmother asked or, sometimes, demanded. Old habits die hard and here was her grandmother making a demand again.

She screwed up her face and tried to concentrate on telling the fungus to come down off the tree.

Nothing happened. The fungus remained unmoved by this awesome display of psychic power.

"Oh what the hell, grandmother, nothing's happening."

Cyndy looked accusingly at the shade of a grandmother standing, smiling at her.

"Hmmm. I don't know, child. That old fungus should just pop off the tree. Tell me just what are you thinking anyway?"

Cyndy thought hard and couldn't answer. She didn't really know what she'd been thinking. Mostly about the total weirdness of what she was doing she guessed.

"O. K. Cyndy, dear baby. Now I see the problem. You're hung up on weird. Well now, it's weird all right, at least by any standard you've ever had up to now. But you've got to learn to let go all your notions of what's real and what's strange. From now on everythin' you do is going to seem a bit weird. 'Specially to anyone who ever sees you in action. I tell you we have to be careful or this could be the death of you and I don't want you cluttering up my heaven just yet, hear me?"

She paused, thinking.

"O. K. my baby. Here's what we'll do."

With that she laid her hand on Cyndy's forehead.

"Now follow my thoughts, girl. Pay attention."

Suddenly Cyndy's mind seemed to light up. It was almost blinding and she squinted before realizing that the light was inside her head and no amount of squinting was going to help.

"Ouch, grandma, stop. You're hurting me."

"For goodness sake hold still or I will hurt you even if you are all grown up. "

Now the light dimmed and Cyndy could see the fungus, although she realized she didn't have her eyes open at the time. Weird, she thought, trying to follow what was happening. What was happening was the fungus appeared to slowly detach itself from where it had grown between the two thick, scaly-barked branches and was just hanging in the air. Too weird, she thought again.

She opened her eyes a bit. Yes, the damned fungus was just hanging in the air. And now it was floating down to settle at her feet. Too weird.

"How'd you do that, grandmother?"

"Don't worry, darlin'. You did it, not me. You did it. I just tuned up your mind a little. Oh, you've got big-time talent, little girl."

Here she started to laugh again and suddenly vanished. Cyndy looked around, startled, then confused, then angry.

"Damn it grandmother. You can't do this. Come back."

But all she could hear was a laughter that became fainter and fainter until it was gone. Only the quiet sough of wind through the leaves above her and the songs of her little finches were audible. Sighing, she picked up the fungus and headed back towards the stable, intent on putting it in a safe spot until she could find out what she was supposed to do with the damned thing.

Chapter Five

The room at 7 Milk Street was on the second floor and was exactly as he remembered it. The house itself, a bygone of the old whaling days, had been built by a prosperous captain in 1798. The room looked out over the harbor and was fitted with period pieces of sailing and Americana. A full-rigged ship breasted a rolling sea on one wall. Another print showed a whaling dory in the full flight of a Nantucket sleigh ride as it was pulled by a harpooned whale, while other dories floated near by, small figures standing, holding harpoons.

Mrs. Tonshirek had seemed much the same too, comfortably into her 70's and many years into her widowhood. An islander for many generations, it was her own great uncle and ship's captain who had built this old house.

She had been so pleased to see Johnathan again, pressing him to come down for a cup of tea when he was settled. He'd do just that. There was nothing like the local gossip to bring him up to date on island happenings. He wouldn't have to do more than say a casual word or two to keep her right on track with what he needed to learn.

He dumped his backpack onto the bed and looked into the mirror of the pine dresser, stooping to do so. Whoever had decorated this room hadn't planned on giants stopping by. He cast a glance at the bed. Well, his feet would stick out, but he was used to that.

The mirror showed its usual image of a large, well formed head crowned with shocking red hair, a legacy of his Scottish ancestors, and blue, blue eyes from the same set of genes. When he visited the Scottish highlands he was assumed to be a local, at least until he opened his mouth. Then, if he let it, his Louisiana upbringing with soft southern accents quickly changed the first impression. Not that a lot of the South remained, as his life had led him to live in many countries over the many years of his life.

Indeed he had a quick ear for accents and could soon mimic locals wherever he traveled. He quickly learned to speak languages of non-English countries. It was a gift. He had a photographic memory. Anything once heard or read never left him. It was sometimes a pain to remember so much, but more often a blessing, one that had saved his life on occasions.

He reached one large hand into his bag and pulled out a leather folder with his passport, driver's license and other official looking papers. He opened the passport and looked at the first page, noting that his office had done their usual good work.

He was described as Johnathan Millar age 39, born in Green Bay, Wisconsin, but raised in Baton Rouge, Louisiana. Some of that was true, but he chuckled at the thought that 39 was the age when many women chose to stall their true birthdays for a few years. Too bad they didn't have his special powers. Then the reality. Although ageless he still had to be careful. His body could be stopped by the trauma of violence, such as a gunshot wound to his heart or brain. Although he could do miraculous things his body remained, at least in this sense, mortal.

His aging wasn't something he really thought of much anymore. It had become impossible for him to age at all since he had visited India back in the late 1800's. That adventure had come about when he hooked up with that most unusual of men, Baird Spalding, who, in turn, had led him to meet the Masters. When Baird had brought groups of interested observers to India, Jonathan had been hired to heave the heavier pieces of luggage, easy for him with his giant's body. When Baird left India for good, Johnathan had been encouraged to stay on to live with and learn from the Masters.

Years of living with these Masters had changed not only his life but the very nature of his body. Now he, while not a Master, had been taught many of their secrets. His body didn't age because he had learned how to turn off the aging genes in his DNA. It all seemed simple to him now, but he remembered how awe-struck he had been at his first meetings with these magical men.

All the Masters continued to live, study and affect some of the events of the world from the boundaries of the Indian subcontinent. Because of his American background, he had been chosen to return to the North American continent. He was the first to take the Masters' mission beyond the old secular boundaries first set up by Jesus Christ.

It was during those so-called missing 19 years that had had scholars speculating for centuries. That was when the Masters had been created in India to carry on the most secret of Christ's teachings, teachings that never reached the scriptures. What little remained in the scriptures had been expunged by jealous Church leaders in the first 500 years after

Christ's life and death and resurrection on this earth. Occasionally there was still an echo of the magic in a verse here and there but the most of original information was gone.

The Cardinals of the Church had reasoned that no good would come of common people knowing they were immortal and capable of living many lives. Too dangerous for the Church to let that kind of news out. Better that men and women strive to be good enough to go to heaven without knowing they would return, and return many times. More control for the Church, more control of the people.

But that was a story for another time, he muttered to himself. First things first. He removed the gun and holster from under his right arm and stowed it under the mattress of his bed. He didn't really like carrying a gun, even if his fictional heroes had carried heat, but sometimes it made it easier to explain his success in persuading people to do his will rather than trying to explain the real source of his power.

The small radio transceiver he put on the shelf by his bed. It looked like any other clock radio, unless you knew what to look for. He carried the radio to help him reach people in the organization he had set up to help him in his New World mission. Only he had the powers. His powers were impressive but even he couldn't do everything.

Johnathan opened the door and went into the hall to check out the rest of the upper floor. It appeared the other four bedrooms were empty. The main bath was two doors down the hall. It didn't matter too much if others were in the house, but it made it easier, not having to do background checks. Even with his powers it took too much time.

Satisfied that he was alone, he returned to his room and sat down for a few moments of intense meditation. As he centered himself, the room seemed to change, filling with subtle music and a light that appeared to swirl around him, then all was quiet. In twenty minutes he was ready.

Taking the stairs down, two steps at a time, he stopped to stoop under the lintel of the door to the upper floor and then stepped out into the main hall. Mrs. Tonshirek met him as she came out of the kitchen with teapot and cups balanced on an old wooden tray. She smiled at him and continued into the large, well-lighted parlor to put the tray onto a carved oak coffee table set before the huge fire-blackened stone fireplace. A soft, even light came through the windows set under the overhang of a generous front porch. Mrs. Tonshirek waved a knobby-jointed hand at him.

"Sit down Johnathan. Tell me what you've been up to since you were last here...how many years has it been?"

Johnathan settled down to enjoy his tea and spin his stories. Mrs. Tonshirek would be spreading them around, he knew, and that would save him a lot of trouble. People would be less curious if they thought they already knew where he'd been these last few years. Yeah, save him a lot of time and trouble. He gave her his best smile and began.

The lovely white steeple climbed gracefully against a background of cumulous clouds in a serene blue sky. Set on the highest point of the island the church gave a full view over the Town of Nantucket and the harbor. Today, as far as the eye could see, the sky was clear and blue, flecked with puffy clouds. Outside the harbor, sails bloomed as boats leaned into the breeze on their journey to and from the mainland. A few came through the narrow harbor entrance to anchor at the town marina. Most boats showed briefly then disappeared below the horizon.

The old church dated from the early 1800's and had been home to sailors for well over 150 years. It was built on the site of an even earlier church that had burned during the great town fire. Lower down the slope were some of the elegant old homes of whaling captains, complete with their widow's walks, outlined in fancy iron or wood railings. During the heyday of whaling the large wooden whalers were often at sea for two and three years at a time. Quite a few had foundered and made widows of their masters' wives.

Lately in the history of Nantucket, the church had taken on the role of sole arbiter of morals for the Island. The services were more and more a description of violence rather than love, while hell seemed more likely than heaven for many. Over the last fifty years the church had also become a center for the hopelessly ill. When Maaiken presided, the sick and halt could expect to become well again. Miracles still happened on this isolated outpost in the Atlantic Ocean. There was even a move on by a committee in the State Legislature to investigate these healings to determine if they were genuine. The more orthodox Churches were interested, too, most scoffing at the idea of these being of any real spiritual basis. Some mainland doctors wanted to do a proper study. The healings of The Poor Soldiers of Christ Church had created something of a stir.

The dwarfish figure of Maaiken Starbroke wrote with vigor as he drafted his sermon for the following Sunday. He chuckled to himself. Damn fine, he thought. He'd keep them trembling with this description of their futures if they disobeyed his edicts. Then he would hold a healing. It was the center of his church, the healing. People came from far and wide now to be healed. Yet no one knew what lay behind the miracles. It was a secret passed down through his family for generations. It was such a great secret that only through a blood oath could anyone share and then he only ever let part of the knowledge out.

No one must know the real source of his power. It was far too dangerous. Thousands had died over the ages for the mysterious object that was kept in the chambers below the church. No. No one must ever find out the real truth.

Finally, setting down his pen he gazed thoughtfully at the far wall, at the bookcases filled with histories of the island, the church and the whaling that had sustained the economy for so many years before kerosene had been invented. Books filled all the spaces except for one—it held an oddly dented Coleman lamp with a broken mantle.

Maaiken rose out of his chair and went to the point where the bookcase joined the right side of the fireplace. Carefully he reached under the fireplace mantel where his finger found what appeared to be a knot in the wood. When he pushed on the raised surface of the knot, he could feel it sink into the thick wooden plank above. At this moment a distinct click sounded and one portion of the bookcase began, silently, to open out into the room. Maaiken impatiently pulled it further open and walked through the space now gaping in the wall. Just as silently, the bookcase swung closed behind him. The bookcase had no more than just completed closing when the door to the study swung open and Jeremy Sloken poked his head in.

"Funny, I would have sworn old Maaiken was in here."

He muttered this thought to no one but a cat that pushed in at his feet. The cat decided not to take notice but leapt up onto Maaiken's desk and started to play with the papers. Taking one last look around Jeremy left with a puzzled shake of his head not noticing the cat. The cat seemed happy with this and curled up in a shaft of sunlight that streamed in through the tall cathedral window and poured gentle warmth onto the surface of the desk.

Grunting, the Sheriff swung his legs out of the car, pulled out the hapless bundle that was Luke, and led him through the door of the Sheriff's office.

"Here, Clem, sling this bundle of worthless shit into a cell and see he makes the next steamer out of here."

Clem looked up with a sigh, stubbing out a cigarette as he stood up from his scarred old desk to grab a fistful of Luke's coat. With little ceremony he shoved Luke through a door at the back of the office that led into the holding area at the rear of the building.

Taylor went through the door to his own office and, with a grunt, sat down heavily in his old, beat-up leather chair. Thrusting his legs against the floor, he proceeded to roll it over to the files against the far wall.

He pulled open a drawer, rifled through file folders, then grunted again, this time with satisfaction as he pulled a manila file folder out of the drawer. Propelling his chair back to the desk, he put his feet up, opened the file and began to read. After a while he began to hum. The door to the holding area opened and Clem came back and then into Taylor's office.

"What are you singing on about now, Taylor? I know you well enough that when you got something really good going, you're like a bathroom baritone. Now what's the scoop? Don't tell me you got something interesting on that bag of garbage in the holding tank?"

"There isn't anything in the world interesting about old Luke there, Clem, except why he thought he could put foot on this lovely, old island and get away with it. Damn the man. How many times do I have to throw him off Nantucket before he learns not to come back? Maybe I better put a boot to him before you put him back on the boat. Nahhh. That would make me sicker than it would him. Just make sure he makes the next sailing."

With that Taylor turned back and continued to read his way through the pages in the file folder. Pretty soon his humming began again. Clem looked as if he wanted to say more but thought better of it and returned to the outer office where he sat at his desk in front of an old typewriter holding a partly finished report. Soon all was quiet except for a ragged clicking of typewriter keys and the slightly off-key baritone coming from the open door to Taylor's office.

Chapter Six

Cyndy carefully set the fungus down on the table in the still room and returned to the house. Hesitating for a moment she pulled a set of keys off the wall, opened the door into the garage and walked out to her new red pickup, glistening beside the bits and pieces of Harley.

She still felt spooked when she drove the new truck but she wasn't about to let the accident stop her life. Still she drove with unusual care, for her. At every side street she looked nervously right and left before driving past. She hoped this would pass in time, but for the moment it was a drag. She'd never felt nervous about anything in her life. She was one who pitied the poor folks who couldn't hack their lives. Now she was one of them. It was a humbling experience. Driving slowly through the narrow streets she finally reached the pride of her life, the Maria Mitchell observatory on Vestal Street.

The first American woman astronomer had been born on this island and the observatory was named after her. It had always been in the care of women. The telescope was an 8-inch refractor and CCD camera, not a large telescope but one still capable of science. Even better, it was an ideal teaching instrument. She had undergraduate students here all summer, helping out with studies and the popular lectures that were given once a week to visitors and islanders alike.

Cyndy's major computer resources were here. She went into the office and began to work on her pet project, variable stars in globular clusters. Soon she was lost in her work, worries about trucks, accidents, dead grandmothers, non-communicating husbands and lost skills as a baseball player all thankfully forgotten. For the moment she was absorbed in her first love, science.

Luke sat in the holding cell, his smelly clothes offending even him. This wasn't working out as planned. He'd never thought of the Sheriff recognizing old Luke when he had borrowed the persona for a disguise.

The real Luke still slumbered back in Provincetown, where he'd wake up soon with no memory of the preceding events. Damn, now he'd have to start taking risks.

He checked the watch on his wrist. Nearing sailing time for the next steamer to the mainland. That fool Clem would be in anytime now if he was to be put Luke back on the steamer. As if prompted by his thought, the door from the office opened and Clem slouched in, carrying the key to his cell.

"Come on you old rummy. On your feet."

With that he unlocked the barred door and slid it open. Luke slowly stood up and started to walk towards the door when he stumbled and reached out to clutch at Clem. The one hand Luke put on Clem's shoulder suddenly grabbed Clem's neck. In a moment he'd found the nerves and pressed them, putting Clem out faster than a good knock with a baseball bat.

Clem crumpled to the floor, unconscious but not damaged. Luke boosted him up on the bunk and covered him with a blanket. With any luck nobody would miss Clem for at least a half-hour, lots of time for him to vanish from the jail.

First Luke locked the cell door, then quickly cracked open the door into the front office and was pleased to find it empty. Fortunately the Sheriff's office was also empty, the door shut. Luke's quick, sure movements belied the look of his disguise. Although the body itself seemed in bad shape, it was all an excellent case of makeup, clothing and his ability as an actor. He smiled, walked to Clem's desk where he dropped the cell keys before quietly opening the door to the rear alley where he stepped out into freedom.

He wondered in passing how poor old Clem was going to explain this one to the Sheriff, not that he cared one way or another. He had handled it with speed and also without damaging the deputy. It was not in his best interests right now to hurt or kill. The object he sought would be well hidden and what he didn't need was the kind of hue and cry that would be raised if the Sheriff thought he was truly dangerous. For the moment the Sheriff wouldn't know what to think, but the persona of Luke would dull his worries for the moment. Walking quickly away from the jail, Luke took a turn off onto a side street and made his way to the safety of the house where he had booked a room before coming to the Island. When he turned in it was at number 7 Milk Street.

Before ringing the doorbell, Luke re-combed his hair and wondered if the suitcase of clothes and supplies had been delivered to Mrs. Tonshirek. He hoped so, as his current wardrobe was a dreadful mess, not made any better by his recent incarceration. He slipped off the coat and reversed it to show a much cleaner surface. Then he took a small, pressurized can from a hidden pocket and quickly sprayed a fine mist over the coat and pants. The nasty odor he had been emitting became less noticeable. There, much better. He smiled as he pushed at the button beside the blue trimmed door.

The soft bell stopped Mrs. Tonshirek in mid-sentence.

"I wonder if that is Mr. St. James? Excuse me Johnathan. I'm expecting another guest, not anyone I know, but a suitcase came about a week ago and I've been waiting for him to follow ever since. He booked a room about a month ago saying he had been given my name from the Chamber of Commerce."

With that she pulled herself out of her chair and headed out into the hall. At the door she pulled it open with a smile that quickly faded.

"Yes?"

"Ah, Mrs. Tonshirek, I presume. Allow me to introduce myself. Reginald St. James. We spoke on the phone and I sent you a month's rent for a room. Did your receive it all right? Oh, and I hope you'll excuse my somewhat shabby appearance but I've been on a walking tour of New England and have had little opportunity to smarten up. I do hope my bag has arrived so I can change."

Luke smiled ingratiatingly and made a little bow. Mrs. Tonshirek, a gentlewoman and kind to a fault, pushed her criticism to one side.

"Please Mr. St. James, do come in. Yes, your bag arrived and is in your room upstairs, number 3, you've got. I do hope you will be pleased with it. And the bath is just down the hall. I imagine you're going to want to hop right in to clean up from your travels."

Here she smiled and waved him inside.

Johnathan listened to the conversation and watched as a very shabby figure of a man with a scraggly gray beard walked past the door to the stairs. Not tall, the new arrival was thin and bony and looked uncared-for. Johnathan's super-senses kicked in and he detected an unpleasant odor, mostly masked by yet another odor, the result of some chemical or mixture of chemicals. Odd, he thought. What's that all about? I think that one needs checking out.

Mrs. Tonshirek came back into the room.

"Odd man. Never seen the likes of him before."

She gazed back at the stairs, then shrugged and sat down again, still eager to gossip with Johnathan.

Upstairs, Luke/St. James now prepared to change persona, closing the door to his bedroom and grunting with satisfaction at the sight of his bag. Quickly he stripped off Luke's old clothes then laid out clean new jeans, shirt, socks and boat shoes. Next he stepped into the bathroom where he turned on the taps and began to relax. Clean hot water filled the tub and steam began to cover the mirror over the medicine cabinet.

Downstairs, Johnathan listened as the clock in the church tower struck 3 o'clock. He automatically checked his Rolex. They agreed almost to the second. That was another of the unusual wonders of the church; the tower featured a four-sided clock that had been built and installed by one of the early islanders. It had faultlessly run the lives of Nantucketers for over 100 years. Johnathan stood and stretched out his back.

"Been sitting too long Mrs. Tonshirek. Guess I should be on my way. Got some business with the Sheriff. Think I'll go on down to his office and see if he's in. Then I'll get a little dinner down by the wharf before I come on back. Be sure to leave the door open for me."

"Oh, don't worry Johnathan. Never lock that front door. But there is a key for your room on your dresser if you want to lock up before you go out."

Johnathan smiled at her and, stooping his way out the door to the hall, ran lightly up the stairs to his room. He listened for a moment, hearing the water running in the bathroom. Probably needed to soak for a week anyway, he thought with a chuckle, remembering the odor of the man.

Then he heard the water swishing and thought maybe this is the time for a little look see. Carefully, these old houses had a lot of squeaky boards, he eased the door to number 3 open and looked carefully around the room.

He noted the pile of old clothes dumped on the floor, then carefully checked the new clothes laid out on the bed. Brand new from the look of them. Strange, who travels with all new clothing? Stepping quickly and quietly into the room, he picked up a wallet lying on the bed and thumbed through quickly. Finding a driver's license, he noted the name and number, then replaced it.

Just then he heard water running out of the tub and quickly slipped back into his own room to think about the stranger. A strange one indeed. He'd have to check further. The door closed, he took down the radio and clicked a button that slid open a small panel on the bottom. Inside were a number of controls. Sliding out the antenna, he typed a message on miniature keys, then hit a send button. In moments details of the man and license were now on file with his office. Sally would start to check out this man with all-new clothes.

Johnathan started to open his door to head back down the stairs when the bathroom door opened. He held the door open just a crack and watched as a man walked past his field of vision. It was not what he expected. For a moment Johnathan was confused. Then he realized the man he now saw was the same build as the ratty, scraggly man who had come up these stairs. It was just that he was now clean-shaven and his hair a new color. Curiouser and curiouser, he thought, walking back to his radio to send these new details to the office back home.

Intrigued but unable to see the man now back in room number 3, Johnathan headed down the stairs where, with a quick salute to Mrs. Tonshirek who was now knitting and watching TV, he headed out to visit with the Sheriff.

The door opened and Taylor walked in, shouting for Clem but getting no response. Guess he's taken Luke to the steamer, he thought. Probably waiting to make sure he doesn't try to sneak off again. Just as he was turning to the door to his office, he noticed a partly typed report sitting in Clem's typewriter and thought that strange. Clem should have finished those reports by now.

With a soft tread for such a big man, Taylor walked over and opened the door to the holding cells. The cell that held Luke was directly ahead. Now Taylor spoke his thoughts aloud.

"Shit, something wrong here. Why's Luke still in that bunk?"

Walking back to Clem's desk he picked up the cell keys lying beside the typewriter and went back into the holding cell. Slamming open the cell door he went to the sleeping figure and stripped off the blanket. Startled, he saw not the straggly bearded Luke but the unconscious face of his deputy.

"Clem? Clem!"

The unconscious face slept on. John gently shook Clem's shoulders.

"Come on Clem. Wake up for Christ's sake."

When he still got no response he picked the radio off his belt and keyed a button that would reach the ambulance center down the street.

"Dick, you there, this is Taylor. I got a problem here at the holding cells. Get your ass over here fast. Something's happened to Clem and he's unconscious."

Making sure Clem was breathing freely, he checked his pulse then went back out to the front office.

The ambulance and the big man arrived together. Dick and the other paramedic raced through the door with their oxygen and first aid bags. Johnathan walked in right behind them and watched as they disappeared through the holding area door closely followed by the Sheriff. He shrugged and strolled after the action.

"What's going on, Sheriff?"

Taylor looked up to see the big man hovering half in half out of the holding cell door. He glared up at him from the cell where the paramedics were busy over Clem's inert body

"We're busy here buddy, wait outside please."

Johnathan obediently went back into the front office and sat down on one of the two hard oak captain's chairs that seemed to limit how many might or might not wait at any one time. With little else to do, he examined the walls of the Sheriff's domain.

One wall had the prerequisite gun cabinet with shotguns, rifles and small arms displayed behind toughened glass and a Yale lock. A bulletin board sported a number of wanted posters, a list of daily steamer sailings from Hyannis and a tide table.

A lone desk near the opposite wall held an old typewriter with a page still in the roller. File folders littered this desk and showed a nasty lack of order on the part of the occupant. Johnathan wondered idly if the man he had observed in the holding cell area was also the sloppy owner of this desk.

From where he sat Johnathan could see three doors, one to the Sheriff's office, one leading to the holding area and one the entrance from the street. Small quarters for law enforcement. Where were all the up-to-date technology of computers, faxes and other paraphernalia? There had to be more to running a Sheriff's department than what was immediately visible.

Then, turning in the chair, Johnathan noticed that the wall behind his chair held a fourth door. Curious, he got up and opened this door to see whether it held lions, tigers and bears. However, nothing sprang out at him but a flight of stairs leading to the upper floor. Didn't look like the activity in the holding pen was going to end soon so Johnathan stepped through the door and climbed the stairs. A second door at the top opened out into an office filled with the missing technology. A young woman in uniform turned to him with a questioning gaze.

"Yes sir? You looking for someone? "

"Sorry ma'am. Just nosy. Waiting on the Sheriff but he's a mite busy so I just thought I'd see where these steps went. Now I see this is where he hides the good looking part of the law enforcement for this island."

Johnathan also noted other desks that had an air of recent occupation.

"I guess you're not the only one who works up here then?"

"No sir, we've a staff of six deputies working this office. That and the Sheriff are the law on this island. 'Course you might like to count in the State Police over on Dunstable road. There're always two of them on regular assignment from the mainland. They rotate every two weeks. New guys come over, the others go back to mainland duty."

At this she gave a small laugh.

"I think they look at it as their holiday time."

This made her give a real laugh. She stopped suddenly and tried to look more serious.

"But if I ever hear that you quoted me I'll see your sorry ass busted for some serious crime, hear? And don't ever let me hear you call me 'ma'am' again, either. Who you think I am, my mother?"

With this serious lecture out of the way she again became friendly.

"So, can I help you or not?"

Johnathan wondered how far he could go, he was getting bored with his own company.

"Well, if it doesn't get me arrested, how about meeting me for a drink after you finish?"

He waited to see what effect this might have. There was no response, just a serious looking over from head to foot and back to head.

"My name's Shirley, Shirley Woodstock. What's yours?"

"Johnathan, Johnathan Miller, Shirley, but most of my friends call me John or sometimes big John, I guess for obvious reasons."

Shirley eyed him speculatively.

"You're new on Nantucket. Don't remember seeing you before and believe me I would have remembered. You're sort of a hard-to-forget kind of guy."

She smiled.

"Don't take this the wrong way but if your offer is legitimate, I'll say OK. Maybe time I met someone other than the local yokels I have to deal with every day."

At this feet sounded on the stairs.

"Oh shit, that's Fred coming back after his coffee break. Get out of here. I'll meet you at the Crawfish around five-thirty, OK?"

"OK Shirl, you're on."

Johnathan turned and stepped back to allow Fred to get through the door, carrying a lidded coffee cup in one hand. Shirley dimpled.

"Thank you Fred. You're not all bad, you know."

Johnathan waved good-bye and went back down the stairs.

"What's going on with the ambulance?"

He could hear Fred's voice but the answer was lost as two doors closed to separate him from the upper floor. Johnathan went back to waiting and counting as two other men and a young woman hurried behind him to mount the stairs. As he watched he realized that these returning deputies would be concerned about the ambulance parked outside.

Now the door to the holding cells opened and the two paramedics rolled a gurney through the door with an unconscious Clem securely strapped in.

"Don't see anything really wrong with Clem but he just doesn't seem to want to wake up. We'll take him in to the Nantucket Cottage Hospital and put him under observation. Far as I can see he seems more alert but he sure ain't coming around very fast. Besides, the docs'll want to see if they can find out what put Clem out anyway."

"Yeah, take good care of him. I need some answers from him as soon as he cares to wake up from this beauty nap."

The Sheriff's voice had an angry edge to it.

"I got an escaped prisoner somewhere on this island and I want to know just how he happened to get out of that cell in the first place. It's just not like the Luke I know to knock someone out. Just not like him at all."

The door from the top floor opened and five anxious young deputies piled into the room and stopped to watch the action. The Sheriff waited as the paramedics rolled the gurney out to the waiting ambulance then turned to look at the Deputies.

"It's Clem, something's happened to Clem and we got a missing prisoner. There isn't anything to be done right now. We'll set up to find the missing man but there's no hurry. He's been gone for at least half an hour or so. We'll just keep an eye out during routine patrol and at the docks. I'll brief you in a few minutes, OK?"

The five returned to their upper rooms. Taylor turned to the patiently waiting Johnathan.

"Well, Johnathan. What're you doing back here, man? Haven't seen you for four or five years as I remember. You still in the Coast Guard?"

Well, thought Johnathan, the old man's still got that incredible memory, that's for sure. He dodged the question.

"Ah, you always did amaze me, how you remember everything, Sheriff. And here I thought I'd have to introduce myself all over again."

The Sheriff looked sideways and smirked.

"Oh, I haven't forgotten you Johnathan, or that bar-busting fight you got yourself into when you were stationed here, either. Hope you got better control these days or I'll have to bust you again. I don't take kindly to people breaking up a good bar. 'Specially not the bar I like to drink in. Hear me?"

Johnathan smiled. The Sheriff tried to be so tough but he remembered the Manx cats and knew the man had a good deal of bluff in him. Not that he'd want to really cross the Sheriff, for Taylor took law and order very seriously and wouldn't put up with real shit.

"Be easy, Sheriff. I'm a good boy now. Haven't had a fight in years and that last one, here, I had to fight or I would probably have had a long knife stuck into me. That boy was seriously drunk and disorderly. He wanted to stick me or almost anyone who even glanced at his girl. I made the mistake of giving her a real look. She was worth it. But what a price."

This wasn't exactly the true story of what happened that night but it had been his cover. The real truth was that the boy with the knife had been one of the smugglers. He had tried to end Johnathan's interest in his activities and just about ended Johnathan's interest in anything ever again. Fortunately, Johnathan had been on alert and had used his own hidden power to deflect the first knife thrust. To cover what had happened he turned and punched the first man he could get next to. This started a general brawl that involved his Coast Guard mates and any friends the knife carrier had planted around the bar. The result had been a mess but it covered his necessary use of power.

For the Sheriff it had been a simple case of drunks doing damage. He had made sure they did time for the damage and also coughed up the necessary money to compensate the Crawfish and get the damage repaired.

Chapter Seven

The phone made its apologetic little bleep and broke Cyndy's concentration. Frowning she looked at the clock and saw that she'd been sitting at the computer for over two hours. Then she turned to frown at the phone. Maybe it was George needing something. She picked up on the forth ring as she continued to watch numbers stream past on her screen. Her voice was abrupt.

"Yeah, hello."

"Cyn, it's Shirley, how's my brainy buddy? Discovered any new worlds today? Is a comet going to destroy us this week or should I buy my lottery ticket?"

Cyndy's voice immediately took a friendlier tone.

"Oh shut up Shirl. What's going on in the world of law and order? Beaten up any bums today? Got your apple from the corner fruit market? How's it for free coffee and donuts?"

Cyndy had never quite understood the motivation that had led her best friend into police work. But then Shirl was probably just as much in the dark about her career choice, so there. They kidded each other every chance they got. It's what they did.

"Yeah, well maybe I should come over and arrest you for loitering near a telescope. Say listen up Cyn, what're you and George doing around five-thirty? I've just said I'd go have a drink with a complete stranger and I want backup."

Cyndy stared at the receiver in her hand.

"Come on Shirl, you never do things like this. I mean a complete stranger who might be the Boston strangler or something?"

"That's why I want you and George to meet me at the Crawfish. Around five-thirty or maybe six. But don't be later because I don't know where any of this is going."

"Let me call George and see if I can get him to quit early and pick me up. Tell you what, if George can't make it I'll just happen past your table and you can flag me down if you still think you need help. OK?"

"Thanks, Cyn, you're a pal. See you."

The line went dead. It had been some time since she and George had had much of a night out. Maybe this was good idea. She dialed George's private line.

The Crawfish had its usual 5 o'clock crowd. Noise swirled around Cyndy's head along with the cigarette smoke as she and George headed for the table where she could see Shirley and a stranger, a big stranger at that. The jukebox beat out some unintelligible noise. Voices were raised as speakers tried to be heard. One table in the corner erupted in laughter, causing her to glance over to see what all the fun was about. Cigarette smoke caught her throat and made tears well in her eyes. She smiled. Nothing like the good old Crawfish. Smelled of fish frying in the back, stale beer in front and attracted mostly locals. Cyndy waved back at a couple sitting over by the wall.

Finally she had made it to Shirley's table. George bumped into her back, his mind still on the program for the banks.

"Sorry, Cyndy."

Shirley looked up, acting sort of surprised.

"Cyndy, what are you doing here? Hey, and is that good old George hiding behind your back?"

Good old George looked over Cyndy's shoulder and waved.

"Johnathan, meet a couple of my best friends. This's Cyndy and her hubby George."

Johnathan looked up ready to be annoyed but instead enjoyed the vision of Cyndy's Irish face framed by her dark auburn hair. His voice was neutral; his eyes still on Cyndy's face.

"Hi. And is there really someone back there?"

He reached his big hand out to where good old George lurked, still blocked by Cyndy and the narrow aisle between the tables. George stuck his hand around Cyndy's waist and grabbed it, startled by how his hand disappeared into the other man's. George muttered into Cyndy's back then acknowledged the hand.

"Shit. Hi, how you doing?"

Finally Cyndy wedged herself around to a chair at the back of the table, George managing at last to follow and sit down in the fourth chair at the battered and stained oak table.

"Cyndy and George Vorester, my new friend, Johnathan Millar. Johnny used to be a Coast Guard here a few years back, didn't you?"

Shirley smiled at her new friend. She also smiled a thin smile at George. Then the strangeness began. Shirley started to lean forward, holding her hands to her head.

"Oh shit that hurts."

Alarmed, Cyndy reached her hand out to Shirley's shoulder and felt a jolt run up her arm. And just as suddenly she could see into Shirley's head and the peach pit thing growing there. It was larger now and looked ugly. She stared at the growth as if challenging its right to be there, and even as she watched it seemed to grow smaller. As she stared, Shirley started to relax her body and straightened up.

"Sorry, everybody. Don't know what the hell that was, but I had the worst pain for a moment."

She smiled at the others. Cyndy was still locked into her vision.

"What's up Cyndy?"

It was George who was now staring at Cyndy in alarm. In fact they all looked at her as she stayed, frozen, her eyes still fixed on Shirley but seeing only her vision. George reached out and grabbed at her shoulder, shaking her.

"Cyndy, snap out of it. What're you doing?"

Cyndy shook her head and the vision dissolved and the smoky Crawfish came into view.

"What?"

"You looked like you were in a trance or something. You OK?"

Then it was Shirley's turn.

"Yeah, Cyndy, you looked like you could see right through me."

Cyndy took a deep breath and forced a concerned smile.

"Are you sure you're OK Shirley? You were saying something hurt and you were holding your head."

Shirley looked thoughtful.

"Yeah, for a minute there my head hurt something awful but it went away. Guess I need another drink."

She waved at a passing waiter.

"Hey Ronny, get me another beer and see what these folks're having."

Meanwhile Johnathan had been watching and wondering. He probed at Shirley, sensing that there was a serious problem here somewhere. The noise and smoke made it difficult for him to use his inner sight. He would have to wait until things were quieter. But one thing he did know, something unusual had just happened. Just what he wasn't quite sure.

He looked thoughtfully at Cyndy. He had sensed the energy that had flowed between the two women. Whoever she was, she was different. Again he couldn't see in the confusion and noise. But his inner sense sounded the familiar alarm and he knew he would have to find out more. What he could see, even with all the noise confusing his senses, was a light around Cyndy's head. What the hell is that?

"Hey, Johnathan, now you look like you're in a trance. Come on, you still with us?"

Shirley was poking at him.

"You worried about me or something? Well don't. I'm healthy as a horse. That's the truth. Whatever it was it's nothing to worry about. Let's enjoy a drink. Well, about time Ron! Thought you had booked off or something."

She gave her large smile to the waiter now back with a tray of drinks for the table.

"And you do what?"

Johnathan looked at Cyndy inquiringly.

"I'm the local astronomer. If you're interested come over to the observatory tomorrow night, I'm giving a lecture. It's simple stuff, mostly for the tourists, but I think you might enjoy it. You get to look through the telescope if it's a decent night."

She smiled at him and he felt an unusual force radiate from her. That, he thought, was a must do. This young woman needed further study and he wasn't being sexist. She was something unusual. He was a student of the unusual.

"And you George, what's your racket?"

George looked at the big man.

"I write computer code, develop new applications, the usual computer stuff."

"Come on, George, you're a big number in the cyber community."

It was Shirley who had leapt to his defense.

"This modest fellow is responsible for CyberGhost, surely you have heard of CyberGhost, Johnny?"

She raised an inquiring eyebrow at Johnathan. As a matter of fact Johnathan had heard of CyberGhost. It was just one of the best-selling computer games that had hit the market in the last couple of years.

"Really, then you are good at what you do."

George tried to look modest.

"Well, I've got some good people working with me you know. A job like that is too much for one guy to hack."

"And you're a Deputy Sheriff, Shirley. So what is it about the law and order business that made you want to do police work?"

Johnathan was always asking questions. It was what he did.

"Oh, her uncle's the Sheriff, John."

George answered for her. Seemed Shirley and George were on much the same wavelength. He wondered where that left Cyndy and George. Shirley gave George a thump on the shoulder.

"That's not the reason, you geek. I've taken all the academy training and I'm damn good at my job. A damn sight better than Uncle Taylor at the computer."

Now George smiled and nodded his head.

"Now that's a fact. If Shirley hadn't gone into this police thing I would've hired her for my company. She's damned good at the computer. Sometimes I think she can teach me a thing or two."

He gave her a look of pride.

Again, George supporting Shirley. Well, well.

"Are you also a computer whiz, Cyndy? Is everyone here deep into computers and I'm the only computer illiterate?"

Johnathan was anything but computer illiterate.

"No, John, I'm just an average user. Need lots of computer power for my work though. Big files to crunch, you know."

Cyndy smiled at him in the gloom, thereby illuminating not only the Crawfish but his whole life.

Johnathan reassessed himself. Was he actually attracted to this pleasant young astronomer aside from the fact that she seemed to glow in the dark, not that anyone else could see this side of her? She might not even be aware that she was glowing a spiritual glow. Probably not. Natural chosen ones often didn't know they had the power at first. He suspected that's what he was seeing, a natural chosen one. He'd check it out later. The bar was too distracting to do it now.

The Sheriff closed the door to the office to plan his strategy. Fred was the only one left upstairs. He didn't know where Shirley had gone. He thought of paging her but decided to wait while he thought on just how he would go about recapturing Luke. Unless the crazy coot had already headed off-island on the steamer Clem had meant to put him on, he had no other way of getting off Nantucket. It was a possibility. But this business with Clem bothered him more than the missing Luke. What could have caused Clem's unconscious state? The paramedics couldn't find any obvious cause, but Clem was out none-the-less. He hoped the docs at the hospital would be able to enlighten him later.

Just how could that under-fed, over-drunk, straggly-faced crook have done it? He could have understood if there was any trauma to Clem's head, but he just seemed to be asleep. No damage anywhere. No needle punctures. Just asleep. Weird.

The Sheriff struggled with facts that didn't add up and decided not to do anything for the moment. He would check with the Steamship Authority folks tomorrow and see if anyone remembered seeing Luke board the 6:25 steamer. It was too late now to catch any of them in the office.

Satisfied with having made a decision, Taylor decided to go across to the Crawfish for a drink before heading home. Then the phone rang. Grunting his frustration, he reached out a ham-like hand and grabbed the offending instrument.

"Yeah, you've got the Sheriff here. Oh, yeah doc, what've you found? What? Bruises around his neck near some nerves that might have made him unconscious? Some kinda Judo thing? Now how the hell would Luke know how to do something like that? What? No, no I don't expect you to know that. I'm just talking to myself. Thanks for calling doc."

Taylor hung up the phone and stared at the wall. Oh well, might as well go get that drink. Nothing was adding up here. Maybe it would be clearer if he looked at it through a beer glass. He punched a button on the phone. In a minute, Fred answered.

"Keep an eye on things, Fred. You've got the place to yourself. If you need me I'm over at the Crawfish. After that try the house. Yeah, OK. See you tomorrow if nothing happens."

Taylor hung up the phone and left, pulling the heavy wooden door shut with a click.

Chapter Eight

It was getting dark in Maaiken's study when the bookshelves silently slid open and Maaiken walked out looking weary. He eyed his desk, seeing the cat still curled up on his sermon.

"Get out of there you foul beast. Get off my sermon."

Maaiken looked for something to throw at the cat. The cat opened his eyes and looked calmly back at the man who had so rudely awakened him. He recognized the bellow and prepared to leap out of danger if necessary. Maaiken, finding nothing but a candle in a pewter holder, picked it up then threw it with all his strength. Unfortunately, his aim was bad, so bad that the heavy pewter base sailed right through the window with a resounding crash of breaking glass.

The cat, seeing nothing alarming coming at him, stretched then leapt gracefully to the floor, taking some care to keep behind the desk. The cat had been a target before. The cat had never been hit. The door to the study was suddenly thrown open.

"What's happening in here, what's the noise?"

Jeremy Slokem stuck his head around the door with an alarmed look on his thin, long-nosed face.

"You OK Rev?"

"Get that damned cat out of this study. How did it get in here anyhow? Did you let it in?"

Maaiken looked accusingly at Jeremy.

"Gosh no, boss. Don't know how it got in."

Jeremy went behind the big pine desk where he could see a bit of the cat's tail and scooped up the beast before it could scoot away. Gently, as he was a gentle man, Jeremy pushed it out the study door. He turned back looking at the broken window.

"I'd better get the hardware guys over in the morning to fix that. I guess it'll be all right for the night. No rain expected or anything."

Maaiken scowled at him.

"Get something and cover up the broken part. I don't want bats or some other enterprising animals in here tonight. That cat's bad enough."

Jeremy turned his lanky body and left to find something for the window. Maaiken sat at the desk and pondered about ways to make the cat pay for its transgressions. He turned and shouted at the door.

"Little bugger. I catch you in here one more time and your nine lives will be history."

With that satisfying thought he turned back to reviewing his sermon. It wasn't until later he noticed he'd forgotten to pull the bookshelf back tight against the fireplace. He hurried over to close it and the latch gave an audible click. He'd have to be more careful. Not that his lame-brained assistant would notice, but it was dangerous for anyone not sworn to know about the secret cavern below the Church. Satisfied no damage had been done, he resumed his review of the sermon.

Jeremy closed the door behind him and stopped for a moment to recollect on what he'd just seen. There was something not right with the bookshelves beside the fireplace; they seemed to have moved. He thought about that for a moment. When Jeremy thought he often thought out loud.

"That'd explain why Maaiken disappears and reappears like a stage magician."

He thought some more.

"There's some other way in and out of that room. OK, I'll just keep that to myself for now."

He let himself out of the side service door and went to a small shed to find some cardboard for the broken widow, still thinking about what he'd seen. First chance he had, he'd see if he could find out more about those shelves.

Luke, or Reginald St. James as he was now, examined his reflection in the mirror and decided that he would pass muster. The one missing item was his pendant. This was a mysterious object he had stolen from a museum in Halifax, where it had lain since discovered at the infamous Oak Island treasure site.

One of the prospectors had pulled up the pendant and a bit of parchment that looked like a piece of an old map when he pulled up a drag sent down a borehole. That and pieces of old wooden timbers were all that had been found. Within days the hole had collapsed and the effort abandoned.

No one knew what to make of the pendant. The Provincial Government had taken it to hold for subsequent study. It had finally been bequeathed to the Provincial Museum and exhibited in a general diorama of Oak Island showing a history of the many digs that had gone on there.

Reginald St. James, archaeologist, historian and sometimes thief, expert in objects related to early Christian history, had realized upon hearing of the discovery that this unusual item resembled pendants described in historical writings, said to be worn by members of the order of Poor Soldiers of Christ. The museum was poorly protected. It hadn't taken an expert like St. James long to find a way to remove the object. He had, in fact, substituted a copy he had made. As far as he knew, the museum was ignorant of the theft.

He took a boot from his bag, and carefully using the blade of a knife managed to separate the heel from the rest of the boot. Nestled within the exposed cavity was a small deerskin pouch. He took it and tipped out the object within.

Exposed to the light, a deep red stone glittered from its setting of gold. Around the stone complex figures were engraved in the metal. Etched into the stone was a figure with wings. The whole object hung from a fine golden chain, the subject of some discussion by expert antiquarians. The chain links appeared to be carved from a single piece of metal. Goldsmiths, when consulted, had been amazed by the intricacy of such work. There was no information on who might have been the artist. There was general agreement that both the object and the chain were extremely old. Just how old had led to many arguments but no answers.

St. James had read old writings that had claimed pendants such as this had a power connected to an object he now believed was on the island, the object responsible for the healing at the local church. For a moment St. James concentrated on the stone within its ring of carved gold. An even color permeated the stone, without deviation. There was no hint of activity, no sign that he was near the subject of his search, an artifact lost from sight for hundreds of years. He sighed and placed the pendant around his neck, sensing a warmth emanating from it.

St. James took a file folder from his bag and extracted a sheaf of dog-eared papers copied from the log of a whaling ship. He began to read the material one more time. The log related the first unusual healing that had occurred on Nantucket in the 1700's. As the log recorded the day in question, it stated that one of the crew of the whaler had sustained a serious injury during the docking; the man's arm had been caught in a hawser just as the ship tightened it at the dock. The master of the vessel had said it was too badly twisted and broken to be saved and called for a surgeon to take it off.

Two mysterious travelers on the ship had offered to help and had carried the fainting victim to their cabin. After an hour they reappeared with the sailor now walking and swinging his previously damaged arm, seeming completely healed. It was a miracle.

The sailor claimed he could remember little of what went on in the cabin but thought that the two men had opened a leather box and taken out an object that they then placed alongside his arm. They had prayed for him, he said, and all the while he could feel the pain leaving him and his arm straightening and becoming whole again. At one time, he said, the whole cabin seemed be filled with a light that came from somewhere near him but he couldn't see where, laying on his side on a bunk with his eyes facing away from the cabin.

He had fallen asleep and was later wakened by the large man with the scarred face and told he that he was healed and could now leave the cabin. He was amazed, he said, and immediately knelt beside the bunk to pray his thanks to God. The two large men had joined him on their knees and all had prayed for some time before the two had lifted him to his feet and, together, had walked him back out to the amazement of the other sailors and the Captain.

The two travelers had subsequently left the ship and gone to speak to the rector of the old Quaker church now known as The Poor Soldiers of Christ Church, one Mordicai Starbroke.

The written history went no further. The large, kindly, mysterious travelers were not mentioned in written record again, except to say they had taken ship not long after and disappeared from sight.

Reginald St. James, an acknowledged expert in the New Testament years, had been searching for one of the most important relics from that era for years; it was rumored to have great powers, not the least among them the ability to confer the power to heal on whomever possessed it.

St. James thought he knew what he was searching for but still, the object in question had not been publicly observed for over 1,200 years. And even that account was vague. The best evidence had been the trail of unusual or miraculous healings that had occurred across Europe at such locations as Lourdes, and then, after a blank period, in the New World. With each healing there was a suggestion of the presence of a venerable object usually concealed but made present at critical times. There was no accurate account of the object. But rumor suggested a long-sought relic from the time of Christ.

St. James had been tracking miraculous healings both in history and rumor to see if he could positively identify a source to explain them. While in New Bedford he had stumbled upon the log of the whaling vessel Columbine. He had become excited by the log's account of the miraculous healing on this very island.

When he investigated further he discovered that during the next 200 years there had been sporadic reports of healing on Nantucket that might be said to be miraculous, but these healings were infrequent and hard to identify positively. Lately the island had become a feature for world media and the subject was miraculous healing. St. James had decided to visit the island disguised as the unfortunate Luke in case he found something valuable, a bad decision as he had found out. He'd had now dropped the Luke persona and taken on his own, a provision he had thankfully set up as a fallback position.

He took out a map of Nantucket and studied it carefully. Now that he was on the island he felt he was close to realizing his lifelong ambition. He could almost feel it within his grasp.

Chapter Nine

Shirley sat at her desk and stared into the computer screen. That blasted headache, she thought. Here it comes again. With a sigh she picked up the phone and dialed.

"Hello, Nantucket Cottage Hospital."

The voice was crisp but friendly.

"Jean, it's me, Shirley, how are things at the bone factory?"

"Hi, Shirl. Things are good here. What's up? Want to bust me for drugs? I've got a cupboard full."

Shirley gave the required laugh. It was an old joke between them.

"No, Jean, think I've got a problem. I need to see one of the docs. Could you arrange something?"

"What's your problem, honey?"

Jean's voice was immediately filled with concern.

"It's just that I've been having shitty headaches lately and last night at the Crawfish, I thought I might pass out."

"Hang on Shirl, give me a minute,"

Shirley heard a muffled conversation and then Jean came back on.

"Can you come in this afternoon, Shirl? Bob's on duty and he'll see you at 2. OK? I want you to come in today, don't give me any shit about being too busy, hear?"

Shirley looked at the duty board and saw Fred, Mac and Marge were going to be in the office this afternoon.

"Yeah, thanks Jean, I'll be there, just have to swing it past Taylor but I don't think he'll object. Fred's here with Mac and Marge. Unless there's a riot on Main Street they'll be able to cover for me. See you."

Shirley hung up the phone and went down to check it out with the boss. At 2 o'clock on the dot she turned her car into the parking lot and found her way into the main reception area. Joan looked up.

"Hi Deputy, I'm guilty. Better put the bracelets on or I might escape."

She smiled.

"Come on, Bob's waiting. I'll take you right in."

With that she led Shirley into an examining room. Bob Hawking, attractive, shaggy and married to Joan for the last two years, looked up from a file folder.

"Hi Shirl. Good to see you. Now, lets see what your problem's all about."

Later, as Shirley sat at her desk, the phone rang.

"Shirl, it's Bob. I've had a chance to go over your tests and discuss them with Jenny Thornton, our neurologist. She wants you back tomorrow, as early as you can get in, say about 8, OK?"

"Shit, Bob, you trying to scare me?"

"No, I'm not, but we think you have something going on in your head that needs immediate looking at so we want to get on with it. So no saying no. Tell Taylor you're checking out sick tomorrow and be here. If you like I'll call him myself and tell him you have to be here or I'll give him a procto exam next time I see him."

Bob chuckled.

"Just the old medical joke, Shirl. I don't think you'll have any trouble. Just be here."

Shirl hung up the phone and felt frightened and alone. She immediately picked up the phone and dialed.

"Hello. Maria Mitchell Observatory, Cyndy here."

"Cyndy, oh I'm so glad you're there. I'm scared."

"Whoa, Shirl, what's happening?"

Even as Cyndy uttered these words she got one of her visions. She could see what the problem was but waited for Shirl to tell her. Shirley explained what was happening. Cyndy said she would pick her up in the morning and go to the hospital with her. Shirley couldn't protest; she'd been hoping that's what Cyndy would say.

The hospital was busy. Eight in the morning and this small hospital hummed with patient care activity. One of the reasons the hospital was so busy lay in the fact that you had to be born on the island to qualify as an islander. Consequently, many Nantucket mothers-to-be, who now lived off-island, insisted on coming home to the Nantucket Cottage Hospital so their babies would be islanders. So many of them did this that it meant the Nantucket Cottage Hospital was kept busy year round and able to keep a larger staff than might have been the case for such a small resident population. The hospital could even afford facilities normally only found in big mainland hospitals. Last summer they had installed their own MRI. It was to this machine that Shirley was led.

Cyndy waited in the lobby and nervously picked her way through a National Geographic dated, she noticed with surprise, August, 1972. Was that possible? She'd heard that medical offices had out of date publications but this was ridiculous.

It was an hour later that Shirley and Bob appeared.

"Now I don't want you worrying, Shirl. Jenny and I will talk this over and we'll see what's what. You got a headache now?"

Shirley shook her head, no. She looked completely shaken.

"What is it Bob, Shirley? What's going on?

Cyndy knew what the answer would be. Her own personal MRI had scanned Shirley earlier. She'd seen the tumor. She listened to their explanations then took Shirley by the arm and gently led her back out to her truck.

"What'm I going to do, Cyn? What'm I going to do? They say I've got this great bloody thing growing in my head. They're not even sure they can do anything about it."

Shirley broke down and began to cry. Cyndy put her arms around her and let her sob on her shoulder. When finally Shirley had subsided into quick gasps and sniffling, she pulled back.

"Look Shirl, you've got to promise me that anything I tell you or do for you is a strict secret between just the two of us, OK?"

"What're you talking about Cyn, what stuff between us?"

"I'm taking you back to your house Shirl and then I'm going home. I think I can do something for you but if George or that dwarf, Maaiken, find out I'll be in deep shit. So, OK? Take it easy and I'll see what I can do."

Shirley looked confused.

"You know a little about what my grandmother taught me, Shirl. Well, I think I have a concoction that may just get rid of that nasty thing in your head. But you can't say anything to anybody. If I cure you they'll all be wanting to know what happened because these things just don't naturally happen."

"But I thought I might ask George about one of those Church cures, Cyndy."

Shirley sobbed again then sat back

"You know how people have been cured up at the Church? Well maybe they can cure me."

Cyndy looked at her friend.

"You want to go to George, that's OK with me, Shirley, you just do that. Maybe it's better that way anyway. Then I won't get into deep shit for curing you. I go curing you they might just lynch me at the Church for being a witch or something. Come on, I'll drive you right to George's office. We'll ask him now."

Cyndy put the truck into gear and drove through the quaint, winding streets with their silvered wooden houses. The occasional brick house stood out, an heritage from the old whaling days.

At Commercial Street, Cyndy parked her truck and she and Shirley walked through the old wooden doors of a building that had housed a cooperage during the whaling years. Now this historical building housed the island's most high-tech business.

The receptionist glanced up and smiled.

"Hi you two, what're you doing here? Cyndy, you want to see George?"

"Yeah, Charlie."

The diminutive woman behind the desk had always been Charlie to her friends, her maiden name having been Charles.

"Shirl and I need to see him pronto. He in?"

"Let me call, I think he has a meeting but I'm sure he'd want me to break in."

Charlie pushed some buttons and spoke into a phone.

"His meeting just broke up, Cyndy, you and Shirl go right in."

Cyndy thanked Charlie and led the way. In a moment she pushed open simple wooden doors to reveal a daunting display of electronic gadgetry. Throughout the large wooden walled room, computer screens glowed on tables and workbenches. At one side a bank of screens displayed images from satellite sources.

One screen displayed a picture of the harbor with the steamer in dock. A second showed the stream of traffic heading up the cobbles of Main Street. George liked to keep an eye on his island as well as the rest of the world. Indeed, the harbor cam and the Main Street cam were hooked into the island's web site, with thousands of hits per year.

The computer on George's desk looked deceptively small, but Cyndy knew it was the most powerful machine in the room. George had designed it himself and it broke new ground many computer companies would have liked to have access to. However, George's interests lay in the programming side of the business. The fact that he could also design leading edge computers was just a means to an end for him, better, faster computing.

"Hey girls, what's going on, why the visit?"

George looked from Cyndy to Shirley and noticed the dark circles under Shirl's eyes.

"Shirley, you look like something's really bothering you. What's your uncle done now?"

He smiled at her trying to get a smile back but failing completely. It was Cyndy who responded.

"George, Shirl's real sick. She needs help and she needs it soon. She's got a tumor growing in her head and it's serious. We just came from the hospital. George, you've got to do something. Can you speak to Maaiken and maybe get him to do a cure? God knows he's cured some pretty sick people."

Cyndy stopped, suddenly realizing she was practically shouting. The silence grew as George looked from one to the other, his quick mind trying to find the right answer. There was only one.

"I'll talk to Maaiken right away, Shirley, don't you worry. I'll go now. You take it easy and I'll call you tonight, OK?"

Shirley nodded still too upset to talk.

"Thanks George. I'll see you back at the house."

Cyndy levered Shirley out of the chair where she had collapsed and led her back to the truck.

"Come on Shirl, I'll take you home."

"No, no Cyn. I don't want to be alone. I'll go back to the office. I'm going to be OK now. George will help me. I know he will."

Cyndy looked thoughtfully at her friend. What was all this confidence in George, she wondered? It was more than she had at the moment. She dropped Shirley at the Sheriff's office and went on back to her own office at the observatory. She wondered about Shirley and George. Was she missing something?

The thought left her as she settled down to review data from her latest observations with the telescope. It wasn't until later that she had another chance to think about Shirley and George. It was then that her newly found psychic skills kicked in. She had just turned off the computer and was still staring at the dark screen. What she suddenly saw left her shocked. An image had appeared to her eyes showing Shirley and George, holding hands across a table.

"Damn," she muttered to no one but her golden lab, Lady, who as usual, had found a place under the computer table where Cyndy was working. Lady looked up but saw no reason to move more than her great golden head that she soon put back down on her paws.

"George and Shirley, they've been seeing each other. I'll be damned. What do I do about that? And, come to think about it, George was speaking up for her pretty good at the Crawfish last night."

Lady looked up again and Cyndy realized she had been speaking out loud. Stroking the dog's ears for a moment, she put the problem aside with one last damn and began to check her notes for the summer student helper who was coming in on the steamer this evening. Each summer saw the arrival of a number of young women undergraduate students looking to get some practical astronomy experience. Her latest arrival would have much to do. Cyndy had several serious research projects underway.

She stopped rubbing Lady's ears. Lady waited hopefully for a moment, giving her hand a nudge. When she got no response she put her head back down and gave a big sigh. Cyndy looked down.

"That's just the way I feel, Lady."

With that she put her attention back to her desk and her notes.

Chapter Ten

It was the kind of darkness that tantalized the eye with bare outlines where buildings and trees should be. Johnathan worked his way around the outside of the church. A fog was beginning to roll in, smelling of the sea, and gradually removing any sign of stars or moon and making the darkness more complete.

Good, couldn't have asked for better, he thought.

He had just returned from the Foredeck, a small restaurant down by New Wharf, where he had enjoyed a dinner of grilled bluefish plus an imaginative garden salad. The fish was the freshest he had ever tasted; a local fisherman had caught and delivered several bluefish just that afternoon. When Johnathan arrived at the church he had decided to wait and take cover in the scrub brush that surrounded the church grounds.

As he watched he had seen all lights go out and Maaiken, himself, come out and lock the side service door. Johnathan had waited for another hour but no one had approached the church, all interior lights had remained off. There was no sign that anyone was in the building.

Earlier Johnathan had spent part of the afternoon with a tour group who were looking at the old building. It was an historical building and was on the official tour taken by visitors to Nantucket. The clock in the tower was one of the most interesting artifacts on the island. Designed and built by an early inhabitant, this complex clock had four different faces, each offering a separate activity provided by animated mechanical figures. Each face went through a ritual, ending up in a beating out of the hours. The clock had been written up in many famous magazines, not the least the National Geographic in 1972.

Now he could hear the clock as its insides ground and groaned. Finally there was a massive stirring as the mechanized action began on all four sides. Taking advantage of the noise, Johnathan slipped down to a side door and began to work on the lock. First he slowed his mind, clearing all other images and thoughts until he could clearly see the inside of the lock. Now his mind grasped at the mechanical parts and caused them to rotate, until, with a click, the bolt slid back and the door swung open under his hand.

It was a neat trick if you could do it. Johnathan knew of maybe a dozen others in the world who could duplicate the feat. He grinned as he rested. It always gave him an adrenaline rush, using this power. It also drained him for a few moments and he had to rest.

He thought of the amazing things that real Avatars could do and did do on a regular basis and it exhausted him just to think about it. He could affect the physical world to a degree but it took great concentration and energy. He'd once tried to materialize objects but he'd found it too exhausting to be worth doing on a regular basis. Maybe with more practice and a lot more spiritual development. Right now he'd have to be satisfied with his agelessness, psychic abilities and the odd picking of locks.

It was a great help to be able to read minds and guess intent, especially if it was someone who might want to shoot or knife him. Maybe he should change his occupation. This made him laugh quietly as he continued to work on breaking into the church.

His visit this afternoon had enabled him to pick out where the alarm sensors and the main control box were located. With luck he'd be able to disable the alarm with his mind, but only because a keyed lock controlled the system. He should be able to turn that lock, too.

He was so sure he wouldn't be disturbed that he relaxed his usual vigilance; he was certain all members of the church had been long gone. The door had just opened to his gentle touch when he stopped, startled. He sensed another sentient being within the darkened building. He froze and listened while his mind probed, to try and locate the life force he could feel.

Johnathan was certain it wasn't in the immediate vicinity, but this changed everything. How could he have missed anyone? Was someone sleeping in the building, maybe a watchman of some sort? Still he listened and probed. If he didn't get to the alarm box with in the next 36 seconds the alarm would summon the police and then he would have to go without finding out anything about the building.

Still he waited until he knew he had delayed too long. He slipped back, out the door, and on down the hill. At the foot of the street he watched as a Sheriff's car went silently by.

Smart, he thought. Want to catch me by surprise, do you? No noise, no siren. All you will find is an open door that looks like it was left unlocked by accident. No sign of a break-in. Nothing to alert Maaiken and his group that someone is looking for answers.

Johnathan reviewed his options. Maybe he'd better ask his friendly astronomer what she might know about the church. After all, her computer whiz kid of a husband was one of the church's leaders. He'd look into that option tomorrow. He stretched muscles that had become stiff during his waiting; a good night's sleep wouldn't hurt. It had been some weeks since he'd allowed himself the luxury of a full night's sleep. Maybe this would be a bit of a vacation as well as a job of detection. The client could wait. Better to look after himself.

With this momentous decision in hand, Johnathan walked on until he found himself once more in front of 7 Milk Street. The light was dim, stars had reclaimed the sky as the fog decided to move on and obscure some other part of the sea.

He lingered to admire the cold brilliance of the constellation above his head, the familiar "W" of Cassiopeia, a beautiful sight under these low light conditions. Even the Milky Way showed as a twisted veil of glowing light. Then he froze as his never-still radar picked up a presence moving toward him from the bottom of the street.

Curious, Johnathan stepped back into the shelter of some bushes and waited. Before long the figure of Reginald St. James appeared, walking softly but without care to the front of the house, then climbing the steps of Mrs. Tonshirek's house to disappear through the door. Johnathan waited for another 15 minutes before doing the same. By this time all was quiet in the house. Shortly after, so was Johnathan.

Back at the church, Fred and Shirley, working night detail, were studying the open side door.

"No marks of any kind, Shirl. Looks like someone just left it unlocked and maybe a gust of air pushed it open, setting off the alarm."

As he spoke a shadow moved in the doorway.

"Shit, Fred, what's that?"

Shirley was in the act of drawing her gun when two bright eyes reflected their flashlights and the church cat came to check on the open door. It then checked out the two Sheriff's deputies.

"Christ, Toby, you shouldn't sneak around when two armed and dangerous deputies are looking for something to shoot at."

Toby took this in with an unblinking gaze, paused a moment to stare down Shirley, then turned back into the church. Really, these people were too much.

Fred closed the door.

"I'd better radio in and suggest someone phone whoever's on the list to come lock up this door. Then we can go get a coffee."

Within a quarter of an hour Maaiken appeared only to claim vigorously that he had tried all the doors before leaving and this one had most certainly been locked when he left.

Fred was unimpressed.

"Well, Maaiken, it ain't locked now so lock up will you, so we can all get on with our lives."

Maaiken glared at Fred and Shirley but did as suggested and left without saying another word.

"Come on Fred, coffee's on me."

With that the two went back to their car and the responsibilities of policing this usually quiet island.

Chapter Eleven

Johnathan woke early the next day and was quickly out of the house, depending on finding coffee and a bun at Island Coffee on Main Street before tackling Cyndy. He thoughtfully ate his way through a blueberry muffin and sipped his skinny latté as he considered just why he had come to this island in the first place.

A client who preferred to be anonymous had contacted the agency that took assignments for him. He had been commissioned to try and find out the truth about the cures that were taking place on Nantucket. It was something he, personally, had more than a casual interest in. There might be something supernatural and that was his field of interest. After all, he was a bit supernatural himself. Well, actually, very natural but science hadn't caught up with the real nature of nature yet, if ever it would.

He grinned. Even if he were willing to give a demonstration of his unusual powers, there would always be some skeptics who would never believe him but would find another explanation. The Great Randy was particularly good at that. An expert at illusion and stage magic, Randy could usually figure out an illusion that would pretty much cover any sort of real supernatural event. And that was it. The majority of the public didn't really want to have the truth. Like the movie had said, they couldn't handle the truth.

Johnathan checked his watch. The astronomer should be in her office by now. He pulled his large frame off the stool, smiled at the woman who had served him and was now watching him, fascinated by his size and cute looks, paid his bill and exited out onto Main Street.

Cyndy looked up in surprise when her secretary said a large, dishy gent wanted to see her. When Johnathan filled her doorframe, she smiled. She had been thinking of this big, attractive man for some time and wondering if she would ever see him again. And here he was.

"Hi, Johnny.... no, Johnathan. That's right isn't it?"

Cyndy grinned in welcome and told him to come in and sit down.

"I didn't think I'd see you again. I know you're not a regular here on Nantucket or I'd remember you."

She smiled shyly.

"You do stand out. May I call you John? Johnathan seems so formal somehow."

Johnathan regarded her in silence, sensing instead with his mind to see what he could pick up.

Suddenly Cyndy looked straight at him, looking puzzled.

"What are you doing? I feel like there're fingers going through my head. That's you doing it, right?"

For some reason, unusual as this was, Cyndy felt no fear but just a curiosity. The big man was not like any others she was acquainted with. She knew this but didn't know how or why.

Johnathan was as surprised as Cyndy. People normally didn't know when he was probing their thoughts. He'd been right. She was a natural chosen one. He thought carefully before answering.

In the meantime a large golden lab came out from under Cyndy's desk and came to stand in front of him, looking at him somewhat suspiciously. Johnathan reached out a hand and let the dog inspect it. Finally Lady came closer and pushed her muzzle up against him. Johnathan smiled and rubbed her ears.

"Well, John, are you going to just stand there and play with my dog? Who are you really and what are you doing with my mind?"

At last Johnathan made up his mind. It was risky but he'd have to be truthful with this one. In fact she could read him just as easily as he could read her if only she knew how to use her powers.

"Cyndy, listen to me for a while and let me tell you some things you don't know about yourself. It's not why I came here but I see I can't talk to you without telling you the truth. Fact is you have powers you don't even know about yet but I know if I try to lie to you, you will know it right away."

Now it was Cyndy's turn to be puzzled.

"Powers? What makes you think I have powers whatever that means? You sound just like my grandmother."

"Cyndy, I don't know about your grandmother but I do know something about your powers and I think you know a little about them yourself. It's true, isn't it? You know things about people that you shouldn't be able to know?"

He watched her puzzled look change to one of suspicion.

"Somehow you've been granted powers that very few in the world ever have. Have you ever used them? Come on, Cyndy, you can tell me."

Johnathan stopped and focused on Lady.

"Let's see. Your name is.... Lady."

Lady looked up and gave a little bark.

"That's right, Lady, and hello to you."

Johnathan smiled into the brown eyes and focused on the doggy mind behind them.

"Tell your mistress I'm a good guy, Lady, that's a good dog."

Cyndy watched this by-play in silence, then amazement as Lady left Johnathan and came over to her and gave a small whimper, tail wagging like fury.

"What are you doing with my dog? How can you make her do something like that? Who the hell are you?"

Cyndy was both angry and a little frightened.

"It's OK Cyndy. Like I said, I'm one of the good guys. You have no idea just how good."

This seemed to amuse Johnathan as he gave a little laugh. Lady barked at him then. Cyndy continued to look angry.

"OK then what's your game, mister? What exactly is going on here? I need some answers and I need them now."

Just then the door opened and George came into the room.

"Sorry, Cyndy, Jane said you had a visitor but this can't wait. I've been talking to Maaiken and he's agreed to do a cure for Shirley on Sunday, during his regular service. Only does these cures on a Sunday, you know, and he'll do it this Sunday. And she'll be cured, Cyndy, she'll be cured. I know that. It never fails. When Maaiken says he'll cure her, he'll cure her."

Johnathan watched, noticing George's obvious agitation. He didn't need to be psychic to see that George was in an emotional state. He looked over at Cyndy and could see similar agitation but not the same somehow. He waited to see what played out here. Maybe this was going to an opportunity for him to learn more about this whole curing business. Cyndy looked as if she might cry.

"Oh George, thank God. I've been so worried about Shirley. She won't let me help her. She wants Maaiken to cure her."

Then she stopped as George looked puzzled.

"What d'you mean Cyndy, Shirley won't let you help her? What kinda help could you give her anyway? You been fooling with those plants again?"

Suddenly George was angry.

"Shit, Cyndy, how many times I do have to tell you, Maaiken'll skin us both alive if you do any healing? He's peculiar that way. He and God are the only ones allowed to heal here, save for the stuff they do over at the hospital. Make him mad and we'll both suffer."

He gave Cyndy an angry glare.

"Damn, I knew I shouldn't have let you make those poultices and things around the house. I thought you were just playing at stuff like your grandmother, but if you think you can cure something as bad as cancer then forget it. Just forget it."

George seemed to notice Johnathan for the first time, although Johnathan was a hard man not to notice, being as big as he was.

"Sorry man. You shouldn't be here when I'm talking to my wife. Do you mind getting out?"

Now it was Cyndy who was angry and loud.

"You get out of here, George, and leave Johnathan out of it. You want to shout at me then it can wait until we're back at the house. You can shout at me all you want to then."

She stopped for a moment and her voice changed to a softer tone.

"In the meantime, thanks for speaking to Maaiken and getting him to do something for Shirl."

Then the hard edge returned to her voice as she fixed her husband with a hard look.

"Just get the hell out of my office, George. I'll see you later."

George took a step forward as if to take some physical action causing both Lady and Johnathan to start up, Lady growling and Johnathan feeling like maybe he should be growling too.

George stopped in mid-step, sensing he was outnumbered, then turned towards the door. He shouted over his shoulder as he went out.

"Just remember what I've said, Cyndy. You don't do healing on this island. Just remember that."

With this last order, he pulled the door shut with a slam.

Cyndy looked at her guest, her eyes now brimming with tears.

"I'm sorry John, you shouldn't have to be witness to a husband-and-wife quarrel. I just can't really talk to him anymore. He makes me so angry. And I guess I'm pretty good at making him angry, too."

She broke off and reached to take a tissue out of a box on her desk. She sobbed a bit then, wiping her eyes, looked back at Johnathan. Her voice quivered.

"Can we have this conversation later? I just can't handle anything else right now and besides, I've got to get this work done before my summer students all rebel and go back to the mainland or something. Can we talk later?"

She smiled a small smile at Johnathan and he felt his knees weaken. What was this woman doing to him?

"Of course, Cyndy. Maybe we could meet later for coffee or something. Would you meet me at the Crawfish later? Maybe around five?"

He realized he was pleading. Not like him. He smiled a little bit sheepishly.

Cyndy came to his rescue, now over her tears.

"Thanks, John, I'd like to talk more. In fact we have to talk more. You've gone and got me intrigued. You're going to have to explain just what the hell you were talking about back there before George horned in. But it'll have to be sometime later. There's too much going on now what with Shirl being ill and getting a healing on Sunday and all. Please. Let it go for now. I'll let you know when I can see you again and talk."

Johnathan realized he'd been dismissed by this neat, young woman and, smiling down at her, turned and let himself out the door, closing it softly behind him. Cyndy stared at the door for several minutes before tossing the wad of damp tissue into the wastebasket at her feet and getting her attention back to the work on her desk.

Chapter Twelve

Jeremy opened Maaiken's door and took a cautious look inside, an excuse ready on his lips. But the excuse remained unused. Just as Jeremy had suspected, the room was empty although he had seen Maaiken enter not more that a half-hour before, and the man hadn't come back out. Maaiken had pulled one of his disappearing tricks, but now Jeremy thought he knew where to look for the miracle.

He walked carefully over to the fireplace, ignoring the cat that had slipped into the room as he opened the door. The cat watched as Jeremy walked over to the fireplace, but had other plans. She quickly jumped up on the great desk and found her favorite pool of sunshine. The pool lapped over an untidy pile of hand-written pages and the cat carefully rearranged them by pushing several onto the floor. Then, with a languid air, she curled up and watched Jeremy pushing and pulling at the bookshelves. Jeremy stopped and thought out loud.

"There must be a spring or latch or something to push."

The cat twitched its ears but pretended to be uninterested. Jeremy, concentrating on the shelves, glanced at the heavy fireplace mantel. It was then he noticed a faint difference in the color of the wood. It looked as if someone was used to putting his hand on the wood. The thumbprint was missing. Missing?

Jeremy reached out and put his left hand onto the discolored area. As he did his thumb naturally fell below the board while the palm and fingers fitted exactly onto the area of slightly different tone. He looked beneath the mantel. Almost where his thumb now lay was a thick knot in the wood. Jeremy put his thumb on the knot and pushed gently, feeling it give slightly. He stopped. He had found it. Jeremy stepped back from the fireplace, stooping to look at the knot in the thick pine board.

"Yeah, that's it. That's what old Maaiken's been pushing to open this wall up. Shit, now what do I do? Maaiken's inside there somewhere and I don't dare open it up now. Better wait and try sometime when he's out."

The cat lifted her head as she listened to all this. So did George from his office. George had just turned on the hall camera in front of Maaiken's office when he'd noticed Jeremy leave the hall area, poke his head in through the door, and then enter with careful steps. George reached out to turn on the study cam. George had planted small cameras in several strategic locations throughout the church disguised as fire sensors. Well, they were fire sensors, too, but equipped with tiny cameras George had designed. They were also equipped to pick up sound and could be set to detect motion.

Now George watched, fascinated, as Jeremy pulled and pushed at the bookshelves, wondering what was up. He also noticed with amusement as the cat strewed Maaiken's papers before curling up in the middle where the sun was strongest. Now he listened as Jeremy spoke to the walls, the cat and, as it turned out, to George.

But, wondered George, what was Jeremy going on about? What was that bit about Maaiken being in there? And what was it Maaiken pushed? To do what? George had never bothered to monitor Maaikin's study fearing that, somehow, the dangerous dwarf might find out. Now his curiosity was getting the better of him.

George watched Jeremy retrace his steps to the door and leave. The cat seemed at peace with all this. After all, the cat had seen Maaiken disappear through those bookshelves many times. She had thought maybe Jeremy was going to disappear too, but instead had watched as Jeremy left the room. She closed her eyes and dreamed a cat dream.

George continued to look at the now silent room. Adjusting the zoom control on the camera, he brought the fireplace mantel into close-up and studied the place where Jeremy had been holding his hand. The camera had excellent definition and clarity. In close-up he could see the slight discoloration that Jeremy had noticed. It was exactly where Jeremy had placed his hand before stooping and peering underneath.

Definitely something there, he thought. Now the remark about Maaiken being in there began to make sense. Whatever was under the mantel might be a latch or spring that opened a hidden door. OK, now I've got you Maaiken. I've always known you had a secret hidden away. Now I know where you are hiding it. He adjusted the camera zoom to a long shot of the room so he could see the bookshelves and desk.

With that accomplished, George pulled his attention back to the work on the screen immediately in front of him, leaving the other screen still showing the inside of Maaiken's study. He would wait and see if he could catch Maaiken coming back into the room.

It was about 45 minutes later when the motion sensor buzzed and drew George's attention to the desk screen with the view of Maaiken's study. He looked over to see a section of the bookshelves had swung open and watched as Maaiken walked through, pushing the shelves back in place as he did so.

George smiled and flipped the switch that deactivated the screen. He was learning things only Maaiken had known up to this time. Mind you someone else was in on this. He'd have to think that out. Jeremy could be dangerous to his ambitions. George did not want anyone else in on Maaiken's secrets. He wanted them all to himself. Whatever was hidden behind those bookshelves, it had to be something to do with the healings. Whatever that was would be worth a fortune if he had it to himself.

He leaned back in his ergonomically correct leather chair and mused. Imagine being able to cure the sick millionaires of the world. Oh yes, that little secret would be worth millions. He wasn't going to let a jerk like Jeremy screw that up. George settled back to writing code again, a serious look on his face.

Maaiken paused, blinking in the bright sunlight, as he came into the study from the cavern below the church. He caught sight of the cat still curled up on his desk. Angry at first, he curbed his rage. He wasn't about to throw anything else through a window. He'd done enough damage with the pewter candlestick. He started to tiptoe towards his desk when the cat, alert from the moment the bookshelves had swung open, prepared herself to spring. Just as Maaiken reached the desk the cat twisted and leapt straight at the man, catching him totally by surprise and causing him to stumble backwards, catching his heel in the edge of the woven area rug and falling, crashing to the floor. Even as he hit he felt his left arm go numb.

Maaiken lay stunned on the floor as the cat, now not threatened, walked slowly towards the open window immediately behind the desk. With a quick leap she reached the window ledge. With another she was gone, landing softly and then walking through the bushes that lined the garden below the window. In a moment she was lost to sight, had anyone been looking.

Maaiken, in the meantime, was trying to get to his feet but the onset of pain kept him anchored to the floor. He groaned then shouted.

"Jeremy.... Jeremy."

Jeremy stood by the door where he had been listening to see if he could hear Maaiken re-entering his study. He had heard the crash and the groan. As he heard his name called he quickly threw open the door and ran to where Maaiken lay, stretched out on the floor, groaning and holding one arm with the other.

The motion detector connected with the study cam buzzed. George was deep into code writing and it was some moments before he shifted his attention from his work to light up the screen that showed Maaiken's office. He watched with fascination. He had missed the beginning of the action that had caused Maaiken to end up on the floor and hit rewind on the data storage device that constantly recorded that specific camera. Recording devices backed up all the cameras he had installed. Now he saw the whole incident with the cat on a second screen. George spoke to the air.

"Silly bugger, why does he chase that cat all the time? Now look at the mess he's in. Wonder if I should go over? I could say I was just looking for some advice for the Sunday service."

While George considered this he watched and listened to the unfolding drama.

"What's wrong, Rev? How did this happen?"

Maaiken groaned and cursed at Jeremy.

"Screw how it happened, Jeremy. What's more important, I think I may have broken my arm. Come here, help me up."

"Broken your arm? I should call 911. Get an ambulance over here."

Maaiken took a deep breath, groaned again, and made himself speak slowly, his voice even more grating than usual with the pain.

"No, Jeremy, don't do anything but help me get up off this floor. OK? Now take it easy, get your arm under my right armpit. It's the left I think is broken."

Jeremy carefully put his arm under the indicated armpit and began to lever Maaiken up into a sitting position, then, finally up on his feet. All the while, Maaiken swore and railed at him to be more careful.

"You sure I shouldn't get you help, Rev?"

"No, I'm OK, thanks Jeremy. Sorry if I got a little excited there. Damn arm hurts like a son of bitch. Look you go on about your business and I'll look after this, OK?"

Jeremy started to protest but Maaiken gave him a push with his good arm and Jeremy went back out of the study, looking behind him with a puzzled frown. When the door had clicked shut, Maaiken slowly walked to the mantel and groaning and grunting, reached the latch and managed to click open the shelves with his right hand. He shuffled through the opening and it closed behind him. George watched and wondered aloud.

"Now what? Where's he gone? Why wouldn't he let Jeremy call an ambulance? Gotta keep an eye on this."

The phone rang.

"Yeah, George here. What Jeremy? Maaiken's done what? Broken his arm? No kidding. He on the way to the hospital?"

George listened while Jeremy explained and asked what he should do.

"Look, Jeremy. Maaiken knows what he's doing. But keep an ear open in case he changes his mind or needs some help. OK?"

George hung up the phone and laughed out loud. The situation was too funny. Then he had a thought and looked serious again. His thoughts became words for only the walls to hear.

"Wonder if this will change his plans to do a healing for Shirley this Sunday? Hope not, the kid needs that healing badly if those tests mean anything. Maybe Cyndy will have to do something for her but I don't know what she could do. She doesn't really know shit about healing, I mean a poultice is one thing but what else could she do that would make any real difference?"

Still musing out loud, George again went back to work, keeping on the alert for more from the Maaiken study cam.

Chapter Thirteen

Maaiken reached the light switch with his good arm. The dim light revealed a set of steep steps that curved down into the semi-darkness. Fortunately the rope rail was on his right; he could steady himself as he carefully started down to the secret cavern hidden below the church.

The steps ended in a freak natural cave that showed signs of having been carved from the rock thousands of years earlier. –The Quaker church fathers had discovered it while digging for a well in the basement of the old church. The leaders had decided then to keep it a secret from the rest of the island. The civil war raging between the North and South was creating great danger for Nantucket and the church elders felt a bolt hole might come in handy if the British attacked the island.

Over the years the space had been improved upon. Even when the first church burned in the great fire of 1846, those few who knew of the cave had managed to keep the secret during the rebuilding. With the advent of electricity, they had extended wiring into the space. The entrance had first been a trap door leading from the original well opening. With the rebuilding the entrance had been hidden behind the bookshelves next to the old chimney in the Rector's study.

Maaiken's family had long been among the leaders of the early church. When the Quaker faith had faded, the Starbroke elders became involved with an obscure eastern sect of religious thought. Over the succeeding years, the Starbroke family kept the secret of the cavern until only the elder in charge knew and passed the secret on to the next Starbroke when it came time to pass the leadership on to a younger man.

This was the state of affairs when, after an adventurous life in the middle east with the Poor Soldiers of Christ, Mordicai Starbroke had come back home and ascended to the leadership of the church, taking over from his grandfather when his own father perished during the great epidemic. It was he alone who knew of the secret cave the year the Columbine made port and the sacred object was deposited into his care by two mysterious men. There had been much fighting and bloodshed among different factions who wanted to own the object. The Poor

Soldiers of Christ finally decided it was necessary to find a hiding place for it until the world was a more peaceful place and ready to receive its great powers.

Alas, as often happens to great plans, the world moved on until the secret resting place of the sacred object was forgotten. One by one the original schemers died without passing on the secret of the hiding place. Now only one person knew of its existence and that person was the head of an obscure church on a small, windswept island in the Atlantic Ocean.

So it came that Maaiken was the only one alive in this modern era who knew the whereabouts of the relic. However, at first even he hadn't known of the power this object could bring, the miracles it could accomplish. Like all accidents, it was a combination of unexpected events that revealed to Maaiken something of the awesome power that was within his grasp.

As he slowly descended into the cavern he remembered how he had first learned the great secret. It had happened when his father had become frail and had decided to pass the leadership to his son. It was then that he had first shown Maaiken the secret entrance to the cavern and then the awesome secret hidden below.

Maaiken had been astonished, first by the oath his father forced him to take, and then by the enormity of the secret. Together, on that fateful day, he and his father had descended the steps to the opening to the cavern. Leading his son the father had stopped at the end of a passage. Maaiken, now aware of a strange force pushing at him, had been puzzled but the puzzle was soon solved as his father placed his hand where it could connect with a small outcropping of rock. As with the bookshelves in the study, a door opened where no door had been visible to the eye.

He and his father entered a small room, dark but for the glow that came from an elaborate table set in the center of the room. Maaiken tried to see the source of the glow, but the darkness made this impossible. The force now was a gale and he felt he had to lean into it. Suddenly he was surprised to find his father kneeling and pulling him down on his knees.

"Be most reverent, Maaiken, you are in front of a relic that came directly from Christ. Without the proper prayers it can be as deadly as it is healing."

Maaiken was dumbfounded; he wondered if his father has failed more than had been evident. Still the thrust of some strange force made him gasp.

"What are you saying, father? How could this object come from Christ? Why that would make it nearly 2,000 years old! What is it?"

The old man stayed silent for a long moment before replying.

"It is the cup passed by Christ at the Last Supper, the Holy Grail. It is priceless. And it continues to glow with the spirit."

"But, but..."

Maaiken found himself speechless at the idea.

"How did it get here? How could that be? What is this strange force I feel?"

The old man was quiet for a while then, when he spoke, it was in a voice Maaiken had never heard before.

"Hush my son. First the prayers or neither of us will live long."

With that he pulled his son to a kneeling position along side of his own kneeling body. A song flowed, sweetly, strangely from his lips. Then a flow of words in a tongue Maaiken couldn't identify. Then just words of praise for God in English.

All the while Maaiken felt the force beginning to fade until he could kneel without feeling as if it would blow him over. He listened as his father spoke to him.

"Our family has been custodian of this spiritual relic since it arrived here back in 1732."

Again the old man faltered, took a breath and continued.

"Legend has it that two of the last Poor Soldiers of Christ brought the Grail here for safety. As the story goes, they were transported here on the whaler, Columbine, returning on its last leg of a three-year journey. The Columbine had stopped in at a port in Lower Canada to pick up water and other supplies.

It was there that two men approached the captain, a man named Rodriguese, and offered to pay him for passage to Nantucket and to our illustrious ancestor, Mordicai, who, as it happened, had spent his youth serving in the same order as these two knights. Seeking safe refuge for their priceless artifact, they chose to bring it to Mordicai Starbroke for safekeeping. Then, as they sailed back, it is thought their ship foundered in a great storm and they and their knowledge of the hiding place of the Grail was destroyed."

He paused, his breathing shaky and labored.

"The Grail has been kept safely here ever since although it has been sought for centuries by archaeologists, historians and others more aware of its power. I fear it is still sought. For that reason, only one member of our family is ever allowed into the secret at a time. The time has come to pass on this great secret and now it is yours to protect."

Maaiken felt his father put something into his hand. In the dim light all he could make out were two small objects with chains.

"Here, when the time comes you will need these amulets. They have the power to protect anyone who ever need handle the cup directly. The original bearers of the cup left them here when they gave the cup to Mordicai."

The room seemed to grow darker. Maaiken felt a chill spread through his body. Such knowledge seemed too much for the young man to bear. Finally his father regained his feet and led the still numb Maaiken out of the room.

As time passed, Maaiken became more used to the idea of a demonstrable spiritual presence within the church. However, it was only after his father's passing and his complete assumption of power and leadership of the church that he had opportunity to further explore the incredible object in the secret cavern.

How he learned the truth happened more or less by accident, as many good things do.

Determined to know more about the mysterious Grail, Maaiken had decided to bring some light into the room where it was kept. As far as he could tell, his father had never brought light into the room. All that could be seen was what was revealed by the glow of the object itself.

Bolstering his courage, Maaiken put one of the amulets around his neck and took a Coleman lamp into the room to finally examine the mysterious box in detail. As he approached the table he put the Coleman lamp on the floor and walked closer.

His first surprise was when the amulet around his neck began to glow. In the glare of the Coleman he could now see the ancient leather box on the table. Even in the light from the lamp a dim, purple glow was visible around the box. As he approached more closely he could read an inscription on the side of the box warning all to beware of directly observing the contents on fear of instant death. Strangely the wording was in English.

Maaiken considered this for some time. He couldn't believe that such a revered object would actually be harmful. However, to be on the safe side, he decided to leave it alone for the moment and turned towards the door, only to knock against the Coleman. Instinctively grasping it to prevent it from overturning, he badly burned his hand.

The searing pain of the burn made him faint. When he finally regained consciousness, he lay quite still for a moment in the now darkened chamber. For a moment he couldn't remember what had happened. The deep purple blue glow cast by the precious artifact was the only light.

At last he pushed up from the floor. In doing so he knocked against the Coleman, now extinguished, dark and cold. The sight of the lamp, only just visible in the gloom of the small room, revived the memory of his contact with the searing heat and the burning of his hand.

He walked through the door to the light of the outer chamber all the while trying to see how badly he had damaged his hand. As he got into the brighter light he could see there was no sign of a burn or other damage. The skin of the right hand was as bright and healthy looking as its mate.

What, he wondered, what on earth was happening? Had he imagined the whole incident? But then he looked back into the smaller chamber where he could still see the outline of the fallen lamp. No, it was as he had remembered. He had grabbed at the red-hot globe, burning himself so badly that the pain had knocked him out. Fortunately, the well-designed Coleman had extinguished itself when knocked over.

Again he looked at his hand, unable to believe what he saw. It was fully healed. Puzzled but too disoriented to think more on the mystery he made his way back up to the church study. It was only gradually that he became conscious of the magnitude of miracle that had happened to him. Only then did he have time to think on this miracle and start to realize just how valuable it would be if what had happened to him could also be made to happen to others.

He would have to find out. He made his plans carefully. The following day he caught the mouser that Jeremy kept in the church. Without a qualm he broke one of its legs. While it screamed in pain he took it down to the cavern and into the most secret room. Almost as he entered the cat began to calm down, its anguished motions and sounds quieting. He watched all this as he set the cat on the floor in front of the glowing object.

Then he waited and watched in amazement as the cat's leg began to straighten. The cat mewed and wiggled, now in some sort of ecstasy. Within minutes the leg was normal, without the ugly bend induced by the break. The cat remained still now, seemingly frozen or in a trance. About fifteen minutes had gone by when the cat slowly sat up and began to lick the previously injured leg. Then, without any apparent difficulty, it finally stood up and began to walk towards the open door.

Maaiken watched in awe. The cat turned to face him. He could swear it glared at him before walking sedately out of his sight. Still Maaiken stood, transfixed, unable to command his legs to carry him back out into the lighted cave. Finally he dropped in front of the faintly glowing object and began to pray as he had never, ever prayed before. If he had ever doubted the presence of God, or the Son of God, he would never do so again.

It had taken him much time and practice, but Maaiken found that this miraculous healing power could be transferred to a small vial of oil. When he used the oil to anoint anyone or, indeed any living thing, with an illness or injury that person, animal or even insect would be whole and normal once more. It was a power that would make Maaiken famous throughout the world. It would also drive him slightly insane. Power can do that sometimes and Maaiken had never been the most stable of men.

For Maaiken it made him more and more cruel and uncaring. He was now formidable, unbalanced and dangerous. He would brook no competition on his island. Oh yes, Nantucket was his island. He only tolerated the islanders, summer visitors and day visitors that supported the island's economy. Only the Island Cottage Hospital was allowed to compete with his curing. Even Maaiken had his limitations. Birthing babies was beyond even his miraculous powers. Besides, it always made him look better when the doctors diagnosed some virulent illness and then found it cured when they re-examined a patient after his cure.

Maaiken limited his curing. It mattered not to him what trauma was afflicting the people or who was in trouble. He only cured one day a week and then he limited his cures to one or two at a time.

He had agreed to take Shirley Woodstock for one of his healings this Sunday. It was important to keep George on his side. He needed his lieutenant's full co-operation to keep others doing his bidding. Doing this favor would ensure that George kept his place.

It made Maaiken laugh to himself sometimes. He was probably the only one who knew of George and Shirley's ongoing affair. Normally Maaiken would have objected but he got perverse pleasure out of knowing how this would ultimately hurt George's wife, the brainy bitch, Cyndy, with all her airs and her grandmother's herb garden. Oh he knew about the herb garden. He knew many things about Nantucket. His spies were numerous. Anyone he cured was his for life.

Maaiken entered the sacred chamber and stood, bathed in the dim purple blue glow. Almost at once the terrible, ragged pain in his arm started to diminish. He sank down onto the coldness of the stone floor and waited, feeling a sense of euphoria filling his body and mind. He lay down. His mind gave over to a dreamy state and he thought he could see his father and mother. But then he saw only a wondrous light and floated away from all care.

It was about twenty minutes later that he came to his senses once more, feeling the hardness of the floor under his prone body. He grunted and moved his left arm experimentally. Oh God! He levered himself up until he was on his knees facing the dim light. He began to pray.

When later he re-entered his study his arm was perfectly normal. Another miracle. It was the first time he'd experienced it for himself since the day he had burned himself so badly. And it had felt so good. Maybe he should break his arm every day. That sense of euphoria could get to be addictive.

He looked around for the cat. He felt like thanking it but it was gone. He wondered if it had left by the door or window. Then he turned his thoughts to tomorrow, Sunday, and how he would stage the healing for Shirley.

Chapter Fourteen

The Sunday dawned a misty gray, with a weak sun struggling to burn off the high fog. The calm air was beginning to give way to a light southerly breeze and the day promised warmth and comfort and lazy hours on the beach or sailing the coastal waters. Offshore, a long slow line of swells came from over the horizon to eventually smash themselves in a glorious roar on the south-side beaches. It was the kind of day off-islanders came to Nantucket to enjoy.

What was planned at the church for this day was another reason so many now flocked to this island.

Out among the rolling breakers a flash of red showed from time to time. The strong arms pulled against the salty, roiling water. Johnathan breathed with the ease of an athlete as he thrust and kicked and propelled his body joyfully and with abandon.

Finally, with reluctance, he turned back towards the shore, letting the flow of the breakers carry him forward until he felt the sandy bottom under his feet. Bracing his body against the force of both breakers and undertow, he staggered and laughed as he finally reached the beach. It was such a wonderful feeling to stretch his muscles and feel the warmth of the sun and cooling of the light breeze. A circling gull laughed along with him, alone on this stretch of deserted sand.

Johnathan toweled vigorously and lay for a moment to let the strengthening sun and breeze complete the drying of his large, well-muscled body. This was such a wonderful world. If only people would realize that and try to preserve it instead of treating it as if there was another world to go to when they had ruined this one.

Too much philosophy for so early in the morning, he thought. He pulled on his shirt, picked up his towel and trudged back over the dunes to where he had left his bicycle.

It was time to be getting ready to attend the church service and to witness the healing by Maaiken Starbroke. Johnathan felt the excitement building. Here was the mystery about to be witnessed. Here was why he had come back to Nantucket in the first place.

As he cycled along the path to the road, his wheels bumping and jolting over small stones, a brown rabbit scampered away from his front wheel and disappeared into tall beach grass. Gulls wheeled in the clear, azure sky and the sun continued to strengthen and heat his body as he turned onto the paved road.

His body glowed and sweat streaked his forehead; his mind toyed with the puzzle of what exactly he was looking for here. He knew whatever it was, a great power, a spiritual power was at work. What he wanted to know was what and how. Specifically, if he could locate the source, he was commissioned to try to retrieve that source for his client, should such a thing be possible. Johnathan didn't think he would actually steal whatever it was. His superiors frowned on stealing. Still, he'd play it by ear and see what was what. The chase was the exciting thing.

Johnathan pulled up to the front of 7 Milk Street. It was still early but there was already activity at almost all houses on the street. This was a town that attended church. But space was limited, what with the sensation caused by the local healing, and Maaiken's wrath at non-attendance was not a pretty sight.

Most of the parishioners were up early to get breakfast into mothers, fathers, children, aunts, uncle, grandmothers and grandfathers and to reach the church ahead of the mob of off-islanders. Seating was guaranteed to the Nantucket congregation but only if in place at least fifteen minutes before the bell sounded in the steeple.

Johnathan hurried to dress and throw a kiss in the direction of Mrs. Tonshirek before remounting his bicycle. He peddled with quick, firm strokes that carried him with amazing speed up to where the church perched overlooking the town.

He was early, it would be an hour yet before the church bells would ring out, but a small crowd had already gathered in front of the closed doors. The Sheriff and a couple of deputies kept watch over the crowd, trying to anticipate and prevent trouble before it could get out of hand. As he watched, Cyndy's bright red truck arrived, reflecting a glare in the new sun. Cyndy and George got out with Shirley and turned to enter the church. Cyndy caught sight of Johnathan, hard not to catch sight of Johnathan, red-haired and standing several inches above the usual crowd.

Cyndy waved and beckoned him over. Jonathan pushed through the crowd and joined her. Cyndy grabbed at his arm.

"Johnathan, you coming to the service?"

Cyndy was smiling and looking relieved, as if she needed a friend. Shirley looked nervously at him.

"Hi Johnny, come to see me get my head fixed?"

She tried to smile but looked more likely to cry. George looked at him as if wishing him to disappear. Johnathan gave him back a big smile.

"Hi George, nice to see you again. Understand you're a senior elder here. I was hoping to catch you up and see if you would be kind enough to get me a seat. I'm real anxious to witness one of the miracles I've heard so much about."

Johnathan was good at the glad hand. His personality could be very forceful. George bent beneath the storm.

"Sure, John, sure. Glad you could be here. Just follow us in. I have to unlock the door and lock it again. Damned crowds of off-islanders, making this into a freak show."

George turned to the great wooden doors and pulled out an antique key that must have weighed half a pound. He inserted it into the 150-year-old lock and gave it a mighty twist. The lock gave forth a loud, snapping sound and gave way under pressure from George's hand.

Johnathan had watched this with amazement, wondering if he could manage such a lock with his power. Somehow it looked too much for him. Lucky there were other doors with more modern locks. Antiquity was a better guard against him than modernity, he decided.

The small group entered. George re-locked the great doors and led his group down the main aisle. Following behind the group, Johnathan entered into the gloom of the large center nave and marveled at the display of ancient craftsmanship. The builders had been master boat-builders and carpenters and the entire church walls had been fitted with a striped pattern of thin boards laid in a repeated pattern to create a spectacular series of cathedral arches down the entire length of the room. Johnathan was impressed. He could feel the loving energy left by these skilled workers. Cyndy looked up at him and smiled and whispered.

"Beautiful, isn't it John? If it weren't for some of the people who run this place I would be delighted to spend more time here. It's just that I can't stand Maaiken. And George toadies up to him so, I feel sick half the time."

George and Shirley were half way down the aisle by this time. George stopped and looked back.

"Are you coming, Cyndy? Hurry up."

His voice had a sharp edge to it. Cyndy immediately looked angry.

"Just go on you two. I'll stay here with John."

George looked like he wanted to argue but then turned and, taking hold of Shirley's arm, led her through a door near the altar. As they disappeared Cyndy took Johnathan's arm and led him down the aisle to one of the front pews. The spiritual beauty of the church made her lower her voice to a whisper.

"I want to see this and I don't want anyone in front of me."

They sat down in the wooden pew as Johnathan continued to admire the detailed designs the carpenters had been able to create using nothing but their amazing abilities with wood. He guessed the woodworking skills had developed from the need to build ships, houses, furniture and barrels and all the other necessities the early settlers and sailors had needed.

"Listen, John, I'm sorry I couldn't talk to you earlier. It's been so hectic. George's quite impossible and my best friend's a total vegetable with fear over her brain cancer. Not that I blame her. Given her circumstances I guess I would be upset too."

Here she paused, looking at her seatmate thoughtfully.

"Now you don't look like a man who gets upset very easily."

Here her voice edged up, making a statement into a question.

"Talk to me, John, what were you going on about in my office on Friday. You were saying things that need explanation. Just what do you know about me and how could you know anything about me anyway? And what was that with my dog, Lady? You some kind of animal trainer or is it Dr. Doolittle?"

She laughed.

"I sound like I need therapy, I think. Is this paranoia or what?"

Her attitude changed once more and she lowered her voice again.

"You said I could know things I shouldn't. Well, it's true, damn it. I've known about Shirley's tumor for days now. I've been able to see it in her head, when I'm not even near her. I also saw it when she was having that headache in the Crawfish the other night. While I watched it, it seemed to get smaller. Mind you I was touching her at the time. But then Shirl said she felt better. Do you think my touching her had something to do with her feeling better?"

Now she squinted her eyes at him.

"I've been told I can heal the tumor, too, but I've not been told how. And you want to know who told me I could heal it? Well, I see things I shouldn't, too. I see my grandmother and she's been dead for three years. And she's the one who told me I could heal the tumor. I mean she visits me whenever I least expect it, and she told me I could heal Shirley, but she didn't tell me how except she made me go find a fungus she said would heal Shirley, and she said it would be safer for me to use the fungus because healing people with herbs and growing things is fashionable or something these days."

Cyndy stopped and drew a deep breath.

"Oh my God. I've been wanting to tell all this to someone and it's just running out of me like water out of a tap. Sorry John, you must think I'm some sort of nut case."

Cyndy hung her head and began to sob softly.

"It's just so.... so.... oh damn it, what's going on with me. Ever since that accident and I popped out of my body, everything has been screwed up..."

Sobbing got in the way of words and she stopped.

Johnathan put his arm around Cyndy's shoulders and pulled her over closer to him.

"Hush now Cyndy, it's all right. What you experienced was a Near Death Experience. That's all. Lots of people have had an NDE. I guess that helps explain some of this stuff you're going through. An NDE can do that to a person. Mind I think that just got you going on something that was bound to happen anyway. My guess is you're a chosen one and that's a fate that's hard to dodge."

Cyndy looked up at him, sobbing now subsiding.

"Chosen one? That's what my grandmother said. What's a chosen one, anyway?"

At this point the door opened near the altar and George and Shirley came out, their heads close together as they talked.

"I think we should continue this later, Cyndy. Try to pull yourself together; here're George and Shirley coming."

Johnathan pulled a handkerchief out of his pocket and stuffed it into Cyndy's hand, then pulled his big frame out of the pew and walked to intercept George and Shirley. They looked up at him, his body screening Cyndy from view.

"Well, folks, what's up? We going to see some fireworks or what?"

Johnathan found himself talking just to give Cyndy time to get back her composure.

"What do you mean fireworks?"

George was indignant.

"This is a very serious religious event. You shouldn't be making fun of it. You're blocking the way; can we get by?"

George tried to push Johnathan to one side but Johnathan was not easily moved. He just leaned into George and spoke sweetly into his ear.

"Sorry mate, don't mean to make light of important religious events. Me, I went to Sunday school as a kid and I know it's wrong to make fun of a serious religious event. How you doing Shirl? Feeling OK?"

Johnathan finally gave in to pressure from George and started to move aside to let George and Shirley get past him. He hoped Cyndy had had time to repair the damage. George grabbed Shirley's arm and dragged her around Johnathan. When he could see up the aisle, it was to find that Cyndy was up near the front doors.

"Cyndy, what're you doing now? Come down here and get a seat. I'll be opening the doors in a minute and that crowd will knock you over."

Cyndy started back down the aisle, smiling at George.

"Why you're right of course, George, I'd better get seated. Johnathan, come sit with me here in the front pew."

Coming up to them she grabbed at Johnathan's large arm and dragged him back to the pew where they'd been sitting just moments before. She lowered her voice to a whisper.

"Thanks, John, you gave me enough time to get my act together again."

She gave his arm a squeeze and Johnathan felt a large thump as his heart took an extra beat. Damn but he was attracted to this woman, no doubt about that. She lit him up like a billboard. Better take it easy, boy. You haven't been in a relationship for a couple of years and there's nothing wrong with your hormones even if some of your genes are twisted a new way.

He grinned foolishly at Cyndy and swallowed. He couldn't believe it; he was acting like a schoolboy. He took a deep breath.

"Let's talk later, Cyndy. Meet me as soon after this service as you can."

Cyndy nodded as George went up the aisle to the doors at the front. They heard the ancient lock give its loud snap and the doors being pushed open. Almost immediately the islanders, who had first right to entry, began to push in with little regard to the sanctity of the church. Quickly behind them came the visitors, the thrill seekers, the curious and even the scientifically inclined. They could hear George shouting to go slow and to be careful. It had little effect on the anxious men and women who had been waiting for an hour or more and who wanted to get the best view of whatever was going to happen.

During the commotion Cyndy leaned into Johnathan, thrust her business card into his hand and spoke into his right ear.

"Here John, take this. On the back, there's a map to my place out on the shore. If it's OK with you we could meet there this afternoon.

George'll be tied up here all day and won't miss me or need me. If you like I'll barbecue us a little dinner later on. We'll have lots of time to talk without distraction."

She smiled into his face, the whiteness of her teeth flashing light in the gloom of the church. He looked deep into her blue eyes and saw her need. He also saw his own need to be with her, a need that overshadowed the fact that he now knew he was to be her teacher.

There are no accidents. Synchronicity, called such by the Swiss psychologist, Carl G. Jung, was the name given to the fact that we experience meaningful coincidences, forces moving us that are not readily apparent. Jonathan now knew he was supposed to meet and know and teach this chosen one. Yet he had never even suspected such an event when he had agreed to come to Nantucket to search out the truth of the healings.

Cyndy looked away from him, shielding her eyes so they would not speak too much to this man, a complete stranger with whom she felt such closeness.

Bells began to ring in the steeple. The church was full and George, with help from Jeremy and the Sheriff's Deputy, had barred any further entry, pulling the great doors shut. Jeremy continued to stand guard as George came back up the aisle to where he had left Shirley standing near the steps to the altar. Taking her by the hand he led her to a space beside Cyndy.

"Now stay here and I'll call you when it's time for Maaiken to bless you with his healing. Don't be frightened, Shirl. It doesn't hurt, you know. Maaiken will tell you just what to do. Relax. I'll be right there beside you."

He smiled at her. It was a tender smile not lost on his wife, who observed all this with furious interest but made no comment. The murmur quieted. Maaiken had just entered, looking severe in his robe of white with the red cross embroidered over his heart. He walked slowly, solemnly to the middle of the sanctuary.

Johnathan watched with interest. This was the closest he'd been to Maaiken since his arrival on Nantucket. It was from this vantage that he could see what a well-formed man, Maaiken was, well-proportioned in all respects. It was only when seen alongside some object of known size that Maaiken's diminutive size became apparent. He was, Johnathan guessed, about 5 foot two or three at best, a quite small man.

But Maaiken made up for his small stature by the size of his ego and energy. Standing in front of the church altar he seemed to swell until he filled the space. When he spoke, his voice echoed throughout the building. The power was easy to see, even if you weren't a gifted psychic. Maaiken projected a big image.

Jonathan sent a quick probe with his mind but drew back immediately as he felt the edge of a barrier. He didn't want to give away anything of his identity. With that first probing thought he had instantly recognized another power that was strong enough to bar his own from entering into the man's mind. There were many with such power; he wasn't totally surprised at finding it here in Maaiken.

Chapter Fifteen

St. James had almost not been able to get into the church. He had miscalculated the size of the crowd and had been among the last to be admitted before those goons had closed the door. He glared at Jeremy. He would have glared at George, too, but George was walking back up the aisle before he could include him in his irritation.

From his position in the back-most pew he could see very little. On top of the distance, a somewhat overweight woman with a large hat obscured what little he might have been able to see.

St. James sat unhappily, trying to peer around the obstruction in front. Finally he just got out of his seat and leaned against the doorframe. Jeremy, under orders to keep order, grabbed at his arm but St. James put out his arm, quick as a snake, and deftly put his hand on Jeremy's shoulder near the neck; he pinched a nerve. Jeremy grunted in pain and staggered back a pace.

"Just let me be, you idiot, or I'll really give you something to think about."

He gave Jeremy his best evil eye imitation. Jeremy stood rubbing his shoulder and looking as if he might still argue the point but, at this moment, the crowded church became silent as Maaiken began the service. From some hidden source, an organ filled the air, gently swelling into a well-known hymn. Jeremy kept still, his back to the door. From there he scowled at St. James but made no other move.

Like puppets reacting to the pull of their strings, the crowd rose as one and a solo voice began to sing the words to "Morning Has Broken." Gradually various members of the congregation followed and by the end of the first verse, most were singing the familiar old song with admirable enthusiasm.

From his position at the back of the church, St. James took a good look at Maaiken. This was the nearest he had been to his quarry since he arrived on Nantucket but it still wasn't very close. He reached in his pocket and withdrew a powerful but tiny monocular which he lifted to his eye. Ah, better. Well at least he could see the man's features clearly. It was an interesting face, well formed but with a mean droop to the lips. The eyes were a misty green and he noticed that Maaiken had his eyes focused on the people in the front pew. That would be where the candidate for this Sunday's healing was seated, he felt sure. He wondered what the reaction would be if he went down to the front two or three pews and just hauled some jackass out. Not a good idea. Make any fuss and the Sheriff might guess who he was, even with his different appearance.

He glanced down at the amulet suspended from his neck but it gave no indication of any activity. Damn thing probably didn't have anything to do with locating the lost artifact anyway. Just a waste of his time to have stolen the stupid thing. He put away the monocular and bided his time, waiting for the service to end and for the healing to begin.

In the front pew, Cyndy had picked up a hymnbook and was adding a full, clear soprano to the general confusion of voices. Shirley had a hymnbook open but was just looking at it. Her mouth remained closed and she looked frightened. Cyndy gave her a poke in the ribs and a questioning smile. Shirley reacted with a worried smile that didn't quite make it and began to sing along with the rest of the congregation.

Now Cyndy looked up at Johnathan with a questioning tilt of her eyebrows and pushed the hymnbook over to him. She decided she was acting as if she was the choir mistress. However, Johnathan responded by picking up on the lines and began singing with her, his clear baritone adding a harmony line. She smiled in approval and they sang together until the hymn ended.

"Very nice, Johnathan."

She had whispered up to him, before turning back to Shirley and quietly saying much the same to her.

Johnathan smiled back. Anything this astronomer did or said made him want to smile. He still felt like a schoolboy when he was with her. He wondered if he was ever meant to graduate. He noticed that Shirley didn't smile back. Well, he was surprised she was standing at all with everything that was on her mind at the moment.

With the end of the music, those standing now sat with a shuffling and squeaking of old wood. Maaiken raised his sternly set face to the congregation. His voice, deeper and more powerful than seemed possible from such a small frame, filled the room. Johnathan looked around trying to see where the speakers were hidden. But then he had a premonition that this voice was not being amplified. The little man had a big voice and knew how to use it with authority. Speaking with the 'voice of authority' was one of the learnings of Shaman.

They could make their voices very loud without appearing to shout, just ordinary voice cadence with shouting strength. Unusual to find this to be one of Maaiken's gifts. Johnathan wondered what the next surprise would be.

Maaiken now read a lesson from the Bible. With that he mounted the steps up to the raised platform of the pulpit and surveyed the crowd. Johnathan thought he must have a soapbox up there, as he appeared to be normal head height, his legs now hidden. Again that incredible voice commanded attention and he proceeded to lay down the ecclesiastical law as interpreted by this old, off-the-main-path church. Much was made of the original founding of the church and the way healing had appeared in the 1700's. It was sort of an oral history, thought Johnathan.

"The ways of the sea have taught us many lessons, and our lessons continue to come from the sea. From the sea came our livelihood and our people and our legends. The sea has kept us isolated from the world and has enabled this church to deal differently with right and wrong, without compromising ourselves with the devil. The sea delivered unto us the power and mystery of healing."

Maaiken's voice boomed, reaching the back as easily as the front. The audience gave him rapt attention.

"The sea today continues to give us our livelihood, but now it is in the form of the visitors that come to us in such numbers and bring their jeeps and other vehicles and clutter up our streets. But we welcome them as always and find it our pleasure to be able to encourage them in the scriptures and in the spirit of Jesus Christ."

He swept his hand in an arc.

"Just look at the crowd here today. Why there isn't a seat free in the entire building. Although I hope and wish that those who attend do so to experience the Spirit, I expect much of it is due to the healing we regularly perform. Much has been made of this healing. Much has been written, much has been speculated on."

He pointed a finger at his listeners, a slight smile brushing his face.

"Whatever your motivation in attending today, I welcome you all in the Name of our Good Lord, Jesus Christ. It will do your souls no damage and hopefully much good to be here, no matter what your motivation."

As Maaiken said this, his eyes swept the sea of expectant faces. He saw a man standing next to Jeremy.

"Why, we must have run out of seats for I can even see a man standing at the very back of the hall. Come here sir, we can't have our visitors standing. Jeremy, bring the gentleman down to the front and find him a chair. Put it there by the end of the first pew."

Jeremy, hearing his name was somewhat startled but obeyed the command. Reginald St. James was also startled, wondering that his wish to be up front should be answered in such a dramatic way. He allowed Jeremy to gingerly take his arm and lead him down the aisle to the front pews, where he waited while Jeremy scurried through the door beside the altar and returned carrying a folding bridge chair.

"Excellent, Jeremy, excellent. Now good sir, if you would just sit there. I assume you will be staying for our healing?"

Maaiken waited for a response until St. James finally nodded and faintly spoke his assent. St. James was embarrassed to be on such public display. He hoped the Sheriff was still on point duty outside.

Maaiken paused now and looked at the group sitting just below him.

"Well, those of you who are here because of our healing, you will not be disappointed. Today we heal one of our own, an islander, a daughter of a family with a long history here going back to our early whaling days. She is a modern young woman and brings great credit to her family and its history. She is a master of the intricacies of the computer and has graduated in law enforcement and is, at present, a deputy Sheriff under our Sheriff, Taylor Russell."

Again Maaiken paused.

"Unlike other institutions or places of healing, we always document the healing that takes place in this church. We do this to silence our critics, to provide absolute proof that our subjects are indeed ill and, finally, to prove that they are indeed cured."

He looked down and his audience and gave another sweep of his diminutive arm.

"Here there is no flummery, no bright lights or band of musicians, no tickets sold or television cameras to sell programming to the world networks. Indeed, let me warn all of you all, we do not allow any visual or audio record to be made of our service. Anyone found with a camera or recording device of any kind will be asked to leave. Our good Sheriff will assist us in this regard. And in case any of you think you can hide a camera or tape recorder in here, we have detectors that will instantly find you out."

St. James sat lower in his seat muttering to himself.

"Oh, shit, the bloody Sheriff is here in the building. Hope he didn't get a good look at me when I was marched down the aisle."

The couple sitting next to him in the pew gave him an odd look then lifted their faces to Maaiken.

"George, would you activate the detectors, please."

Here, George rose from his seat beside Shirley and walked to a small panel under the pulpit. There he opened an access door and pushed some buttons. George had designed the system at the request of his senior elder, Maaiken, some years earlier. It was simple and fool-proof. It incorporated ideas that would have had attracted outside interest. Instead he just patented the ideas, built the detectors and kept on with his true interests, designing new computer applications. He had several such patents, the result of his own personal needs, but declined to commercialize them. The moment George pushed the final button, a small, melodic sound issued from some hidden source.

Maaiken smirked at his audience.

"Well, we seem to have some visitors who have disobeyed the promise they made to gain entrance to the building this morning. Those of you who have recording equipment may now leave."

Maaiken waited. He was in no hurry to finish; in fact he relished this part of his service and was content to drag it out as long as he could. No one moved in the church.

"I warn you, if you don't voluntarily remove yourselves and your costly equipment, it will be substantially damaged and cause you undue expense. Believe me, I dislike to cause harm and wish you to save you all from unexpected loss of money."

Again the suspenseful wait. Finally there was a shuffling and several embarrassed looking men and two women rose from their seats and began to walk towards the doors. Maaiken directed his next words to the Sheriff who had just entered at the back of the hall.

"Sheriff, if you wouldn't mind, just see that these men and women leave the property and don't try to re-enter. I thank you."

He looked down to where George waited under the pulpit.

"George, would you now let your wonderful detector complete its job."

He looked up again to the sea of faces.

"This is a last warning to any of you who have still remained and have recording equipment of any kind."

George rather enjoyed this part of the process. His ingenious circuits would identify and destroy any electronic circuits except those in electronic watches, pacemakers, hearing aids and such other necessary electronics. He could also disrupt cell phones but thought it better to leave that control alone as he knew some of the hospital doctors were in the audience. The system was so sophisticated in operation, yet rather simple in concept. At this last instruction another man leapt up and ran up the aisle to the applause of those remaining.

The melodic sound still keened in the expectant air. George lifted the protective cover and pushed the red button beneath. There was no visible effect but the melodic sound suddenly ceased.

"OK Reverend Maaiken. The device has been activated and there are no more recording devices able to operate. The sweep indicator has ceased. Those who may have been tempted to test our skills will be most disappointed when they try to use their equipment again. It will take some expensive fixing to make it operational again."

Here George turned and looked at the congregation.

"Sorry folks, but you were warned."

Attention now returned to Maaiken standing above the crowd in the pulpit. A few looked somewhat crestfallen. George still watching the congregation saw some of these faces and knew it was the look of those expecting a large repair bill. He smiled to himself. It happened every service. No matter how much they were warned, some didn't take it seriously. He walked back to stand beside the first pew, near Shirley and, as it happened, St. James. Maaiken took back control with his next words.

"I ask all of you to be quiet now as we are to do the Lord's work here and cure this very ill young woman. And just so you may join in the process, let me describe what the illness is so you will better understand and be amazed at the Lord's work done here today."

The silence in the church was absolute. Maaiken pointed at the first pew.

"A few days ago, Miss Shirley Woodstock who is seated just below me here in the pew next to where our Congregational President, George Vorester, is standing, complained of severe headaches. Subsequently, internist, Dr. Bob Hawking and neurologist, Dr. Jenny Thornton examined her at our excellent Nantucket Cottage Hospital. Through the use of their remarkable Magnetic Imaging Resonance machine they were able to see and record a serious tumor growing in an inoperable point in Miss Woodstock's brain. This is the serious matter that has lead us to take Miss Woodstock into our healing this Sunday."

At this point solemn organ music filled the church and George turned to help Shirley stand. Shirley, looking pale and unsteady, held tight to George's arm, stumbling a bit as he lead her forward and up the chancel steps toward the altar. The altar was overlaid with a plain white cloth along the length of which were embroidered a series of crosses in a deep, rich red. Candles flickered in ornately carved golden holders at each end of the altar. Occupying the space in the middle, was an ornately embroidered silk cloth that appeared to cover some object.

Finally George and Shirley stood together before the altar. Maaiken pushed some switches in the pulpit and the lights in the main body of the church slowly dimmed, leaving only the area around the altar illuminated softly from lights hidden above. Then he descended the few steps down from the pulpit and strode importantly toward the pair, his small stature not immediately noticeable until he reached the waiting couple, where he then could be seen to be a good head shorter than either of them.

He halted, and extended his hand. Shirley placed her hand in his and allowed him to lead her slowly around the altar until they stood half hidden from the congregation, looking more like a mother with her child pulling at her. Still the simple and solemn notes of music hung hauntingly in the air.

Unseen by the audience, Maaiken stepped up on a small platform until he and Shirley were face to face. George had turned to face them, careful to move to one side so not to obscure the view of the expectant audience. There was an intense hush within the entire church.

Turning to the altar Maaiken now removed the embroidered silk cloth to reveal a small, ornate, crystal vessel decorated with a simple cross in gold and capped with a golden lid encrusted with gems that sparkled in the overhead lights. This beautiful, diminutive container held a viscous liquid that seemed to glow with its own light. Maaiken pressed a switch and suddenly all lights were extinguished. A murmur rose from the expectant audience. The container shone with an unearthly, blue-violet radiance that seemed to pulsate as if with a life force of its own. Maaiken waited dramatically. He turned to face out into the church, his face illuminated by the glow from the container. His voice filled the room.

"What you see here is the mystical power of God, the healing and sacred power of God, radiating and shining and giving evidence of the Power and the Glory."

The lights above the altar slowly came back on to dimly illuminate the pair as they faced each other. With great care and reverence, Maaiken put the glowing vessel back on the altar before turning to face Shirley.

"Shirley Woodstock, do you believe in the power of God Almighty, and in the sacred love of his son, Jesus Christ, to heal you of all ailments?"

Shirley stood, transfixed, unable to say a word.

"I say again, Shirley Woodstock, do you believe in the power of God Almighty, and in the sacred love of his son, Jesus Christ, to heal you of all ailments? You must answer me, Shirley. Do not be afraid. You are in no danger. There is nothing here that can harm you. There is only the love of Jesus come to you to heal you of the dreadful disease that has crept into the tissues of your brain. The power and love of Jesus is here, now, to heal you."

Maaiken great voice grew louder, more demanding.

"Once more, Shirley Woodstock, I ask of you, do you believe in the power of God Almighty, and in the sacred love of his son, Jesus Christ, to heal you of all ailments."

Shirley swayed, her lips trembled, a whisper came from her lips.

"Yes, I believe."

"Well spoken, Shirley. Now come with me to where we can be seen by these witnesses to God's love."

Maaiken again took Shirley's hand and the two of them walked around to the front of the altar and faced into the darkness of the church. Maaiken stood with his back to the altar, Shirley facing him. Turning, he reached for a red cushion, which he placed on the floor between them.

Once more his voice boomed out.

"Kneel before me, Shirley. Kneel and pray to God and to Jesus for healing. Pray quietly, but pray with love, pray in earnest. Continue to pray as I prepare to anoint you with God's great healing."

With that Shirley sank trembling to her knees to a prayerful attitude. Maaiken turned back to the altar where he put his two hands on the crystal container. For a while he just stood silently. He, too, was praying. Maaiken, more than any of the others, was mindful of the presence of God during these moments; he alone knew where the magical healing originated. He prayed, he prayed sincerely. A stern and grumpy custodian of the islanders' morals, he felt only love at this moment as the power emanated from the vial into his hands and through his body. As often as he did this ceremony, he never got used to the feeling, the euphoria. For this moment even he was humbled in the presence of God's power. The amulet hanging from his neck gave out a dim, reddish glow.

Out in the main body of the church, the congregation was watching and listening in quiet awe. Two watchers were most attentive. St. James from his seat in the chair leaned forward, excitement making his pulse pound. So intense was his focus on the events at the altar, he failed to notice that the amulet that he wore was now illuminating itself. Johnathan, seated next to Cyndy, also leaned forward, and extended his vision by probing with his mind.

His first impression was of great power. He literally reeled back with a grunt and shuttered his mind from the radiation pulsing at him from the altar. Cyndy looked at him in concern.

"Are you OK John?"

"Don't you feel it, Cyndy? I reached out with my mind and was almost blown away. Don't tell me your mind hasn't felt it, too?"

Cyndy smiled. Johnathan might be a powerful mystic but he hadn't grown up within the spiritual power that now radiated at them and at the entire audience. The first time she had experienced this awesome power, she had fainted. However, for some reason unknown to her, instead of becoming worse, subsequent exposure had been strengthening to her, and now she basked in the warm, sweet waves of love she could feel emanating from the small crystal container. She loved it. Others complained about feeling nauseous, sick and disoriented but Cyndy continued to feel better and better the longer she was at one of Maaiken's healings. George had said he never got used to it. Cyndy had wondered why she was different in this way. Now as she wondered a voice spoke quietly in her ear.

"It is because you are a chosen one."

She looked to see if Johnathan had spoken to her but he was engrossed in the happenings at the altar. She looked around for some other source. Just then the scent of apples reached her nostrils as she heard a giggle. Then she knew her grandmother, the irrepressible grandmother, was with her. The voice continued in her ear.

"This is so nice for Shirley, don't you think, Cyndy?"

Cyndy looked wildly about, her attention diverted from the scene at the altar, but she'd seen it enacted many times before as she attended these healing services with George. She whispered into the air.

"Please, grandmother I can't really talk to you now."

Johnathan looked over at her.

"Did you say something, Cyndy? If you don't mind I'd like to watch what Maaiken's doing right now."

He looked away again, trying to observe Maaiken as he stood in the dim light at the altar. St. James was having his own problems. While he strained to see the action up at the altar, his vision kept blurring. He felt vaguely ill and hoped he wasn't going to leave his breakfast on the floor. Around him others were having similar difficulties, two at the back had already stepped out of the big doors. Two or three more were stepping on feet as they struggled out of the pews. St. James became aware of the amulet, warm against his chest, and put one hand on it. Immediately he felt better.

Shirley remained kneeling on the red cushion, George standing beside her, keeping a steadying hand on her shoulder. Finally, the strains of organ music ended, the church was in silence, except for shuffling feet as more members of the audience felt the need to escape to the outside.

Maaiken turned slowly and walked back behind the altar where he reverentially picked up the glowing flask. Holding it at full arm's-length he slowly walked back to stand in front of Shirley's bent form. George backed away, shielding his face from the full radiance coming from the liquid. He gasped and turned to step down to the front pew where he sat beside Cyndy. He coughed and struggled for breath. Cyndy eyed him in concern. This happened every time George participated in these ceremonies. She wondered why it affected him so badly while Maaiken seemed to glory in it. Another mystery, she thought.

"One we'll discuss later, dear."

Cyndy shrugged, trying not to answer. Her concern now was for her friend, Shirley, forgetting for the moment her anger at the apparent closeness between Shirley and her husband.

Standing at the altar, facing Shirley, Maaiken put his hand on her head. The Church filled with his voice.

"Shirley Woodstock, I now enjoin the illness in you to leave you. This abomination that has attached itself to your brain has no power in the sight of the Lord."

With these words, Maaiken held the glowing vessel over her and, carefully, allowed a single drop to fall onto her head. For a moment nothing appeared to happen. Then with a shriek, Shirley staggered to her feet, staring into Maaiken's face before slumping once more to her knees and then, like a child going to its nap, lay flat out with her head supported by the cushion. She didn't move.

Maaiken held the flask above her head. Once more a single drop fell onto her head, a slow-motion glowing trail seeming to follow its descent. Shirley's head now was bathed in the unearthly blue-violet radiation. She didn't stir. She was unconscious, in a trance, unaware of her surroundings.

The rest of the church seemed to also be in a trance. No one shuffled; no one even seemed to breathe. It was deathly quiet until the organ began to play its simple air once more.

Maaiken turned and retraced his steps as he replaced the crystal chalice on the altar and covered it with the embroidered silk cloth. Then, turning once more to the body of the church, he spoke in his large but solemn voice. As he spoke, the lights came up in the church to help the departure of those who had chosen to remain.

"I would ask all of you to now leave. Miss Woodstock will be taken from here to our Nantucket Cottage Hospital where she will undergo another complete evaluation of her condition. George, if you would, come here and help me rouse our Shirley. Dr. Hawking, would you please have your ambulance people come in now."

Dr. Bob Hawking nodded from the row where he had been sitting, a fascinated observer of the recent ceremony. He spoke into his cell phone, one of electronic devices that had not been decommissioned by George earlier. Moments later, two paramedics wheeled a gurney from a side entrance and gently persuaded a dazed Shirley to lie down and be wheeled to the waiting ambulance. Dr. Hawking accompanied her, checking her vital signs even as the ambulance drove away toward the hospital.

Inside, Johnathan paid some attention to the man who had been seated in a chair at the insistence of Maaiken Starbroke. He was aware that it was the same man who had changed his appearance at the Bed and Breakfast on Milk Street. He also knew much more now that his office had been able to trace and identify the stranger. Knowing that the man was a noted archaeologist and historian dealing in the early Christian years, he wondered why he was here and why had he arrived at the house in a disguise. More to check out, he thought. Then he turned to see his seatmate getting up in some agitation.

"I have to go make sure Shirl's all right. See you later John?"

"Yeah, Cyndy. I'll meet you about four at your sea-side place."

With that he turned and followed St. James out the church doors.

Chapter Sixteen

Reginald St. James walked quickly away from the church and crowd. In the noise and confusion he didn't notice the man on a bicycle who followed him down the hill and into town. Traffic was heavy for the island; Sunday and the healing service brought out almost everyone. Many were now heading for the beaches, or restaurants, or bars, or just home for a mid-day meal. The streets were crowded with the jeeps and four-wheel drive vehicles just referred to during the church service. Many cyclists also navigated the narrow streets. Sidewalks were filled with the happy Sunday faces of families, couples and individuals like St. James. No one paid any attention to the big man as he rode slowly some distance behind his quarry.

St. James needed time to think about what he had just witnessed. He didn't know what he had witnessed, that was the problem. During the service he had been aware that his amulet was warming up. Indeed, he remembered how much better he felt once he put his hand on it. Still that might mean nothing at all. He still wasn't sure just what the damned thing actually did.

He needed to get next to Maaiken. That would give him an opportunity to probe and explore. Maybe something would break open enough to give him a handle on just how Maaiken worked the effects and the healing. Oh yes, the healing, he must find out if there really had been a healing. He suspected the healing would be authenticated by the docs at the Nantucket Cottage Hospital, as the others had, but he had to make sure. That would be the first order of business. But only after he took some lunch.

St. James turned under a large blue parrot and into the restaurant he was just passing. He didn't care what he ate at this point. He just needed to take in some calories for energy and then get on with his investigation. Johnathan, now loping along behind St. James, having leaned his bike into a space between some stairs, paused, wondering if he should continue into the restaurant, then thought, why not.

He, too, turned into the Blue Parrot, wondering what they served. He hoped it wasn't parrots or other birds. When he studied a menu while waiting to be seated, it turned out that birds were indeed the order of the day here at the Blue Parrot, but they that were chickens, not parrots. The restaurant he had chosen was a fast-food franchise noted for its southern fried chicken.

He looked into the dinning room and spotted St. James seated by himself in one corner of the partly filled room. Johnathan checked his watch and saw that it was already past 2:00 and assumed the rush was over for a noonday meal.

"Yes sir."

An attractive, blond-haired, green-eyed young woman smiled up at him. Her ears were adorned with plastic blue parrots, her left bicep, which was very visible, as was much of the rest of her in her brief tank top, sported what appeared to be a tattoo of a blue parrot. A badge was pinned to the cloth of the tank top. A blue parrot in full flight across her breast read Tiffany. Johnathan pointed at the tattoo, smiling his best goofy smile.

"Tiffany, I can't believe any franchise could get their servers to be tattooed with blue parrots. That thing real?"

"No way mister, no way. If you like I'll get you a transfer and you, too, can show your friends your blue parrot tattoo. Put it anywhere you like. Betty over there has one on her left breast and just a little bit of it peaks out. Makes the boys want to see more."

She giggled. There was something really attractive about her giggle but Johnathan had other matters on his mind.

"Wonder if you can seat me at the table near that scrawny guy who just came in ahead of me."

He lowered his voice in a conspiratorial way.

"I'm sort of keeping an eye on him, official business, you know."

"No I don't know, what do you mean? You some kind of cop? You don't look like a cop. So what are you, anyway?"

She smiled.

"You're not like, gay, or anything like that? Going to pick up a date? He's not much. Try a real date."

She vamped for him, giving him a coquettish smile. Then her smile froze and she spoke over her shoulder.

"Hi Mr. Skillen. Excuse me just a minute mister then I'll show you to your table."

Tiffany turned to pick up menus and tableware as Johnathan looked to see Mr. Skillen, a sour looking man in a Blue Parrot apron, frowning and then walking back behind a door that led to the kitchen. As soon as he had left, Tiffany smiled again and waved Johnathan to follow her.

"That's the boss. He doesn't like it when I flirt with the patrons. Silly man. Why's he think I stand out here every day? Well, it's not for the big bucks he's paying me, I'll tell you that. Here's your table. Your waitress will be Betty. Do you want to think about our conversation?"

Tiffany looked hopefully at Johnathan who gave her a smile in return.

"You mean about Betty or about you?"

Here Tiffany glared at him.

"Just kidding, Tiff. Truly sorry but I've got other demands on my time or I would be very tempted. Thanks anyway. You made my day, believe me."

He laughed and got a laugh in return. Tiffany went back to her post and Johnathan began to look through the menu. He also looked over at St. James whom, he noted, was in the process of ordering from a tall brunette with just a bit of a blue parrot showing where the swell of her left breast showed, thanks to her own skimpy tank top. Tank tops appeared to be the order of the day at the Blue Parrot.

All in all, I bet the boys do want to see more of that parrot, he thought. He waited while St. James brusquely ordered. He didn't seem to appreciate the blue parrot. Sad, thought Johnathan. The man has no soul.

Then Betty came to his table.

"Hi Betty, how's your parrot?"

Betty looked at him and laughed.

"I usually get that question from the younger set, mister. You set up by that Tiffany? I'll have to throttle her when I get the time. So what's your order?"

He could see Betty was all business and guessed that Mr. Skillen must be somewhere watching their table.

"Don't worry, Betty, your secret's safe with me and I won't even mention it to the boss."

Betty looked surprised.

"Thanks, you are quick now aren't you. So what can I get for you?"

Jonathan gave her his order and then turned to look at St. James, who appeared to be talking to himself. Excellent, thought Johnathan, as he quickly centered himself, then tuned into the thoughts that were crowding St. James's mind. At this range, it was a piece of cake for him to overhear thoughts. Piece of cake as long as the individual didn't take just ordinary precautions to block. St. James wasn't blocking. Soon Johnathan heard St. James muse to himself about checking out to see if

Shirley had actually been healed at the Church. Or even if a healing could happen so quickly.

Then some images of meeting with Maaiken and trying to get him to talk about the artifact that must have arrived back in the early 1700's. Was there a written history of the event on Nantucket? Maybe he'd check the local library and the whaling museum. There was a lot of old whaling memorabilia, some of it might date back to the arrival of the mysterious artifact. St. James's thoughts then jumbled and Johnathan lost him. Betty had come back with their orders and he and St. James settled down to eating.

Well, thought Johnathan, wonder what this artifact is he's going on about. First I've heard of something arriving here in the early 1700's that's related to the healing. Guess I haven't done my homework. But I'll just guess the object in question is related to the early days of Christ, that's his specialty, after all. Johnathan settled down to his southern fried chicken and was pleasantly surprised at how good it tasted. He spilt catsup on his fries and mused on.

The ambulance with Shirley and the doctor rolled to a quiet stop at the Nantucket Cottage Hospital emergency entrance where they were met by neurologist Jenny Thornton.

"Come on Shirley. I've got the MRI set up and waiting for you. I'll just take you there in this wheelchair."

With that Jenny and Shirley disappeared into the Imaging Department. Bob followed along after giving his wife Betty a kiss and a hug. They were an affectionate couple. Soon after, Cyndy arrived at the parking lot, skidding her truck to a stop and jumping out. She was out of breath when she arrived at Betty's desk in the lobby.

"How's Shirl, Betty? She get here OK? Where is she?"

"Slow down Cyndy, everything's under control. Bob and Jenny are with her now in the Imaging Department. Relax and get a coffee. Get me one, too. I'm all alone here this afternoon and I can't get away from the telephones. They're ringing off the hook. Lots of people want to know how Shirl's doing. Her uncle's rung up twice already."

Cyndy went down to the cafeteria and brought back the coffees. Then she sat and started to read the ancient National Geographic again.

It was an hour and a half before Bob returned to the lobby. Cyndy had already read about baboon families two times and had tired of the subject. Grateful for an interruption, she turned to Bob.

"Bob, how's Shirl?"

Bob gave her a gentle smile.

"Better than I would ever have believed, Cyndy, better than any one could have hoped."

Here he pulled her up and gave her a hug. Betty watched carefully from the reception desk.

"I can't believe the MRI scans, I can't but I have to. It's bloody incredible. The tumor we detailed in the last scans is already half the size it was and you can almost see it shrinking. God, that Maaiken can have my vote no matter what a grumpy old bastard he is. Right now I'd vote for him for president."

Bob stopped and went over to Betty. There were tears in his eyes as he hugged her and then just held on.

"Betty, it's another miracle courtesy of that magician, Maaiken."

Here he turned back to face Cyndy but keeping hold of his wife.

"You best go home now Cyndy and come back after dinner to see Shirl. She's sedated and sleeping now. Later you can celebrate with her. She'll want to celebrate. She deserves to celebrate. Now that I think about I'm going to celebrate. Soon's you're off that desk, honey, we're going to go have a drink and wonder a little bit about God."

Here he gave another hug to Betty, waved at Cyndy, then turned and walked back into the ward.

Betty smiled at Cyndy.

"See you later Cyn. I think I'll just sit here and have a good cry."

Cyndy went back out to the parking lot, found her red truck with its door still half open and got in. She sat quietly, thanking God and praying for her friend. Then she put the key into the ignition and drove back to her house. As soon she opened the door Lady ran out and squatted. Cyndy had a moment of guilt, thinking this great friend wasn't getting her usual attention.

"Sorry Lady, old pal, but our friend Shirl's been sick and is getting better and I'm afraid I just plain forgot about you waiting back here for me with your legs crossed."

Lady, now that immediate problems had been taken care of, came lolloping back and nuzzled at Cyndy's hand. Giving her dog a hug she turned and together, Cyndy and Lady re-entered the house. Cyndy went into the kitchen and began to put together supplies she would later take to the beach house for the promised barbecue. Lady helped by getting under her feet as often as she could. Finally Cyndy stopped what she was doing and grabbed up Lady's leash and led her into the woods at the back of the property. Together they began to jog up the path.

Having decided to work off some of his southern fried chicken, Johnathan liberated his bicycle from between the stairs where he had left it and began pedaling his way back up to the church. As he approached up the hill, he could see several cars were still in the parking lot. Among the cars he could see George's Harley, now restored from a bunch of parts to glistening beauty ready to bellow its special Harley thunder.

Johnathan continued to the manse where Maaiken lived, alone now that his father had passed away. Maaiken had never married, and was the last of his line. Johnathan, who had done some homework, knew that the authority for the church would have to pass on to a non-Starbroke for the first time in over 200 years. If there were any arcane knowledge, he would have to pass that along, too. That might just put George in the running to be privy to whatever secrets were hidden somewhere in the church.

He circled the manse, a large two-story wooden building built about the same time that the church had been rebuilt in the late 1840's, after the great fire. It had a deep veranda running around three sides of the building. Beautiful stained glass windows ran up both sides of the entryway. A ship's lamp hung over the doorway. Six gable windows hugged the hip roof and over all was the widow's walk. To one side of the walk an elaborate wrought iron, sailing-ship weather vane kept track of the wind as it shifted.

Johnathan braked his bike, paused to view the scene, then decided there was little to be done here. He turned his bike toward the beaches and pedaled leisurely toward the property that Cyndy owned near the water. It would take him about an hour to ride that far.

Meanwhile, back at the church, George and Maaiken were closeted in Maaiken's study. Maaiken poured coffee into two mugs from a jug that Jeremy had just delivered. George had walked over to the bookshelves near the fireplace. Maaiken looked up, annoyed.

"What're you up to George, come here and sit down. I've got things to discuss with you."

George plucked a volume on scrimshaw from the shelves.

"Nice collection you've got here, Maaiken, as I know for a fact this book's out of print and worth about two grand. Are the others as valuable as this?"

As he said this he leaned on the fireplace mantel and tried to see what his camera had seen the day before. Maaiken looked even more displeased.

"George, put that book back and come over here. We need to talk. Got serious problems and you, maybe, are going to have to find a solution."

George finally acceded to Maaiken's urging and put the book back on the shelves. He had been unable to see much on the mantel and vowed to come back when Maaiken was elsewhere.

"OK, what is it Rev? I thought the service today was brilliant. You should be running a tent show. I could put you in a tent with two thousand paid guests each week and we could make a fortune."

George was smiling as he said this but Maaiken erupted in fury.

"You're a fool, George Vorester. A damn fool. Don't you have any idea of the spiritual nature of the work we do in this church? Don't ever forget, this is a church and we do God's work here. We have a lot to do. That miserable bunch of sinners out there have little idea of how to behave in God's presence. Did you see them trying to sneak their video cameras in today? And it's like that every service. They have no respect."

He scowled into his steaming mug.

"And don't think I don't know some of them were our own parishioners. Oh yes, there was Doug Gibley and his wife and they had to leave or face having their camera destroyed. And they weren't the only ones I recognized, who should know better. That's what I need to talk to you about. It's about time we disciplined some of these sinners."

George watched carefully. Maaiken's face was red with anger. His eyes burned with rage and he pounded his small fist on the table.

"I've decided, I'm going to have them put into purgatory.

George winced. Purgatory meant that no one on the island would be allowed to have anything to do with the members so named by Maaiken. No one could speak to them. When the Gibleys or others sent to purgatory tried to buy groceries, they would be denied access to the store. Anyone doing business or just caught talking to them would also be put into purgatory; it would be as if they didn't exist. In order to be able to eat those in purgatory were allowed two meals a day in the church kitchen. They had to learn lessons and recite them to get fed.

Any children who might belong to the parents in purgatory were parceled out to other parishioners to be loved and properly cared for until such time as their parents were removed from the living dead list. Finally, if any of those in purgatory tried to leave the island, the Steamship Authority wouldn't sell them a ticket; the staff were all members of Maaiken's church and wouldn't dare.

"Come on Maaiken, time's moving on. You can't be so autocratic with people any more. What if the papers got wind of it? There would be hell to pay, a media circus for sure. You've always treated Nantucket as your own fiefdom, your kingdom, as your whole fucking family has done for generations. Well, I think you've got to stop it or we'll have the law down on our heads. Yeah, just think what would happen if they got a lawyer involved. You think you can run the courts, too?"

"You finished George?"

Maaiken was icy cold now. Only his eyes continued to burn in anger.

"You think you're big enough to take me on? Is that it? You want to inherit my post here, don't you? You want to risk getting an illness and not have access to our healing? What do you think would have happened to our Shirley if she didn't have access to our healing? Think about it George, she was going to die and nobody could have saved her except me, and the healing only this church can provide. Would you like to have lost your little lady love?"

George stopped what he was doing and stared at Maaiken.

"You dirty old son of a bitch. What do you mean my lady love?"

Now Maaiken was smiling a cold smile.

"Oh, I know most secrets on Nantucket, George, I have my ways."

"You mean you have your spies, don't you, Rev? Got everyone so scared of you they'd turn in their own mom or dad, now wouldn't they?"

George took a deep breath and counted to ten. He'd have to be careful. This was one mean son of a bitch and he could do great damage to George's reputation, maybe damage more than that.

"Yes, well, George, I know more than you think, more about that smart little wife of yours for one thing, the astronomer who wants to be a witch. I'll tell you now and don't forget it. If I ever find she's been doing more than curing her friends of so called female problems, I'll make sure she never ever does it again. If I find she's doing worse things that I've had some hint of, like giving her friends plants to help them keep from having babies, well, I won't stand for it. That will be her end, George, her life will be forfeited."

George just stared at this mad munchkin.

"You see, George, it is of utmost importance that nobody else in this community is seen to have the power of healing. This is what our church does, nobody else. I won't stand for anyone getting in my way. Healing has to be seen as coming from this church or coming from a source for which I have given approval."

His calmness was frightening, like a large storm seen just over the horizon.

"For your information, I had my eye on that grandmother witch of hers. Plenty of times I was going to send her to purgatory or worse but she was a wily old bird. Just when I thought I had her, I couldn't get anyone to testify against her. Now she's dead and buried at least I don't have to worry about her anymore."

At this pronouncement, the papers on Maaiken's desk rustled although the windows were closed and there were no drafts in the room. Maaiken glanced curiously at the desk. The papers subsided. A faint scent of apples filled the room. Maaiken stirred uneasily then continued to speak to George.

"Oh, I can and do allow the hospital to play healer and birth the babies and fix broken bones for tourists, but the serious healing is spiritual. It's connected to Christ. This church has Christ's own healing, brought here from the dim beginnings of Christian history."

Suddenly, Maaiken, who was standing, glared threateningly at George. His incredible voice grew in volume. George instinctively winced and barely stopped himself from covering his ears.

"OK George, I've just said something I vowed to my father never to divulge except to my successor. Well I'm getting a bit long in the tooth and I don't have family. It looks like fate has intervened and you just might be my successor. How do you like that, huh George? Only trouble is, if you want to live a long and productive life, you better agree with everything I'm going to tell you."

Now he was less threatening and more business like.

"You're already President of the church board. It has been in my mind you should become involved in the secret of the healing. Now, you are going to have that chance, indeed, you have no alternative. But I tell you again, cross me or ever tell anyone what I'm going to tell you and you are a dead man."

His eyes were like two cold and frozen pools.

"What I'm about to tell you never leaves this room. I will swear you to secrecy and, believe me, if you ever break that vow, you will simply die."

While he was saying this Maaiken had opened a drawer in his desk and withdrawn the crystal flask he had used during the healing ceremony with Shirley. George vaguely felt his usual nausea and swallowed hard as he watched Maaiken play idly with the elegant little container. Inside the viscous liquid rolled gently around. It appeared to be still glowing but it was difficult for George to tell in the bright light of Maaiken's study.

George looked at Maaiken trying not to let the force he could feel make him flinch. He said nothing although in his head he said to himself, Maaiken, you little runt, how could you even think you could harm me. Then he looked at the liquid and wondered.

"How'm I going to die, Maaiken? You gonna take out a gun and shoot me or something? What do you think you are, the Mafia for God's sake?"

"Hush, George. God's listening. God is part of all this. You'd better listen. If you need persuading, I'll just have to give you a demonstration."

Maaiken grinned an evil grin when he said this and held up the elegant little flask. George did flinch now and felt a chill run down his spine as he sat down and began to listen. Outside Maaiken's study door another pair of ears was also listening. Jeremy had his head pushed up to the door.

Two people were hearing a deadly secret. Either one was now at risk. George and Jeremy shared a common threat. George had been warned, and whether he took the warning seriously or not at least he was aware there was danger. Jeremy, on the other hand, was convinced he was outsmarting the Rev. and could only think how he was gaining valuable information. He had nothing to warn him of how dangerous this could be. Dark clouds were forming over his head. He was oblivious to all but his greed and glee. He listened and as he learned of the secret hidden below, he made up his mind. When Maaiken and George left he would strike.

Chapter Seventeen

Johnathan slowed his bike and looked down from the dunes to the gray weathered cape cod that nestled alone, held in the arms of a small bay stretching around it, sheltered from the road by the dunes and facing into the ocean.

The house was set on a rise of land that fell off to the beach immediately below. There the Atlantic sent swells that gently crested, then crashed onto the sand of the beach some 500 feet from the front of the house. He wondered if it was high or low tide at the moment and how far a storm might send the waves towards the house. But the house looked as though it had weathered many storms, so he decided not to worry.

From his perspective he was viewing the back of the house. A drive led down to a sheltered back door and, off to the left side, to a garage that looked somewhat newer than the house. Along the right, a graveled path disappeared as it led to the front of the house. Beach plum and bayberry bushes formed the outer edge of the path.

A large enough space had been cleared and graveled in front of the garage to accommodate several cars but only Cyndy's bright red truck was in sight. As Johnathan coasted down the drive from the crest of the dunes, he could hear quietly plucked chords of a guitar drifting from the open window that he assumed looked into the kitchen. Then a dog barked, the screen door banged open and Lady came bounding out to meet him, barking and wagging her tail completely out of time to the music. In self-defense, Johnathan tipped his bike onto the gravel and dropped to one knee to greet this friendly dog. The screen door banged open once more and Cyndy, dressed in blue designer jeans and a bright red knit top, stepped out to view her defender who, with front paws on Johnathan's shoulders, was trying to lick his face, Johnathan dodging and laughing and reaching to pull on Lady's ears.

"A fine defender of a woman's virtue you are, Lady. Get down from Johnathan and behave."

Jonathan smiled back and felt his usual weak-kneed response to seeing the woman astronomer. He covered up his confusion with a heave that sent Lady rolling back as he picked up both himself and his bicycle and walked to where Cyndy waited.

"Hi John, welcome to my little retreat. This was part of my grandmother's legacy to me. Did I tell you she left everything to me, including our house in town with its incredible herb garden, and this beautiful little retreat on the ocean? Come in and see what a marvelous gift she gave me."

Cyndy held the screen door open in invitation. Lady came up to him, taking his hand in her mouth and trying to pull him forward.

"Easy, Lady, easy. I'm going to come in."

Johnathan, parked his bike against the wall near the door and followed Cyndy's slim form and Lady's waving tail into the cool interior, feeling the ocean breeze as it blew in from the open front windows and door and exiting through the back.

"Natural air conditioning, I see."

She looked back smiling at him, once more inducing long-forgotten feelings of adolescent shyness, and continued to lead the way, avoiding Lady's bouncing excitement as they walked through the kitchen with its old-fashioned gas stove and cooking pots hung from hooks.

Once through the kitchen door a small dining room opened to the right with an antique, pine-topped, maple-legged extension table, overhung by a cranberry-shaded oil lamp, and set about with six pine chicken-coop chairs. An old pine flat-to-the-wall cabinet held dishes and small china pieces. Finally they walked into the living room with its great windows looking directly out to the beach and ocean, and comfortably furnished with soft, over-padded chairs and sofa, all in various shades of faded glory.

Outside the sliding door on the weathered deck were canvas-covered beach chairs and a round wooden table topped by a bright green and white umbrella. One corner of the deck held a propane-fired black cast-aluminum barbecue. Steps led down from the deck to a rocky ledge with more steps to the sandy beach below.

"Settle yourself John, I'll get us a couple of beers."

With that Cyndy disappeared back inside the house. Johnathan pulled one of the beach chairs out from under the shade of the umbrella to sit in the full sun, close enough to the front railing to put his feet up. He drank in the beauty of the rolling breakers and warmth of the sun. Cyndy found him with his eyes focused on the infinity of the horizon, slowly breathing in the soft salt air.

"Don't fall asleep on me, John. Here, you're probably thirsty after peddling out from town. It must have taken you an hour or more unless you're a Tour rider. Mind you the temperature is just right and the humidity is low for this time of year."

She handed him a Sam Adams, then paused, looked at him as if seeing him for the first time. The Sam felt refreshingly cold in his hand and the cool liquid cut slightly at his throat as he tilted the bottle and took his first sip.

"You're a complete stranger to me, John. Why do I feel as if I know you? I mean I told you things in my office I've never told anyone, especially my dear husband, that lech who seems to have something going with my best friend. I feel like I'm in a soap opera."

She gave a sigh.

"And I'm not sure, but I'd be happier if he did run off with Shirley, except Shirley's always been my best friend."

Another, deeper sigh.

"Some friend."

Another pause while she rubbed Lady's elegant head. Then she looked at him solemnly, her faded-blue eyes misting. He hurt inside.

"Who are you John? You some kind of alien or something? Did I miss a UFO landing? I know you fucked with Lady's mind back in my office like I've never seen anyone do with a dog before. And I know Dr. Doolittle's just a book, not about a real person."

A tear slid slowly down her cheek.

"And then you go telling me I'm some sort of chosen person. I thought the Jews were God's Chosen People, 'least that's what I learned in Sunday school. Oh my God, listen to me, I'm babbling. Three science degrees and I'm babbling. Sorry John. But really, who the hell are you?"

Cyndy pierced him through with her blue-eyed stare.

Johnathan thought and decided. For once he'd tell the truth. It had been a long time.

"Think you can stand the truth, Cyndy? I wonder?"

He was quiet for a moment, thinking how he could begin.

"I've told so many stories about myself that I confess, I'm sometimes confused as to just who I really am. But for you, Cyndy, for some reason for you, I'm going to tell a story that I've never told anyone before, the true story about me. You'll find it's unusual. In fact it's so damned odd, you probably won't believe it anyway. Can't say I'd blame you either."

He stopped to take a pull from the neck of his Sam Adam's, beads of moisture running down the bottle.

"Tell me Cyndy, with all your education, did you ever hear tell of a man called Baird Spalding?"

He waited. She looked puzzled. He continued.

"I guess you're a bit young for that. Well, It's a very long story of which I can give you only a brief synopsis. It started when I was a boy. I had a hero, man named Spalding, Baird Spalding. He was a major media sensation in his day. But media in his day was a different kind of fish."

"What do you mean, different, John? Just when was this? You make it seem like it was the last century or something."

"Bingo, Cyndy, you're not just a pretty face. The man I'm talking about was born in 1854. By the time he became a media story, I was just 17, big for my age even then. The year was 1894 and I'd been hired by a travel company to lug baggage and be the roadie for a most unusual group of eleven men on a trip to India."

Another pause to sip his Sam Adams. Cyndy's face was a gathering storm.

"What happened on that trip is really another story, one that has been public record for many years, but, briefly, during that trip we all met and lived with a group known as the Masters. Baird went on to give many lectures in America about these incredible entities and the adventures we all had traveling with them. For years Baird Spalding was one of the most sought after speakers of his time. Strange to think, but now he is all but forgotten except by what is considered by some to be a lunatic fringe, the new age groupies."

He smiled.

"And me, well I was never officially a member of Baird's party. In all the excitement somehow I managed to get myself left behind in India and adopted by these Masters. Now that's a story. Sometimes I think I should write it into a screenplay and sell it for big bucks. Anyway the end result was that these incredible, gentle, wonderful entities, the Masters, subsequently taught me some of their secrets."

He paused, remembering.

"The Masters taught Baird how to levitate. What do you think of that? He only ever used the power once and it caused such a riot that he never did it again, except in private and, occasionally, for very close friends. They taught a Scotsman named Hume how to do it and he did it all the time."

Now he paused again, sensing the gathering storm. He looked over at Cyndy who was looking pale through her tan. She grabbed at her bottle and took a gulp. Johnathan watched her closely; he could feel her anger. Then he began to notice that the scent of bayberry, which had been hanging heavy in the air, had been replaced by the refreshing scent of apples. That was puzzling. There were no apple trees on the island that he was aware of. He continued his narrative.

"I can see this is disturbing you some, Cyndy. Do you want to know just who the Masters were, well who they are, actually, because they still exist and do work in this world?"

Then the explosion.

"Wait just a darned minute mister."

Cyndy jumped to her feet, startling Lady who was lazing under the shade of the umbrella. She was breathing hard as if just returned from a 10k run. Her cheeks were flaming, her eyes narrowed and accusing. She raised her fist as if to strike him. John put out a big hand and gently enveloped hers. She struggled for a moment, then turned and looked out over the ocean, still breathing heavily.

"I can do numbers you, you... I'm an astronomer remember, and if you were 17 in 1894 that would make you... Oh my God! You can't be... you'd have to have been born in... in 1877. You'd be more than 100 years old. Oh give me a break, what kind of fool do you take me for?"

She turned back to glare at him, now rigid with fury. Then she, too, smelled the scent of apples. She looked wildly around. Johnathan watched and wondered what she was looking for. A baseball bat maybe, he thought. She'd probably like to give him a belt. Well, this sort of thing can be a bit of a shocker. Probably why he never ever told anyone about this part of his life. Cyndy was getting more and more angry.

"Damn you mister, Johnathan, whoever you are. I thought you were my friend and now you just turn out to be a lying son of a bitch."

"Cyndy, Cyndy, what have I been telling you about your mouth. Very unpleasant to hear a well brought-up young woman using that kind of language."

Now both Cyndy and Johnathan spun around trying to find the owner of the voice.

"Grandmother, what's with you? Why're you here? Why now?"

Then she felt like a little girl and felt guilty.

"Don't you see what you're doing to me, grandmother? Just when I want to be bloody mad at this lying..."

"Easy, easy little darlin'. Don't get your knickers all knotted."

The bodiless voice hooted with laughter.

"You used to think that was pretty funny when you a little bit of a thing. Any mention of knickers or other underwear words used to make you laugh and laugh."

"Oh yeah, grandmother, well in case you hadn't noticed I'm a big girl now and your spoiling a good mad on. This... this..."

"Nice man, Cyndy, try handsome big galloot. Only thing makes me sorry I'm not in the physical anymore is when I see a good-looking man, and this is one good-looking man."

Johnathan didn't know why but he was embarrassed and he couldn't even see whom he was being embarrassed by. Oh, he knew a spiritual manifestation when it complimented him, but he was puzzled at one showing up now. Apparently there was more here that he had supposed or suspected. And apparently it belonged to the surprising Cyndy. Not only a chosen one but comes complete with traveling spirit-guide, he thought.

"Yes, Johnathan, I'm Cyndy's old granny. At least I was before takin' off for the pleasant spiritual world. Because of Cyndy's unusual gift I have been commissioned, isn't that a nice word, commissioned, to help her get started on her spiritual quest. Didn't know when I was alive that she had this gift. Well, it was precipitated by that danged car crash. Maybe she wouldn't ever have wakened up to her gift for healin' if she hadn't gone out of body and all. But then I didn't know you, of all people, a disciple of the Masters, would show up here, too. Were you also commissioned to help her?"

By now Johnathan had gathered his wits together and, centering within his sixth chakra, cleared his mind, opened his third eye and clearly saw the wise old blue eyes looking into his own.

"That's better, Johnathan, maybe you could teach this sweet brat of mine how to do that and then I wouldn't have to keep using up ectoplasm just so she can see me when I'm visitin'."

Cyndy was getting another burst of mad going but this time aimed at both her invisible grandmother and Johnathan.

"Hey, you two, remember me? It's rude to talk about someone in the third person when they're standing right here in front of you. And where the hell are you anyway grandmother?"

She swung around to face Johnathan.

"Can you really see her and I can't?"

Johnathan nodded.

"Its not all that difficult, Cyndy. I can help you learn how to do it. Like I can teach you many other things you're going to need to know if you plan to take up your role of chosen one, teacher and healer."

"What role? I'm an astronomer, remember? That's my role here. That's where I'm a teacher, too. And I don't know anything about healing, not real healing like Maaiken does in his church. Oh God! I'm so confused. I feel like crying. Damned female weakness, crying, but that's how I feel."

Tears were beginning to cloud her eyes. Each tear tore a hole in Johnathan's heart. He wanted to reach out and comfort her but felt awkward and unsure.

"Oh, go ahead, Johnny, give her a hug and tell her to get a grip on herself. We've got some serious talkin' to do here and I can't have her weepin' like a baby. Happens nearly every time I show up. I'm getting a complex."

She raised her voice and it was like a strong wind sweeping over the deck.

"Stop it Cyndy, darlin'. Just stop all this weepin' and wailin' every time I show up. Get a hold of yourself, now."

Johnathan felt a push and stumbled, catching Cyndy for balance. He hugged for a moment and felt her return his hug before pushing him away.

"No hugging around here until I get some straight answers, OK? Now where the hell are you, grandmother, and are you going to show yourself to me?"

Johnathan, with his heightened awareness, watched where the grandmother stood just behind her granddaughter, a shimmering mist. Cyndy eyed him narrowly, then glanced over her shoulder.

"Now you're looking at her again, aren't you John. You see her and I don't? How do you do that, John? Talk to me John!"

Cyndy strode over to where he had sat down again and perched, with his feet up on the railing, and kicked at the chair. The chair gave a lurch, spilling Johnathan onto the deck where he lay and began to laugh. Lady ran over to get into the game and attacked him with her tongue. Cyndy just gave him a look that didn't know if it should be stern or give way to the laughter beginning to bubble up into her throat.

It was then that Lady suddenly backed off her killer attack and began to bark at the space beside Cyndy. Johnathan watched as the mist took on solid form. Cyndy spun around to watch the space where Lady's bark was aimed. To Cyndy's eyes the empty space slowly filled with the loved form of her grandmother, hair streaming back in the wind, a wicked smile on her ancient lips. The sound effects this time were more like air released from a punctured automobile tire. Lady was prancing up and down and trying to leap onto the new arrival only to apparently bounce off an invisible wall.

"OK now, grandmother, it seems I'm the only one on this planet who can't see you except when you pop or swoosh into a body. I thought I was a chosen one. Why don't I see you like Lady here who, far as I know, isn't chosen for anything, or Johnathan... John do get up off that deck... like this large oaf of a mystic?"

Johnathan eased his over-large body up off the silvered boards of the deck and walked over to where Cyndy stood frowning and looking unhappy.

"That's some of what I wanted to talk to you about, Cyndy, time you learned how to use your gifts. You can see your grandmother in this reality or in spiritual reality, just like Lady here who doesn't know she shouldn't see into the spiritual so does it anyway. Or like me, who has learned to open his third eye whenever necessary to see beyond this world."

He smiled his real smile at her, no time for goofy now.

"You just haven't had time yet to know you can do these things; these are natural things for you to do. Fact is this is just the thin edge of what you can do. Fact is you can do more than I can ever do. It's just that I know what I can do and do it. However, I happen to know that your power will eclipse mine in a very short time."

Cyndy's grandmother had eased her way over to where Cyndy stood and now put her arms around her.

"Let me give you a good hug, little darlin'. Why waste perfectly good ectoplasm if I don't use it to give my girl a hug?"

Cyndy turned and put her own arms around the thin wispy figure and gave a sob.

"Oh grandmother, I thought I would never be able to hug you again."

"Cyndy my darlin', hush up. Enough already. When are you going to barbecue? I haven't had the chance to eat solid food for about three years now."

She grinned her wicked grin.

"Besides, we need to talk about you and getting you up to speed. It's a real blessin' having Johnathan here to help. He is a very powerful mystic who can help you find your own center and power. And we have little enough time to get you ready. Things are happenin' even as we speak that are going to test you to your very limits. And, I might add, your limits are very narrow at the moment."

Her eyes, a startlingly sky blue compared to Cyndy' washed out blue, speared Johnathan.

"Johnathan, you're goin' to help with all this aren't you?"

"And when did I think I had any say in this matter?"

"Right, you don't really, not if you want to keep on the right side of God and we all want that. Without it we don't have power. Even you Johnathan with your agelessness and mind powers, even you would begin to lose these vital powers if you were to go against the wishes of God. Well, you know when I say God, I mean the power of the spiritual reality, which is the only reality that counts."

She gave her characteristic giggle that he had heard before she became visible.

"Do you know what all the healin' on this island is about?

Johnathan shook his head no.

"I was commissioned to come here to find out about the healing and I haven't yet got a clue. I watched Maaiken this morning. Whatever was in that crystal chalice shut me down completely. I couldn't see past the power radiating when Maaiken took it out from under its cover. What was that anyway?"

Cyndy looked puzzled.

"If it's about Maaiken's ability to heal, I've seen him do it many times. George always wants me in church on a Sunday morning and especially when there's going to be a healing. Of course I would have been there anyway for Shirley and he did it just for Shirley this morning. I know that it's remarkable but is there more than what I can see, grandmother?"

"Well, yes and no child. If we get your power up and runnin' you will be able to see the truth. Right now you're about as blind as Lady over there."

Lady looked up and barked.

"Oh you're right Lady, sorry. She's much more blind than that."

Again she giggled, then looked serious.

"Sorry about the giggle but I think some things are just so funny. But, funny or not, things are happenin' in that church that need a lid put on them. I fear the power that can heal so well is corruptin' Maaiken, making him more dangerous than usual. If he loses control completely his healin' can turn to killin'. That temper of his may just blow completely."

She turned and pointed.

"Come on, let's get busy. Cyndy sit down on the deck. Go into your lovely lotus position and get your mind empty. Johnathan, sit beside her and start to focus on her mind. I want to get her power to recognize itself. You can be a catalyst."

As they moved into position in the bright sun, Lady came over and nuzzled at Cyndy.

"Go Lady, go under the umbrella and stay out of the sun. It's too hot for you and I don't want you getting heat stroke."

Lady put her head down in a sulk and moved away.

Johnathan began the process to clear his mind, center on his sixth chakra and peer through his third eye into Cyndy's mind. As he did so Cyndy jerked her head.

"Ouch! Easy John. What are you using, a shoe horn?"

She settled back again. Johnathan, startled out of his meditative state, muttered an apology, recomposed himself and more gently observed Cyndy through his altered state. As he did so he felt a warmth that surprised him. He felt like a Peeping Tom, not wanting to know or feel Cyndy's personal feelings and thoughts. But that feeling of warmth stayed with him; it was a feeling that was meant for him whether Cyndy was aware of it or not.

He sighed, he felt as though he was falling in love and that was a complication he didn't want to deal with. His life had been so complicated for so long, He didn't know if he could ever be normal enough to fall in love. Oh, his body had responded to women before, but there had never been the complication of really caring. Just as well, he thought, it's no fun watching someone you love grow old while you remain the same age forever. Also you have to somehow explain your youthfulness. He had had to move into new societies and communities to lose contact with those that grew old. It had meant a lonely sort of life, but he'd become used to it. Finally he muted his mind, yet kept a constant watch over his new friend.

Soon the only sound was the wind-softened noise of waves breaking on the beach and Lady scrabbling as she scratched hard to reach a point behind an ear. Cyndy began to feel as she had during the moments just after her crash. She felt as if she were lifting out of her body, then realized she and Johnathan were somehow sharing a single point of consciousness and in front of them the grandmother sat, blue eyes now blinding, piercing, entering her total being. Then there was an explosion of light and she was alone in a void, frightened but then feeling a reassuring sense of love and compassion. Hearing voices singing, she even for a moment thought she might be hearing the very voice of God. At this moment she ceased to feel anything and surrendered herself to velvet blackness that obliterated everything.

There was no sense of time passing but Cyndy slowly opened her eyes and looked at Johnathan, still seated beside her, his eyes anxiously watching her. To one side her grandmother was sneaking an Oreo cookie and obviously enjoying this long-lost pleasure. The sun seemed to have jumped through the sky and now was sitting lower down over the ocean. Strange, but it was getting towards dusk, it must be at least seven o'clock. Her body felt stiff. She listened as Johnathan and her grandmother spoke. Then she realized that neither of them was moving their mouths. She listened and watched fascinated. Johnathan smiled.

"Welcome home, Cyndy."

The words sounded in her head but Johnathan still just smiled. Then she heard the grandmother.

"This is what it's like when you have your power turned on, dearie. Isn't it fun? And this is just the beginnin'. You've no idea what you're capable of now. Oh no, you've no idea. Why, you just throw out that telescope of yours. No need of mechanical devices for you. Now you can personally go visit the planets and stars. Just think of the papers you will write then. The others will have to use their telescopes and spectrometers and polarimeters but even then they are going to have a hard time understandin' what you are going to be tellin' them in the future. If you still want to be an astronomer, that is. You might very well decide to become a full time healer; you can heal now just by envelopin' others with your energy and spirit. Oh well, that's for the then. For the now we need to eat so let's light up the barbecue and put on those steaks I know are in the refrigerator."

She smiled proudly at her granddaughter.

"Oh and if you want to talk using your mouth then go right ahead. It's probably better, then you won't confuse the locals by seemin' to be a mind reader, even though that's what you are now, you poor mixed up little darlin'."

Cyndy felt totally confused. Johnathan leaned over and put his arm around her. He felt his pulse quicken. He felt Cyndy's sudden awareness of his feeling and her quick, now speculative look.

"Easy Cyndy, you're just experiencing your new power. Don't be frightened."

Lady came over to forgive her and licked at her face. Cyndy realized she could understand Lady's concern. It was as if Lady was actually speaking to her. When Cyndy reached out to the dog it was with a new understanding of life, her life, the dog's life, the life she could now sense around her as the tree and plant energies moved into her consciousness. She also wondered about this realization of John's feelings toward her. Somehow she wasn't surprised. She must have sensed it long before her powers had expanded. She now considered her own feelings; did she have feelings for Johnathan? Then she blushed; Johnathan must know what she was thinking.

"A little at a time, Cyndy, it's confusing at first. It's like you've been deaf and now you can hear. It's like you've been blind and now you can see. It takes a little getting used to. Take it just a bit at a time. As to whether I know what you're thinking or not, well the first thing we'll teach you is how to cloud your thoughts so no one, not even your granny or I, will be aware of them. And, just so you don't feel too embarrassed, I'll confess to thinking about you more than anyone ever before. I may even be in love with you. Now let me get the steaks while you begin to better understand what has happened to you."

Johnathan levered his large frame up and disappeared into the house. The grandmother smiled at her protégé.

"Isn't he a sweetie? I'll go start on a salad. Just sit there and be a lazy good for nothin' little darlin', you darlin', and think about Johnathan and think about how screwed up your orderly little life has become."

Laughing and laughing, the grandmother stood up and walked by Cyndy on the way into the house, stooping and kissing her forehead on the way.

"I do love you Cyndy dear. Now your life's going to be different. But not to worry, Johnathan and I will help you sort it out."

Chapter Eighteen

George and Maaiken had left the study some two hours ago. George, reeling with the new information, and Maaiken somehow relieved that he could at last talk to someone of the great secret in the dark caves below the church. Maaiken had promised to show George the hidden spaces below on the following Monday.

Jeremy had remained and was still sweeping out the church when Maaiken and George were leaving. Maaiken had told him to lock up when he left. However, he had never left. Now the sun had set and he was standing in front of Maaiken's study door. The door was locked but Jeremy, as custodian, had keys to all the doors including Maaiken's study. He took a deep breath and put the key in the lock, clicked it open and felt the door give under the pressure of his hand.

Pushing open the door to the darkened room, he put his hand on the light switch, then stopped. There was a glimmer of light; something was emitting a violet-blue glow on the big wooden desk.

Just then he gasped as a body pushed past his legs. He knew it was the cat but his nerves were stretched. He aimed a kick at the cat, very unlike him under ordinary circumstances, but the cat was past and gone long before his kick reflex got into action.

He looked curiously at the desk. He knew what it must be. He'd seen it in the church earlier that day. What he hadn't known was that Maaiken, having used the container to help terrorize George, had forgotten to put it back into his drawer. Indeed, under more ordinary circumstances, Maaiken would have returned the precious container and its glowing fluid to the cave below. As it was he'd been carried away with bending George to his will and had set it down amongst his papers and forgotten it.

Now the cat, curious by nature, jumped up onto the desk looking for her usual bed among Maaiken's papers but was attracted to the strange object. Cautiously, she approached the glowing vessel, put out a paw to swat at it, then leaped into the air with a screech, landed on the floor and fled the room, scrabbling through Jeremy's legs to get out the door.

For Jeremy it was almost too much. But he finally got his heart rate down to something near normal, clicked on the lights and entered into the room, walking toward the desk, his curiosity as great as the cat's. As he got closer he began to experience a feeling of discomfort and stopped for a moment wondering if that fish sandwich at noon might have been less than fresh.

He swallowed and continued to close the distance to the top of Maaiken's desk, fighting off feelings of nausea.

Now he was close enough and could see it clearly although his vision was being effected by his feelings of nausea. It was the slim crystal vial with its elaborately carved and jeweled gold cap. The last time he'd seen it was in Maaiken's hands during the healing in the morning. He bent down to more closely inspect this unusual object. His head began to ache and his muscles throbbed.

He straightened up for a moment as he wondered if this was the secret that Maaiken hid in the space behind the bookshelves. He had seen Maaiken using it on Shirley. He had since heard that Shirley seemed to have been another in series of miracle cures. But as he looked at it he thought there must be more to the secret because there was very little of what ever it was in the container. He paused for a moment, wondering why the cat had screeched and left in such a hurry.

Then he leaned over again, put out his hand and picked up the delicate crystal vial. As his hand closed on it he felt a surge of energy bite at his arm as if he'd just touched a live wire. He jerked his hand back with a curse but found he couldn't let go of the vial. His hand was locked around it and he had no control of the muscles, his arm was rigid.

The energy continued to build, running up his arm and into his chest, his breathing became labored, he moaned terribly, his legs trembled, his face became white and sweat jetted from his pores and streamed down his face, soaking the collar of his shirt. Slowly he sank to the floor, his whole body now beginning to twitch as muscles lost control. His bladder voided. His bowels loosened and a stench filled the room. Within minutes all movement had stopped.

The crystal vial survived Jeremy's collapse, still locked in the death grip of the janitor's hand. A faint violet-blue glow was visible where his hand shadowed it from the lights above.

Jeremy was dead.

The thin figure of a man skulking along the side of the church was barely visible in the darkening dusk of evening. St. James had taken this evening to see if he could get into the church and look around.

As he looked up at the cathedral windows above his head, searching for some easy access, he was startled by a flood of light suddenly illuminating his hiding place. He ducked back among the bushes.

"Damn, I thought the place would be empty by now. I saw Maaiken and George leave a couple of hours ago."

St. James listened, hearing a voice speaking before realizing it was his own. He remained still for several minutes, waiting, not wanting anyone looking out the windows to see him. As he strained to look at the windows they remained clear of any figure or motion. One window was raised slightly and, before the lights had come on, he had heard a screech that sounded like a banshee but was most likely made by a cat somewhere in the room.

Now he heard a curse followed shortly by a terrible moaning. What, he wondered, could be going on in that room. He waited, curious, still wanting to get in and look around.

The moaning had stopped. There was complete quiet now but the lights remained on. Wondering about his next move, he detected a faint, foul odor.

Still wanting to get into the church, St. James moved slowly and with caution through the bushes along to the side of the church to where he could see a plain white service door well-shadowed as the outdoor lights were dark. He approached the door and tentatively tried the doorknob. Somewhat surprised, he found it turned easily and the door cracked open. Inside the entrance hall a small wall fixture dimly lit the area. Beyond, he could see a hall and a door to a room that streamed out light.

He entered quietly, guessing that the well-lit doorway down the hall was the same room with the windows that had lighted up earlier. He listened then started to creep toward the doorway when he stumbled over a small body in the corridor. It was a cat. He looked at it in the dim light and could see that it was a very dead cat. He stopped, now nervous, wondering if he should go forward. Surely the church didn't just leave dead cats lying around. Something was seriously wrong.

Still driven by his need to know more, he again crept towards the open door, pausing from time to time to listen. There was no sound. Finally he had reached the door and peered around the frame. He gasped. In front of the massive desk over by the windows the figure of a man lay sprawled, unmoving. He recognized him, the doorkeeper from the church whose neck he had pinched when threatened with expulsion. The same man, he remembered the name Maaiken had used, Jeremy, who had taken him to the front and found him a chair. The foul odor he had perceived from below the window was stronger here, making him take shallower breaths. He looked about the room, obviously Maaiken's study. There didn't appear to be anyone else in the room.

St. James pondered his next move. This didn't appear to be a good night for exploring. A dead cat in the hall and a dead man in the study. He turned to go, then, on impulse, walked to the desk and, taking out his handkerchief to cover the telephone receiver, picked it up and, using his pen, poked out the numbers 911.

The telephone answered on the first ring. A young woman's voice sounded in his ear.

"911 emergency response, how can I help you?"

St. James thought a moment then said abruptly and in a voice different from his own.

"Just found a dead man in the Poor Soldiers of Christ Church. Thought maybe you'd like to send someone."

Before she could respond, he quickly put down the phone and, as quickly, turned and hurried into the corridor and out the service door, stepping over the body of the cat on the way.

Blue lights flashed as the first car arrived with the two deputies stepping out. Two other cars and an ambulance crowded in behind the first arrival. Quickly a group of men and women had assembled in front of the church when Maaiken arrived, breathless, demanding to know what was happening. It was Fred who answered him

"Don't know, Reverend Maaiken, we just got a 911 call to say there was a dead man in your church. Don't know who phoned it, he hung up before we could ask any more questions, so you know as much as we do. I'm glad you're here Reverend, now we can explore the property together."

Maaiken strode up to the main doors and tried them but they were locked.

"Come, the service door at the side, we can get in that way."

Just then another car skidded to a halt and the Sheriff stepped out.

"OK, what's going on here? I just got a call about a dead body in the church. Anyone been in yet?"

"No Sheriff. We're just about to go in. The Reverend here's going to open the side service door."

It was Fred who spoke up. He'd been first on the scene as his car had been on patrol nearby.

"Then let's get our asses into the church and see if there's anything to the call."

With this the sheriff led the group around the side of the church. The side door was in darkness.

"Funny, these lights should be on. It's the last thing Jeremy does before he leaves."

Maaiken took out his keys to open the door but realized it was, in fact, slightly ajar.

"Lights out and the door open. What's that man thinking? I'll have to have words with him."

Maaiken pushed the door fully open and walked into the dimly-lit entrance hall. Immediately he could see that the door to his study was open, lights streaming into the hall.

"I locked that door before I left. What's going on here?"

He pushed his way through the congestion in the entrance hall and immediately tripped over a small bundle of fur on the floor.

"What's this?"

Maaiken reached out and pushed a switch on the wall, immediately flooding the area with light.

"It's that damned cat. It's dead."

Now he turned and hurried to the door of his study, closely followed by John and his deputies. Maaiken stopped suddenly at the door, taking in the scene before him, smelling the stench of death.

"Oh my God, Jeremy..."

Taylor shouldered him aside, then stopped, confronted by the body and the smell in the room. Then he started forward only to stop when Maaiken shouted at him.

"Sheriff, stop. Don't touch that body. Every one keep back. The thing that killed Jeremy can kill all of you if you touch it."

With that he pushed past the puzzled Sheriff and reached down to the body.

"Stop right there, Maaiken. You're interfering with evidence at what may be a crime scene."

Maaiken stopped momentarily to turn and stare at Taylor.

"You don't understand, Sheriff, that vial in Jeremy's hand. It's what's killed him and it's deadly to anyone here but me. You must let me take it before anyone else is harmed. I'll explain it all to you, but I must secure that deadly vial first."

With those words he again turned to the body, stooped down and gently pried the vial out of Jeremy's rigid grip.

Taylor watched but made no more protestation. Maaiken turned to open his desk drawer and took out a small but elaborate silver box decorated with hieroglyphics. He opened the box, inserted the vial, and quickly shut it again.

"There Sheriff, your men can enter now. You and I should talk. You see, in a way I'm responsible for what's happened here tonight. Due to my carelessness and to Jeremy's stupid curiosity, we've had a fatality. I carelessly left this vial unprotected on my desk. I don't know what brought Jeremy in here; he was never to come in here when I was out of the church. However he did, he picked up the vial and the intense power of the contents killed him. The irony is that the power in the vial's contents can heal any illness, and yet it can kill, just as you see here."

Maaiken looked down on the body.

"Dear God, bless this man. Take his spirit gently into your bosom and give him your love."

Maaiken was weeping now, tears coursing down his face. He turned back to the Sheriff.

"You should arrest me for negligence, Sheriff. This is all my fault. Even that cat out in the hall, somehow it must have touched the vial. Curious little cat, it was always jumping up on my desk. It infuriated me but I wouldn't have wanted it to die like this."

Taylor watched. He had never seen Maaiken so disturbed. Normally this man was cold and autocratic at all times. Now he had collapsed into normal human grief.

George parked his car in front of the garage and climbed wearily out, leaning for a moment on the hood before turning and heading into the house. He listened to the silence, no dog barking at him, no hello from the kitchen or elsewhere in the house.

He kept thinking of his meeting with Maaiken and the incredible information he had been given. God, he practically had his hands on the discovery of the century, even millennium. The power to heal any illness. And the source of the power? That's what really kept his mind at full throttle, unable to stop. He pulled open the refrigerator door and grabbed a cool bottle of Sam Adam's, popped the cap and poured half of the bubbling brew into his throat, swallowing and then gasping but feeling better with the cool feel of the liquid now coursing down to his stomach.

"Where are you Cyndy? Damn it why aren't you here when I need you!"

He stopped, realizing he was shouting at an empty house. Then he remembered Cyndy telling him she was spending the afternoon out at the beach. He wondered for a moment if he should go there and then stopped. What would he tell her, anyway? He didn't want her to know what he had learned. This was his secret. When he was ready he would tell her just enough, but not the real secret, not how to produce the healing whenever he wanted. No. He had to think. He decided to go to his office. He always thought better there anyway. Besides he could peek into Maaiken's study and other places and keep track of matters until he decided how to handle the situation.

It took only a few moments to pull off his suit, shirt and tie and get into jeans before going out the door and into the garage. He pulled his Harley out and kicked it into action. With the characteristic Harley growl he swept out of the driveway and onto the street on his way to Commercial Street.

The office was in darkness, the staff off for the weekend and no overtime pressures currently keeping anyone chained to their computer. Snapping on lights as he went, George entered his office and quickly entered commands on a keyboard that brought the church cams onto his screen. He checked the clock. Just going on 8.00 p.m. Time to get some hours in on the new application for the banks. He settled in, keeping one eye on the church cams. Time slipped quickly by.

Suddenly the buzzing of the study cam alerted George's attention. He glanced at it only to see a darkened room with light spilling from the door and a figure of a person standing half in and half out. Then there was a flurry at the door and something small brushed past a figure. Almost immediately the small furry figure of the church cat could be seen as it leapt onto the top of the big pine desk. There was a faint glow in the middle of the desk and George immediately identified it as the vial Maaiken had been showing him earlier, obviously forgotten.

As George watched, the cat put out a paw and batted at the vial, then screeched and leaped from the desk and was gone from his sight.

The door continued to open and the lights came on to show Jeremy now coming into the room. George watched apprehensively as he saw Jeremy come closer to the desk, pause, then stoop and put out his hand. George shouted at the screen.

"No, no, you fool, leave that alone."

But his shout only echoed around his room. On the screen he watched in horror as Jeremy picked up the vial then staggered back and slowly sank to the floor. Even as he watched, the body began to twitch and jerk then become still. And he was spared nothing as the moaning sounds of Jeremy's pain reached his ear through the study cam mike.

"Oh my God!"

George sat in shock not knowing what to do.

Even as he debated phoning the Sheriff's Office another cam buzzed and another screen opened to show a man George recognized. He had seen him earlier come from the back of the church at Maaiken's invitation to sit in a special chair provided by Jeremy.

Intrigued and forgetting Jeremy lying in the study, he now watched as the man as he cautiously walked up the dim hall, stumbling over something on the floor, then continuing until he had reached the door where he peered in.

George could see the scene from two cams, as the study cam picked him up as he began to enter, while the hall cam provided a back shot of the action.

He saw the shock on the stranger's face as he first caught sight of Jeremy's body lying on the floor, still clutching the crystal vial in his right hand. The stranger walked over to study the body, then, taking out a handkerchief and covering the phone, lift it from the cradle and used a pen to dial 911.

"Just found a dead man in the Poor Soldiers of Christ church. Thought maybe you'd like to send someone."

He hung up immediately. The man's voice sounded clearly through the study cam mike.

Quickly now, the man left the study without disturbing anything else and the hall cam caught him as he left through the side service door.

Only minutes went by before the door opened again and Maaiken entered followed by the Sheriff and several deputies.

George sat, his work forgotten, as the scene unfolded before him. He was surprised by Maaiken's obvious remorse for the accident that had taken Jeremy's life. He had never seen this side of Maaiken, always assuming him to be cold to all human misery.

Finally he pulled himself up from his chair and went out into the gathering darkness and his Harley. He had much thinking to do. Maaiken had never revealed the deadlier side of his secret, only the healing. Now what could be done in this world if you possessed deadly force as well as incredible healing? People might confuse you with Jesus. He could be the next Messiah.

His mind dwelt on these thoughts as he wheeled the big bike towards his house. It might explain why he failed to see the truck, just leaving the docks and heading into the island to make a delivery. The moment became a roar of broken motorcycle and screaming brakes and finally the quiet of death, of life suspended, of destiny changing.

The phone in Cyndy's office was answered by her grad student who was working on a paper due to be read at next Monday's public lecture. The shocking news left the young woman momentarily stunned. Then she dialed Cyndy's cell number.

Out at the beach house, Cyndy and Johnathan had just finished up their barbecue meal. As mysterious in going as she had been in her appearance, the grandmother was now absent once more. Just a "time to be leaving you now children," a wave of her hand and a slight sound like a door closing in the distance, and maybe a slight burping and giggle, and she had simply become more and more transparent until there was nothing left to see.

Johnathan hung up a tea towel and paused to admire the scent of Cyndy's hair that just happened to be in front of him as she stretched up to put the last dishes into a cupboard.

As if she had eyes in the back of her head she reacted.

"You know I can read your mind now, Johnathan. What are you doing, anyway?"

She laughed and turned to him, then, suddenly, was enveloped with emotion, not hers, and felt a trembling in her heart chakra. She took a quick breath, stepped back a pace, bumped into the sink and stopped short.

"Sorry, Cyndy, I'll just have to be more careful and shield my mind. I'm not used to being with someone with your powers, young lady."

Johnathan couldn't remember when he had felt so free and so young. This new friend was causing him to feel emotions he'd thought were long gone from his life. He slowly reached out to pull her closer. She, in turn felt an unaccustomed weakness in her knees and let herself fall toward him, her arms reaching around his middle, her face buried in his chest. For a long moment they stayed close, locked in an embrace. Johnathan just held on and tried not to breathe too fast. Cyndy simply let herself go into the moment.

A strident peal broke the silence.

"Oh, damn, sorry, John, that's my cell phone. Only my grad student has this number and I'm sure she wouldn't be phoning me if it wasn't important."

She quickly reached up to kiss his cheek then pulled away, walking out of the kitchen to where the cell phone made its demanding noises on the table in the dining room.

Johnathan, still lost in the moment, heard her gasp and went to where she stood, pale, cell phone pressed to her ear, listening to the voice on the other end. Finally, she put the phone down and turned towards him.

"It's George. He's had a terrible accident on his motorbike. He's in the hospital. They don't know if he'll live. Oh, John..."

Johnathan stepped to where she still stood leaning on the pine table. He took her hand in his.

"Come on Cyndy, we'll go now. If you like I'll drive."

They quickly turned out the lights, locked up the small house and went to her truck. The bright red pick-up started immediately. Johnathan turned it in the graveled lot and drove up the drive and onto the asphalt road back to town. Cyndy sat quietly beside him, eyes on the road, mind numbed. In his mind he could hear her pain and confusion. Her pain became his pain as he drove toward the Nantucket Cottage Hospital. The knowledge of their newly bonded state gave him much to consider as he drove with controlled haste, ignoring the 'Thickly Settled' signs and posted speed limit.

Chapter Nineteen

It was twenty minutes later when Johnathan turned Cyndy's truck into the Nantucket Cottage Hospital parking lot. In all that time Cyndy had sat, frozen, her mind almost totally stalled. Johnathan had carefully screened his mind so that she would have privacy to deal with this situation without revealing herself to him.

He parked the truck, then went to Cyndy's door and opened it. Cyndy looked at him with a blank stare, as if she didn't recognize him. He gently took her arm and eased her out of the seat. She staggered as he put her on her feet and he quickly put his arm around her, holding her until she seemed to return to this reality.

Johnathan watched her take a deep breath, focus on the hospital doors and take a quick step forward. He caught her as she stumbled. He didn't relax his hold this time but supported her as they went up the two steps to the small entrance and through the double doors into the hospital reception area.

The first person he caught sight of was a thin young man with long dark hair caught back in a ponytail sitting behind the reception desk. The man leapt to his feet and came out from behind the desk to grab and hug Cyndy.

"Cyndy, we've been waiting for you. Bob and Jenny Thornton are with George in the OR. I don't know how long they will be. There's talk of flying George to Boston where they have a large neurology department. Sit over here while I get you a coffee."

His eyes looked questioningly at Johnathan. He smiled and nodded.

"I'll sit with her. Sorry I don't know your name. She hasn't been saying much since she heard the news. We were out at her beach house when her grad student phoned. We came straight away."

Johnathan took an unresisting Cyndy by the arm and led her to the chairs set out in one corner of the reception area, near a window that looked out into the parking lot.

The young man followed, looked at Johnathan and put out his hand.

"Sorry about George. My name's Art by the way. I man the desk here most nights. Actually I'm studying medicine at Harvard and this summer night job usually allows me lots of study time.

He looked around almost in awe.

"I was born right here in this hospital."

Art gave a little shrug, smiled at Johnathan, then went to Cyndy and took her hand.

"Cyndy, they took George straight to the operating room, Jenny and Bob are both working on him. He's suffered terrible head trauma. He wasn't wearing a helmet when the truck hit him. He lifted right off the bike and took much of the force of landing with his head. His vital signs were feeble at best when the ambulance arrived. They're trying to stabilize him now and relieve the pressure on his brain."

Just then the doors to the entrance flew open and Maaiken strode in, a small fury of a person, eyes blazing, mouth a thin mean line.

"Where is he, Arthur? How is he? What's going on? What's happened to George?"

He turned toward Cyndy and Johnathan.

"Cyndy?"

Cyndy turned to look at him, her blue eyes taking on signs of awareness for the first time. When she spoke her voice became stronger, her words crisp.

"Sorry Maaiken, we just got here. We don't know any more than George has sustained severe damage to his head from a motorcycle accident. He's in the operating room with the neurologist."

The arrival of Maaiken seemed to galvanize Cyndy so she was more her own self again. At least she was talking and making some sense.

It was Maaiken who now seemed unable to deal with this news. He stared at the floor then back at Cyndy.

"But I need George at the church. We've had a terrible accident there and I need George to help me deal with it."

Maaiken surprised her. He was almost pleading.

"Maaiken, George may be dying. He can't help you now. You'll have to deal with the church yourself. If you need George so badly you'd better go heal him with one of your miracles. He's going to need a miracle as far as I've heard."

Cyndy stopped, turned away, lost her momentary calm and began to sob quietly. Johnathan watched her with care, unable to think what he might do to help.

The hospital entrance was the focus of a number of people coming and going. Art had to excuse himself and go to talk to some recent arrivals who were looking for a patient. A muted speaker asked for Dr. Rollands to come to room 223. Then the front doors opened again to the arrival of George's father, looking white-faced and scared.

Cyndy calmed at once at someone else's need. She got to her feet and went to him, leading him to a corner where they sat and talked in low voices. Johnathan felt awkward, wondering if he could do something to help but not knowing what. Although schooled in many mysteries, he was not a healer. He wondered if Maaiken might really be able to do a miracle cure for George.

Johnathan glanced over to where Maaiken was standing, then pacing, then stopping and staring around, looking unusually out of control for the man who controlled so much on this island. He walked over to him and held out his large hand.

"Reverend, we haven't been introduced. Johnathan Millar. I was in your church when you were working on Shirley Woodstock. It was an amazing performance."

Maaiken swirled around to stare up into Johnathan's carefully benign face. He anger came up like a cloud from an atomic burst.

"Performance, performance... that was pure spirit at work, whoever you are. Never call my work in the church a performance."

He stopped, choked by his own rage. A blood vessel on his forehead was enlarged and pulsating. His lips trembled.

Johnathan shielded himself from the energy that radiated at him. His smile remained friendly, even goofy, as he stood his ground.

"Sorry, Reverend, meant no harm. It was just so moving to watch you as you called on Jesus and God to help Shirley be cured of her mortal illness. And then to see the results confirmed by the hospital MRI, well, I'm just so impressed at your unique ability to heal. You must be in demand all over the world. There are so many people who are desperately ill and who have vast wealth, people who would pay you very well to heal them."

Johnathan had pitched his voice to its most soothing cadence and his words were having just that effect on Maaiken. His breathing started to calm and the fierce light went out of his eyes. He looked suspiciously at Johnathan.

"Who are you again? What did you say your name was?"

Johnathan still stood with his hand extended. He left it there.

"Sorry, Reverend. I meant no disrespect. This must be a most stressful time for you. My name is Johnathan. I'm a friend of Shirley Woodstock. That's why I was so concerned and impressed by your healing. Shirley is such a vital and lively young woman, to see her struck down so suddenly and then to be cured just as suddenly, well, I'm quite blown away by the whole process, spiritual as it is."

His hand stayed unanswered. He finally lowered it.

"I'm just wondering how you can do these miracles. Indeed, I've read that your father was considered a miracle healer, too, but he never demonstrated this power as you do on such a consistent and successful basis. Or in front of so many people."

Johnathan had deliberately refrained from mentioning his friendship with Cyndy, being aware just how much Maaiken disliked her. Acknowledging a friendship with Cyndy would just turn Maaiken off completely, and he wanted to learn more.

Maaiken was now under full control and looking speculatively at Johnathan.

"Don't I remember you from some years ago. Weren't you here with the Coast Guard detachment? As I recall, you were involved in a fight in a bar that left one man desperately injured. He was in the Nantucket Cottage Hospital for a month before he was well enough to leave and then there was something about his being a foreign agent. I remember the FBI coming to Nantucket to investigate and finally take the young man off-island."

Johnathan was unprepared for this burst of memory.

"Well, yes Reverend, but I'm surprised you would remember that little incident so long ago. It was all cleared up and I wasn't really involved except to have the bad luck to be in the bar when a fight broke out. I had some difficulty getting out of there without getting injured myself. Why would you even remember an incident like that?"

Maaiken had roused Johnathan's curiosity.

"That man, the one who was injured, he was also trying to find out how people get healed in my church. He was trying to steal my secrets. Well I don't forget people like that or anyone that might be associated with that sort. That's why I'm curious about you, mister, what did you say your name was?"

"Millar, Johnathan Millar, Reverend. Yeah, I was lucky to get out of that bar without getting a knife in my ribs, but that's old history. I've left the Coast Guard now and run a little business on the mainland. Just here for a visit to see Nantucket again."

Jonathan's goofy smile was getting a bit tired but he left it on his face.

"You said something about a terrible accident at the church. Can you tell me what happened? Can I help in any way?"

Maaiken looked up into Johnathan's innocent face and lost his earlier anger. He looked almost human. A sad expression took over where anger had previously dominated.

"Kind of you, Johnathan, but I doubt you can do anything the Sheriff and his deputies can't handle. One of my staff was found dead in my study. He was an old member and I feel responsible for his accident. If I hadn't been careless Jeremy would be alive today."

With this mysterious message Maaiken turned and went out the double door entrance. Johnathan followed him out.

"I'm serious, Reverend, I would like to help if I could be of any use. I'm pretty good with handling the press, for instance. It's what I do for a living. If there's going to be media interest in what's happened, maybe you would like someone who has good media contacts to help fend off the curiosity this might arouse."

Maaiken turned back to stare into Johnathan's face.

"I hadn't thought of how this might appeal to those wolves in the media. You have media contacts? You know how to handle the press?"

Johnathan nodded. Maaiken stood, looking at Johnathan, studying his face. He seemed to come to some decision. He bobbed his head. When he spoke, it wasn't the old autocrat. Disaster had robbed him of his sense of absolute power for the moment. Instead he now sensed another disaster.

"Are you free to come with me right now? If there is going to be media involvement we need to get on it right away."

"Give me just a moment to let my friends know where I'm going and I'll be right with you, Reverend."

Johnathan turned and re-entered the hospital, going over to where Cyndy was still talking to George's father.

"Cyndy, sorry to interrupt. I'll get back in touch with you later. I'm going over to the church with Maaiken to find out what's happened over there. Remember who and what you are. Be careful. Don't let your guard down even though you're in shock for the moment. They'll be a while with George anyway, I'm sure. We'll talk later this evening."

Cyndy looked surprised at this, frowned, then smiled at him, nodded and turned back to the older man, taking his hand and speaking softly. George's father sat slumped, dejected, worried and still pale.

Johnathan slid his big frame into the driver's seat of the red truck. He gave the seat a shove, trying to clear more room for his long legs, but to no avail. The seat was already pushed back as far as it would go.

Finally accepting the futility of the exercise, he grumbled under his breath and started the engine, grinding his way into first gear and shooting gravel out behind him as he hurried to catch Maaiken, whose taillight was just disappearing though the exit to the main road.

The ride was short, distances on Nantucket were all relatively short. Maaiken pulled in behind one of the Deputy Sheriff's cars, its lights still strobing blue. Pulling in behind Maaiken's Saab, Johnathan caught up to him at the service entry door.

Maaiken pulled Johnathan by the arm to get him down to conversational height and explained what had been found in his study. He still sounded shocked that his carelessness had resulted in the death of one of his own staff. They went into the entrance hall and up to his study door. The room seemed full. The Sheriff and three deputies were standing, watching, as two men from the local mortuary put Jeremy's body into a body bag and lifted it onto a gurney. Johnathan moved aside to give the gurney room as it squeaked by; one of the mortuary men looked to see which wheel was causing the racket.

"Shit, got to get that wheel oiled when we get Jeremy back. We wheel this thing down a church aisle, the family would kick us out."

The gurney continued its noisy passage until the two disappeared out the service door.

The Sheriff looked up to see who was in the doorway and frowned, looking belligerently at the odd couple.

"What do you want, Johnathan? We're mighty busy here and it's none of your business, far as I know."

Maaiken intervened

"I've brought him here, Sheriff. He's going to help me with the media who'll be descending on this place as soon a whiff of this gets out. Now leave him be."

Maaiken was back to his old commanding self. The Sheriff backed down, grumbling but doing nothing to cross the diminutive leader of the church.

"OK, Maaiken, OK. Do as you like. Didn't know you were a PR guy, Johnathan, you continue to surprise me."

The Sheriff turned back to his deputies.

"Guess we've done all the damage we can do tonight."

He turned and looked at Maaiken again.

"Maaiken, I'll need to see you tomorrow, down at the office. We've got some forms to fill out and some swearing to do to complete the formalities. Don't see where you have any real liability. So you left out some lethal mixture or something. It was a locked room. Jeremy got himself into trouble you never meant for him. Same for that darn cat in the corridor. Curious, just like Jeremy, I figure. Got itself into serious trouble. Just for the record, Maaiken, how'm I gonna describe whatever that stuff is that killed the two of them?"

Sheriff John looked at Maaiken, slanting his head as he did, his eyebrows arched quizzically.

"For your information, Sheriff, that is a special gift from God, Himself, that He provides to help me heal these good people each Sunday. It's my special anointing oil. Trouble with it, it makes people real sick if they aren't used to its power. Well, you've felt that yourself in the church, haven't you? I've noticed you ducking out when I bring it out. You feel it and you get out of the church. Many do.

The Sheriff nodded.

"For the right recipient, under my guidance and my prayers to God, it heals. Otherwise it can be deadly, real deadly."

"Yeah, well make sure you lock that stuff up proper now. I don't ever want a repeat of this evening."

Taylor turned and strode out the study door followed by the deputies. Those in the church could hear him telling them to button their lips about this case. The voices dwindled and soon the Sheriff's cars started up and the blue strobing stopped, leaving an eerie sense of darkness, even though the study lights were blazing.

Johnathan pulled an antique captain's chair up to the desk and sat gingerly, hoping he wouldn't break it. It creaked a bit but took his weight without further protest. Maaiken went behind the desk and then appeared as he perched on his especially elevated black leather office chair.

He'd just got settled when the phone rang. Shaking his head, he picked up the receiver.

"I'll wager I know who's on the other end of this."

With that he spoke quietly into the receiver.

Johnathan took advantage of the interruption to look around again, especially eye-balling the bookcase. There was nothing out of the ordinary that he could see. He decided to take a risk and closed down briefly while he centered himself and probed with his mind, passing through the bookcase and was surprised to find himself in a darkened area with steps leading downward.

The sound of the phone being slammed back on the cradle jerked him back into ordinary reality. He opened his eyes to see Maaiken staring at him with a puzzled expression.

"You OK, you seemed so still for a moment I thought maybe you were asleep or something. Am I keeping you up?"

Johnathan smiled his usual goofy smile.

"Sorry there, Reverend, just lost in thought, that's all. Nothing to get excited about. Was thinking about putting together a news release so we'd have something when the media start asking questions. That way we'll all have the same words to sing off the song sheet."

Maaiken considered this and nodded his tiny, perfect head.

"Well, we'll need something soon enough. That was the Washington Post, can you believe it. How the hell did they hear about this so soon? They've got reporters flying in, due to arrive almost anytime."

He paused and shook his head at this thought.

"Anyway, let me tell you all about the accident. Seems Jeremy, you remember Jeremy, he was in the church while I was doing a healing for Shirley Woodstock? Well, poor Jeremy, got curious I guess and his curiosity got him killed."

He then explained how he'd left the vital vial of glowing, healing oil out on his desk instead of locking it up in its usual secure, shielded storage place. Jeremy, it seemed, had picked it up and the extraordinary power of the healing oil jolted his heart until it stopped.

He fingered the amulet with its carved red stone as it hung around his neck, vying for space with an ornate cross. His voice became dreamy for a moment.

"I have special protection, something no one else could possibly have or even know about. Also, I've developed some immunity to the power, probably from long association. However, I know it affects others badly. Only those I'm healing can withstand the power and I believe that's because it's accompanied by sincere prayer. There is sanctuary in prayer. Poor Jeremy, he didn't know about the power and how to make it work for the good of our fellow man."

"You make me curious, Reverend, what is the source of this power?"

Maaiken looked cross at Johnathan.

"Look, your job is to help me out with the media. I don't need or want to answer your questions, understand me?"

Maaiken was standing now, a furious scowl on his face. Johnathan stared back, using some of the force of his mind.

"Easy Reverend, easy. I'm just here to help and if I'm going to do that I need a computer or typewriter. I need to get some words down on paper before these investigative reporters arrive."

Maaiken looked dubious but nodded in agreement.

"There's a computer on my secretary's desk. Come on, I'll show you."

Maaiken led Johnathan out to another office door. Inside were filing cabinets and a cheap gray metal desk with a Dell computer, Hewlett Packard bubble jet printer and an AGFA scanner sitting in an orderly row. An umbrella hung from an old oak clothes tree and framed pictures of small children shared desk space with the computer equipment.

"You know how to run one of these things? Confess I never took the time to learn, too many other things for a church leader to do around here. That George now, he knows all about these technical things. He's a bit of a genius, I'm told. And that girl, Shirley Woodstock, she's also a computer expert. George has told me about her. Wants to hire her for his own business."

Here Maaiken stopped, looked sad.

"Poor George, looks like he might die too. And I need him here. He's supposed to be my heir to running the church. Why I've even told him the most secret things."

"Why don't you heal him, Reverend? This should be right down your street."

"It can't be done outside the church. It just doesn't work outside the church."

"Why's that Reverend?"

"Because, because... you don't need to know why. This is church business. Get to work and draft up something for these fool reporters."

With that Maaiken turned and stomped out. Johnathan thought it must be hard to stomp when you're a midget. He laughed, then sobered. He had no right to be so critical, after all he was supposed to love his neighbor. He knew the rules. If he weren't careful the Masters would be pulling him back to India. Right now he had no desire to go back and leave Cyndy. She had become more important to him than anything else. He had to see this through and find out where it was all leading.

Strange though, why Maaiken couldn't heal George outside of the church. Another mystery to unravel. He set to work, turning on the computer and booting up the word processing program. After that he started to compose his news release.

As he worked, one part of his mind wondered at this latest mystery. The healing was restricted to the church. That, he supposed, meant there was something here in the church that made the healing possible. The glowing oil was not the primary healing agent. There was something else. Something hidden. He remembered the glimpse beyond the bookcases. Something hidden in the secret space behind and below the bookcases?

He would have to find a way to get beyond the bookcase. But he would have to be very careful. Look what happened to poor old Jeremy. He might not age but he was vulnerable.

When he had finished composing and printing out a copy of his news release, he tried the phone on the desk but he couldn't get an outside line. He experimented with dialing 9 first but to no avail. He wanted to find out what was happening at the hospital. Finally he got up and went looking for Maaiken.

Maaiken was still in his study. He looked up as Johnathan knocked and entered. He had been writing in a large, leather-covered book. He looked somewhat sad.

"Births and deaths in the parish. I was just recording Brother Jeremy's passing."

"Well, here's a take on the news release. If you have time, take a look at it and tell me if you want anything changed. I suggest you leave it the way it is unless I've stated something inaccurately, OK? Now I need a phone, I want to check up on the situation at the hospital. I want to find out how George is doing."

"Use the one on the secretary's desk. You need to dial 112 to get an outside line. My line here is the only one that is a direct out."

Johnathan nodded and left, finding his way back to the desk where he had been working. As he walked down the hall he thought about the puzzle. Somehow he had to get into Maaiken's office and through the bookcase. Just as he was entering the secretary's office he heard Maaiken's door closing. He had deliberately left it open when he walked out. Now he wondered why Maaiken had bothered to get up and close it. He felt a little spurt of excitement. Maybe Maaiken was going to open up the bookcase. He turned and hurried back to stand quietly in front of the closed door.

He listened but there was no sound. He tried the door but it was locked. He quickly centered and let his consciousness project through the door. Now he could see into the room. It was empty. He turned his attitude so that he was facing the bookcase. It was just closing. Slowly, he let himself move forward to the opening, then stopped. Something was wrong. He quickly became one again with his body. Now he was in the physical again and found himself with his hand on the door, looking at the blank panel. It was a phone ringing. That's what had spooked him into coming back to the physical body. He hurried back to the secretary's office. One of the lines was blinking. He picked up the receiver and stabbed at the button beside the blinking light and spoke into the phone.

"Church of the Poor Soldiers of Christ, Johnathan Millar speaking."

"Johnathan, oh Johnathan I'm so glad I found you."

It was Cyndy; she was sobbing.

"What is it Cyndy, what's happening? Are you all right?"

"It's George, they tell me he's dying. I feel so bad for him. I don't know what to do. We've had our problems but I didn't want him to die, Johnathan, I didn't want him to die."

There was fresh sobbing in his ear and Johnathan's heart felt ready to break.

"I'm coming back right now, Cyndy. I'll be there in ten minutes. Hang on, I'll be right there."

He hung up and raced out of the office heading for the service door. He had no way of reaching Maaiken wherever that little man had gone. Cyndy's grief-stricken voice sounded in his mind and there was only one place he had to be.

The little red truck raced through the darkened streets. Fortunately there was little traffic and it was only minutes later that Johnathan swung into the hospital parking lot, skidding the tires and throwing open the door to hurry into the hospital entrance. He could see Cyndy standing with George's father. They were both crying and holding on to each other.

As he stood for the moment, not wanting to break into the grief before him, he felt a gentle tug at his mind. At the same time the familiar scent of apple blossoms and he looked to find Cyndy's grandmother but found only a shimmer of light. She was not in a physical body. Then her voice found his mind as she whispered.

"We need to talk Johnathan, we need to get Cyndy out of this shock and thinking. Do something, boy, she needs you, and I need to talk to her. Think of something but get her where we can talk."

There was a sharp urgency to the usual placid voice Johnathan associated with the grandmother. He took her at her word and went directly to Cyndy and George's father. Gently, he took both their arms and led them into the small chapel built next to the reception area. Once inside he settled them on two chairs. The room immediately had a soothing effect on them both. They sat back and gradually stopped their tears and sobbing. Johnathan whispered into Cyndy's ear.

"Cyndy, I need to speak to you privately. Could you please break away for a moment? I know that George's father needs your comfort but it's urgent that we speak in private."

Cyndy looked at him, her eyes reddened by her tears, for a moment almost not recognizing him. Then her eyes focused and she nodded and leaned over to the older man taking his hand in hers.

"Allan, you sit here for a moment, I have to go and take care of some business. I'll be back soon and maybe we'll be able to see George then."

She got up out her chair, moving slowly as an old woman. She reached out and leaned on Johnathan's ready arm. Together they walked out of the Chapel door into the busy reception area. Leaving Johnathan she went to speak to Art, still sitting in the receptionist's chair. After a whispered conversation, she returned and took Johnathan's arm again.

"Come with me. Art says to use Bob's office if we want some privacy."

She pulled him towards a set of doors that led to a series of offices set aside for the medical staff. Finally she opened one of the doors and they went into Bob Hawkin's office, a small but neatly furnished room with a chintz curtained window, a small, antique pine desk and a set of filing cabinets against one of the walls. Pictures of Jean and Bob on a sailboat, grinning at a dance, at the beach, and other happy moments graced walls and desk. A small couch and leather chair formed a conversational grouping with a low oak table holding some magazines. Here she sat and pulled Johnathan down to sit beside her

"What is it John, what's so urgent? Have you heard something about George? Is that why you wanted to talk to me in private?"

She looked nervously at him as she asked this question. He wanted to hug her but resisted. What she didn't need right now was his emotional attachment to further complicate her feelings. Just then a slight tearing sound brought their attention to the chair behind Bob's lovely old desk. It now held the graceful, gray-haired, blue-eyed wraith of a grandmother. She smiled at them before casting a hard glance her granddaughter.

"Cyndy, dear Cyndy. This is so hard for you. I know how you're feelin'. Mostly guilty you didn't love him more, George I mean. Well girl, now's the time to do somethin' you have been preparin' for your whole lifetime. Except you didn't know that's what you were doin'. You thought you were preparin' to be an astronomer. Well just put that thought out of your head for the moment. There are more serious issues ahead for you."

"What are you going on at, grandmother? Make sense, please. What issues? George is dying, don't you know that?"

"Yes dearest girl, I know that. What I want to know is what are you goin' to do about it? Do you want to save his life?"

Cyndy looked confused.

"Now what are you going on about. Of course I want to save his life. Only I can't now can I? Only Maaiken can do stuff like that and he says it only works in his church and how am I going to get George to the church? The only thing keeping him alive right now is a bunch of machinery. And they can't move that to the church now can they?"

Cyndy was indignant, hurt, wanting to cry. And her grandmother was driveling on with nonsense. She swiveled and scowled at Johnathan, his heart groaned under her angry stare.

"Well John do you know what's going on with my usually sweet old grandmother? Does she make sense to you?"

Johnathan thought he might just know what her grandmother was getting at. Was it possible?

"Of course it's possible, Johnathan. If Cyndy weren't so emotionally confused, she'd know it too. You can't do it. I can't do it. Even that mighty midget and his healin' and anointin' oils can't do it. Oh, he can heal anythin' that's just broken, but he can't stop the angel of death from taking his due. But, Cyndy, well, Cyndy's different. Cyndy's rare. She can heal. She can stop death. She might even bring life back if it has slipped away."

Cyndy was staring at the two of them. Her mouth kept trying to make sounds but only succeeded in making strange strangled noises.

Finally one word did make itself heard, then whole sentences.

"Stop it, stop it the two of you, especially you, grandmother. What are you saying? I'm like God? I can stop death? I can revive a dead person?

"No Cyndy, darlin', you aren't God. But God has given you a God-like gift. That's why you're goin' to have to make up your mind what you want to do now with your life. You can go upstairs, give that George a hug and he'll revive. Not that he deserves it all that much. And if you do, you'll be branded a witch or worse. So what's it to be. You gonna be an astronomer all your life or are you gonna take up your true callin'? Sorry to spring all this on you so sudden like, but it's all George's fault. If he'd paid more attention when he was drivin' that Harley of his well, I could have eased you into all this. As it is, George is going fast and even your powers will be unable to recall him soon."

Cyndy looked like she might faint. Johnathan reached out and put a large, strong arm around her. When she leaned into him, he felt he might faint too.

"Come on Cyndy, listen to your grandmother. I felt your power before, at the Crawfish that night, and wondered then. I knew you were different. But I didn't realize just how different. Now you're going to have to decide what you want your life to be."

"I just want my old life back. I hate what this accident has done to me. I want to do astronomy and I want to fall in love with you, maybe, but I don't want to be a Savior to the world. That's too much. Surely you see, Johnathan, it's too much, too damned much."

She let go of his arm and sank back into the couch, her body now quiet. Her mind numbed by all that had been said. Then her mind kicked back into gear, her voice now indignant.

"So, grandmother, just how do I do this magic? How do I save George's life? Tell me, how do I learn to do all this? Is there a save-a-life school somewhere?"

"You don't have to learn anythin' but to ask God's help. If you mean to save George, then all you need do is go to him and put your arms around him, put your hand over his heart and pray for God to heal and save his spirit. That's all darlin'. You really know all this but it hasn't had time to come to the front of your mind."

Her grandmother suddenly got out of the chair, came around to the front of the desk, and reach down to pull Cyndy up from the couch.

"Come on darlin', time's wasting. Your destiny calls. What are you goin' to do? Let George slip away and feel guilty all the rest of your life, or are you goin' to go and save his sorry soul?"

Cyndy swayed. It was all too much. The room started to spin out of control. Then she felt her grandmother's hand as it slapped her face. The shock and sting suddenly brought everything back into focus. She took a deep breath. Without knowing where it came from, she felt a sweet love fill her body and it felt as if she might float right off the floor. She turned slowly to face her inquisitor.

"If half of what you've just told me is true, then I have to go to George. I need to know if you're telling me the truth, although suddenly I feel strangely different and full of a new power I didn't know I possessed."

She straightened up, looked at Johnathan, felt a rush of affection and blushed. She must save her husband, but she realized suddenly she was in love with another man and she didn't even know anything about him. She smiled at him; her sense of loss now turned to joy. Johnathan looked at her with concern. Then he felt her spirit reaching out to him and he felt her joy, too.

"Later, Johnathan, we have to talk. Right now I have to do the only right thing I know. Let's go find George and try out this strange power you think I have."

Together, Cyndy and Johnathan walked out into the hall and up the stairs to the ICU. As they entered, the duty nurse nodded to them and waved her hand to where a small cluster of gowned nurses and doctors labored over the figure of a man encumbered by tubes and wires and flashing, beeping machines. A ventilator on one side wheezed breath into the inert body. Several intravenous bags were slung from stands, their tubes ending where an arm was tied to a board.

There seemed a sense of fighting for a lost cause. Those who watched the beeping, flashing monitors, who monitored oxygen intake and fluid outflow, kept looking for other treatments, other drugs that might slow the progress of this soul from this world to the next.

But the vital signs were obviously weakening. The fight was going to be over soon. The abused body was losing its fight to stay alive.

Cyndy looked frightened. Johnathan held her hand. Together they walked to the bed, the caregivers parting to let them get close. Cyndy took one last look at Johnathan then put her left hand on George's chest over his heart chakra. Her other hand she held just above his bandaged head. She made a small sign of a cross before letting her hand rest gently on the bandages. She closed her eyes and prayed to God to restore health to this body, to let it begin to heal.

Johnathan could feel the power surge from her hands into George's wracked body. And still she stood. It happened almost instantly. The heart monitor showed improved beating. The oxygen monitor showed more oxygen being taken up by the blood. The ventilator suddenly had less to do to assist with his breathing. Color began to suffuse George's waxen face. In total all his vital signs suddenly began to improve.

One of the doctors moved to study the various dials and image panels. He looked at the blood pressure reading, the heartbeat, the oxygen monitor. He looked startled. He looked at Cyndy, still standing, eyes closed in supplication and prayer, hands still firmly on George's chest and head.

Finally, Cyndy took a deep breath, opened her eyes and turned to Johnathan.

"God says he will be OK, John. I think we can safely go now."

They both turned to the door. One of the doctors came after them.

"What's happened here? What did you do? I don't understand. George was in the process of shutting down, dying, and suddenly he is beginning to look the picture of health."

Cyndy gave him a shy smile and continued with her arm now tucked into one of Johnathan's, leaving the doctor standing, staring after her. Together they walked through the door and out into the corridor and down the steps to the floor below. Cyndy went immediately to George's father who still sat, abjectly, where they had left him in the chapel. She spoke quietly to him, his face looking stunned, then incredibly happy. He hugged her and left to go the ICU. Coming back to Johnathan, she put her arm back into his; they nodded at Art, and continued out the entrance and into the parking lot.

Cyndy suddenly sagged. Johnathan's large arm supported her and gently deposited her on the passenger side of the red truck.

"My God, John, I did it. God did it through me. I don't understand but the power came through me and started George on the path to live again. He won't die now. I know he won't die now. I need a drink. Take me home and come in with me. I don't want to be alone for a while. I need to talk to you about what happened in there. She was breathing as heavily as if she had been running for miles.

Chapter Twenty

They drove to Cyndy's house through quiet streets, put the truck into the garage and proceeded into the house. Cyndy led the way to the little room off the more formal living room, a small study complete with a Franklin stove in one corner. Wide floor-to-ceiling windows looked out on the famous herb garden. An overstuffed sofa and chairs were set around a coffee table. Cyndy sank into one of the chairs and took deep breaths. When she spoke it was in a voice that would take little to turn into hysteria

"I don't really understand what I just did, John. I mean, I understand that somehow I have acquired a power I never dreamed existed. I just stopped a man from dying. I did it by virtue of putting my hands on his body and praying to God. What have I become? I feel like God. I was taught that only God or Jesus can deal with life and death. I'm just an astronomer. I like astronomy. I want to go back to my observatory and my students."

She was crying again, softly, head bowed. Not hysteria, just quiet sobs that punctuated her words. Johnathan sat quietly, letting her talk out her feelings, ready to step in if needed but seeing no need, yet. Lady had come in to see what was happening and went to Cyndy, where she whined and tried to get up and lick at Cyndy's face. Cyndy pushed at her but Lady was insistent. Finally Cyndy just buried her face into Lady's neck and continued to sob gently. Still Johnathan didn't stir. He knew a good helper when he saw one. Lady was just the right friend to hold Cyndy's hand.

Finally the sobs slowed down, then stopped. Cyndy peered at Johnathan over Lady's gentle neck. Her eyes were red; tears had left luminous wet trails down her cheeks. But there was a new spark now, one he hadn't seen before.

"Sorry, John, for letting go like that. I just needed to get it out so I can deal with this new reality, whatever it is."

She sighed deeply, hugged Lady for a moment, then straightened up. It was just then the phone rang. The strident sound broke the silence that had been with them since leaving the hospital.

Cyndy glanced at the weight-driven wall clock, noticing the hands indicated the early morning hour of 2:35. She looked at the phone but it didn't stop. She finally picked up the receiver. After her first hello, she did nothing but listen while her face became pale and her breathing more labored. Johnathan watched, too tired to try to bridge the distance to the receiver with his mind, but alarmed at Cyndy's face and reaction to whoever was on the other end of the phone.

"Thanks, Art, thanks for calling and warning me. No, no, I'll be OK. I'll think of something. Take care. You could be in trouble for calling. Be careful. Keep a low profile and don't worry about me."

Cyndy put the receiver down, staring at it then lifting her head to fix her washed-blue eyes on Johnathan.

"You won't believe this, Johnathan, but Maaiken seems to have finally, certifiably gone crazy. He's found out that I stopped George from dying and he's furious. He's been heard shouting that no one can stop people from dying, not even him. He's been calling me a witch that needs dealing with. Art just called to tell me. He's terrified because he's an islander and knows what power Maaiken has on Nantucket."

She paused.

"Almost everyone owes him a big debt for healing someone or other of their families. They have all sworn to uphold him and that church of his. Either that or face being ostracized and unable to do or buy anything or go anywhere. Now Maaiken's after me. He's promising to treat me just like the witch I am, or so he says. John, I'm frightened. You can't believe the power he has here. No one will stand up to him."

Johnathan knew they were both too tired to deal with a new emergency. Yet one more seemed about to break over them. He pushed his shoulders back then let them slump forward again.

"This is the 20th century Cyndy. No one can deliberately harm you because he or she thinks you are a witch. Not even that madman Maaiken. I admit he seems to be able to control the folks around here but you can't really be afraid he'll harm you now, can you?"

Johnathan smiled at her from across the room. If he hadn't been so tired he would have stood up and given her a hug. Oh what the hell, he pulled himself up out of the chair and started towards her. It was at that moment that he heard a chanting and shouting.

He had heard sounds like that before in the early part of the century, when crowds had lynched a black man down in Georgia. The sound sent a trill of fear though him and energized his lazy body. He took two quick strides to stand beside Cyndy.

"Hear that sound? That's a crowd out of control. Or maybe in someone's control, like Maaiken's. I don't think we want to hang around here for the moment. Grab Lady's lead and let's get out of here."

Cyndy looked at him with fear in her blue eyes then began to react, running into the kitchen where Lady's lead hung from a peg on the wall then walking quickly to the front door and opening it. The sight that greeted her sent her reeling back and slamming the door. A crowd was gathering in front of her house. Just turning into her walkway were five men with silk stockings over their faces and carrying baseball bats.

Even as she closed the door a window broke in the living room and a large rock skidded onto the floor.

"Shit Cyndy, out the back door. Quickly!"

Johnathan grabbed Lady's lead from Cyndy's nerveless fingers and snapped it on her collar. Then he grabbed Cyndy's arm and dragged her and Lady towards the door to the garden.

Fortunately, a high wooden fence secured the herb garden. But, as they ran out of the kitchen door, Johnathan heard a smashing sound as someone attacked the gate built into the street side of the fence.

Almost at the same time another crash came from the gate to the woods.

"Quick, John, follow me."

Now it was Cyndy's turn to grab Johnathan. She led him to the stables where she stored her herbs to dry in the hidden still room. They were barely inside the wooden building when the front gate smashed open and a stream of men raced into the herb garden.

Cyndy pulled at a hook set into one of the thick roof support beams and the wall beside them slid back to reveal steps to her grandmother's basement still room.

Pushing Johnathan through and dragging Lady, she turned and slid the wall section back into place.

"What's this, Cyndy, where are we?"

"Easy John, follow the rope railing down the steps to the basement."

Johnathan felt out in the darkness, his hand coming into contact with a heavy ship's hawser, his feet stumbling as they found the steps, his mind still too numb from fatigue to see without his eyes. He was aware that Cyndy and Lady were ahead of him in the darkness. Cyndy's voice whispered in his ear, her breath warm and moist.

"We're in my grandmother's old still room. It's where she made her potions. I still use it. Now be quiet."

They heard a commotion and shouting as the men they had seen spread out looking for her. The sounds of window glass breaking were muted by the thick floor above them. Feet pounded into the stables. Voices cried out in frustration as their hiding place went undetected.

"There's nobody here. Where the fuck's she at, boys. She's got to be here somewhere. That fancy red truck's in the garage. Motor's still warm. She's got to be around here somewhere unless she rode outa here on her broom."

A voice shouted from another location.

"No sign of anyone in the house, Ray. We been through all the rooms. No sign anyone's been here all day. Just the truck in the garage. She got another car, you think?"

"Don't know but she's got that little house down at the beach. Maybe that big guy she was with had a car. Ruddy, you and Andy and some the boys get yourself down to the beach house. Maybe that's where she's gone to ground. Rory, you and the rest get over to the observatory. She's got to be at one place or the other. She sure as shit can't get off the island. You find her, get her quiet and bring her out to the church. You find the big guy, don't mess with him, he looks like trouble, just shoot him."

The noise intensified, then gradually died down as trucks on the street roared to life, squealing tires as frustrated men sweated inside, angry, frightened, in the grip of mob hysteria. Cyndy, Johnathan and Lady waited quietly, Lady wagging her tail in the darkness, thinking this was all some kind of game.

"They're gone for the moment, John. What'll we do now?"

Cyndy's voice sounded thin in the dark and her body trembled against his side. Johnathan gripped her gently and held her to him. She responded and put her arms about his waist.

"I don't know what's going on exactly, Cyndy, but Maaiken seems to have whipped up a more than just a lynching kind of crowd. The crowd is crazy for the moment, but there's another element out there. Real thugs. Where do you suppose the Sheriff and his deputies are? Surely they must be aware of what's going on. They couldn't be a part of it, could they?"

"I don't know what to think John, except I can't believe Taylor would be a party to anything like this. There's a phone down here. Is it safe to use?"

"Who really knows anything but sure, dial 911 if you can see to do it. Try to get the Sheriff's office."

The ringing was answered by a rough voice.

"Yeah, what's your trouble? Services're down for a while. You need the ambulance? I can patch you into the Paramedics. You got a fire? I'll connect you with the fire station. You want the Sheriff, well the Sheriff's office is closed until further notice."

Cyndy quietly put the receiver down.

"I can't reach the Sheriff, John; they're in control of the 911 service, too. Sounds like they've taken over the Sheriff's office. Wouldn't be surprised if John and the rest of the deputies weren't in their own holding cells. Now what?"

"We're safe for the moment, Cyndy. Take a deep breath and relax. I'll think of something, just give me a minute."

"I just had an idea, John. George has a sailboat out at the Marina. If we could get to the boat, we might be able to get off this island. What do think?"

"Won't be easy to move through the streets let alone reach your sailboat and get her rigged in the dark. I might try to get back to my room at 7 Milk Street. At least I have a gun in my room and it looks like a gun wouldn't be a bad idea right now. But what I need more than anything is some rest. I can't use my powers when I'm this tired. I'm just another guy, Cyndy, until I get a chance to recharge."

Cyndy squeezed his hand in the dark.

"What if I take a look outside? Do you think it's safe yet?"

"Wouldn't be surprised if they didn't leave a watch on the house. But if they're there they'll only be covering the front of the house. I think we could chance going out the back way and through the woods. Only thing's it's so dark tonight with no moon, I don't know if I can find my way."

"Then I'll just have to light the way for you Cyndy. My goodness, darlin', what a to do. And just because that Maaiken's finally snapped, lost what little sense he ever had. Can you believe it? You've threatened his little fiefdom. And is he a sore loser."

The apple scent was unmistakable.

"Grandmother, oh thank God you're here. Those men were so angry I was frightened, frightened for me, for John, for Lady. I thought they wanted to kill me. I was sure they would hurt Lady if they found her. And there's no telling what they might try to do to John."

A small glow of light appeared, suspended in the air without obvious source. Johnathan looked around the shadowy room, the long counter with grinding and mixing bowls, jars on shelves that ran three sides of the room, herbs suspended for drying from the beams above their heads. He gave a speculative look at the light that glowed, trying to cast his mind to the source but failing.

"It's all right Johnathan, you're much too tired right now to use your psychic abilities. Just rest your mind. Better yet, try to put it to findin' a solution to our dilemma. How are we goin' to get our Cyndy safely out of this mess? Or you either, of course."

There was a serious note to the usually laughing voice.

"Maaiken has started somethin' that won't rest until someone has died, I'm afraid, and I don't want it to be our Cyndy. Or you either, of course."

This time the voice couldn't quite help giving up a giggle.

"Why do I put you last all the time, Johnathan? You are vastly important to the world and the grand scheme of things. I know that and all I can do is worry about my little girl."

"Well, if it helps, I'm also worried about your little girl. Those men were armed and dangerous. They have no good in them. I don't know where Maaiken came up with them but with men like those as ringleaders and with his hold on the rest of the island, anything can and probably will happen. We have to get Cyndy and me off this sandbar and damn soon. We can't stay hidden here forever. They'll probably bring dogs next."

He paused and thought.

"Can you get us out the back way, grandmother? Where does the wood end up? Maybe I should try to get to the gun that's hidden in my room at 7 Milk Street. And there's one more thing. I need to find out what Maaiken has hidden at the church. I think if I could find and take whatever it is that gives him his power, then I could put this little show of force down. If Maaiken lost his power base, his supporters might go back to their day jobs."

Again he paused, yawned and hung his head in exhaustion. The grandmother didn't answer.

"But first we all need some rest. Let's bunk in here for a few hours and see what the day brings."

Cyndy looked at him with concern.

"Oh John, you're dead on your feet. Come on, I have some blankets in a box over here. Let's all get our heads down for a few hours.

There's a little toilet and washbasin behind that door in the corner. Thank you, grandmother, for providing the essentials."

The grandmother made no reply.

In moments, Cyndy and Johnathan were lying side by side, now holding on to each other. The little light continued to glow for a while, then extinguished. Lady was already curled head to tail and asleep on her own blanket.

Johnathan kissed the top of Cyndy's head and then put his own head down. Before long, the only sound was Lady kicking after some dream rabbit and long deep breaths from Cyndy and Johnathan.

Grandmother made no sound, but then she rarely did unless asked.

Johnathan was the first to stir. He had developed a particularly accurate internal clock. The room itself was the darkness of complete night. His clock suggested otherwise. It's five o'clock, he thought to himself.

Cyndy stirred in his arms. From her position and his it appeared neither had moved much more than whatever muscles it takes to smile contentedly. Johnathan rearranged his face to a more serious look. As he thought, another thought crept into his mind. It was Cyndy, now awake and showing her new power by inserting her thought into his mind with an ease that both surprised him and gave him momentary pause.

"Good morning Cyndy. You are getting too strong for me, I may not able to block you much longer."

"So what did you want to hide from me anyway?"

She gave him a hug and then pulled herself up from the floor.

"'Scuse me, big man, but little me has a need greater than your love."

A ball of light slowly emerged, hanging in the air, suspended above Cyndy's head.

"Is that you or your grandmother doing that?

"I seem to be able to do all sorts of wonderful things, John."

Cyndy gave him an impish grin in the gentle light.

"I'll just leave it here in the middle of the room while I visit the facilities."

With that the ball of light moved to the center of the room and hung, just below the roof beams. The luminescence was easy to look directly into, yet it illuminated the room to the very corners.

When Cyndy had returned, and John had made the same journey, they stood, holding hands and looking into each other's unusual eyes.

Lady came to join them and Cyndy disengaged one hand to rub her ears.

"Lady has needs too, John, I'm going to have to take her outside. Do you think it's safe?"

Now rested, Johnathan centered himself and let his mind project up and out of the stable building. He was aware of the dampness of the dew, the few remaining stars slowly extinguishing in the growing dawn. His consciousness expanded slowly towards the front of the house, finally pausing with its perspective now the street from the front of Cyndy's house. He was then aware of two facts. One was that a truck parked in front of the house held two sleeping men. The second was the presence of Cyndy, beside him in spirit. He turned his perception to where he felt her presence. He was amazed to find himself looking into her eyes as if she were in the physical body.

"I don't understand this, Cyndy, but you are as real to me right now as you were standing next to me, body to body."

"But we are standing next to each other, John. Our spiritual energy looks the same to us as our physical bodies. Strange, isn't it? But that is the notion of ourselves that we have imprinted and so that's the way we continue to perceive each other. I suspect this would fade away and we would see each other as light energy if we stayed in this form for long. But I would know your identity no matter what form you take. You'd know mine too, I'm certain."

Johnathan looked around then back to Cyndy.

"I think it's safe to let Lady out into the back yard. Just shush her with your mind if she wants to bark or anything."

They returned to their physical bodies and smiled at each other. Cyndy took Lady up the stairs and opened the wall. John followed and stood with her as Lady dutifully performed her functions.

"Strange, John, I feel so much closer to nature. I can feel the movement of the insects in the grass. I can hear their crunching as they eat. It's amazing."

"It's the same experience you would have if you were a Kundalini experiencer, Cyndy. Ask me again sometime and I'll tell you all that a lovely man named Gopi Krishna experienced. Too much going on for a lecture right now."

It was time to move. They quickly returned to the hidden still room, picked up the blankets, stored them back in their box, then went back to the stable entrance. John probed with his mind but could find no sentient life forms other than a family of mice feeding by the corner of the garden at the rear entrance to the garden.

Together, they stepped over the broken gate and followed the path into the woods. Disturbed, the mice scurried away. Cyndy led the way, looking briefly over her shoulder at Johnathan.

"This is better than trying to find our way in the dark. I know this part of the island better than anywhere else. Grandmother and I came out here often to gather herbs and other things."

"Where's it come out then?"

"This bit of wood ends at the mile road, that's the road to the Cliff community. It's a pretty little row of houses that were once fishing shanties. The old fishermen wouldn't recognize them now, though."

"Then what, Cyndy?"

"Well, we can get to the church pretty easily, it's about a half hour walk. I need to end this and the end has to be at the church. It's where it all began and it's where it's going to end, one way or the other. Now that I seem to have come into my power, I think we need to have this out with Maaiken. Maybe, between the two of us, we can induce him to be reasonable."

They walked along, quickly, their footsteps muffled by the grass and leaves on the trail.

"Small hope for reason, I'm afraid, Cyndy. You threaten all Maaiken's power, his empire, here on Nantucket. He's insane you know. Whatever power he's been working with, it's drained his mind of all reason. You're the greatest challenge he's ever faced. It may not be as easy as you imagine. He stopped me from probing him at the church yesterday. He has power too. We'll just have to see which of us is the strongest."

Cyndy was quiet. Lady kept up with their brisk pace, putting off any investigating of tempting odors until another time. Finally they reached the Mile road walking along the verge to one side.

Once they heard a truck approaching and hid in the bayberry bushes at the side of the road. Fortunately, at this early hour there was little traffic on the road.

After about twenty-five minutes of quick walking, the hill with its church came into view. Several trucks were parked in the church parking lot. Cyndy stopped and Johnathan pulled up quickly so as not to run her over. Lady looked at Cyndy, waiting for instruction. She, in turn, looked at Johnathan.

"Now that we're here I don't know what to do next."

"We need a diversion, something to get them out of the church and into their trucks."

"Did I hear my name mentioned?"

Both Cyndy and Johnathan looked around in surprise. Standing behind them, rubbing Lady's ears was the stealthy grandmother.

"I think I might get a diversion going for you two."

Lady gave a low bark.

"Sorry Lady, you three. Indeed I think Lady should come with me. What do you think, Lady?"

Again a low bark from Lady, who seemed to appreciate the need for discretion.

"What are you going to do grandmother? Be careful with Lady."

"Hush darlin', I wouldn't put our Lady to any harm now, would I Lady?"

Lady wagged her tail but didn't bark this time.

"What we're goin' to do is set off the fire alarm, then Lady is going to run into Maaiken's office, get Maaiken to recognize her, then run back out. Hopefully Maaiken will tell the men to catch her because he'll think Lady can lead them to you. I'll be there to make sure nothin' harms her. I think we can get the men out of the church, at least for a few moments, long enough for you to get in. Here I go."

With that the grandmother gathered up Lady's lead and walked out across the road where she skirted the parking lot and came up to service door at the side of the church. The door stood ajar. There was no noise within.

Quietly she unhooked Lady's lead and grabbed at her collar, disappearing as she did so. The collar pulled forward on Lady's neck and she let it guide her forward until they were opposite Maaiken's open study door. The grandmother's voice whispered into Lady's ear.

"Go, Lady."

A quick tug propelled Lady into the study where Maaiken worked at a paper on his desk. Hearing a sound he glanced up and was transfixed for a moment by the mysterious appearance of Cyndy's dog. Maaiken knew Lady well, since George had often had her in the truck when he and Cyndy came for Sunday service.

"What the hell. How'd you get here? I know you. Where's your witch of a mistress? What am I doing talking to a dog?"

Then he shouted.

"Rory, get your sorry ass in here. The witch must be close by, her dog's here in my study."

The sound of feet running and Rory came into the room.

"What's the matter, boss?"

He saw Lady wagging her tail.

"Where'd the dog come from? What's going on?"

He paused.

"That's that damned witch's dog, boss?"

"Get the boys out of the church and find the witch. That's her dog, all right; I'd know it anywhere. She's got to be around here somewhere. The dog never goes anywhere without her. Get going. Find her."

At this moment the strident jangle of the fire alarm began to sound.

Maaiken looked puzzled.

"Now what the hell? Get out of here and look at the enunciator board. See what detector is sounding off. The church can't be on fire. And close that door. Keep that dog inside the church."

As Rory turned first to locate the enunciator board, then spun in response to the second shouted order, Lady darted through his legs and then the doorway, sending him reeling off balance and into the wall. By the time he had regained his balance, Lady was well on her way out into the hall and, racing down the corridor, slid out of the still open service door.

"Get after her, man! No, no. First find out why the fire alarm is going off. Leave the dog. I can't have the church burning down. Get all the rest of the men and get going."

He gesticulated wildly.

"Send someone after that damned dog. No, no. Get the men and find her, I'll look after the fire alarm."

Maaiken was sputtering in his anger, his mouth beginning to shower spittle as he shouted his contrary orders.

Rory, looking confused, hurried out of the study and raced out into the main body of the church where a half dozen men lounged in the pews.

"Come on boys, the witch is somewhere around here. We just saw her dog. She's probably outside."

With that Rory ran for the main church doors, followed by his men.

Outside, Cyndy and Johnathan watched and waited.

Suddenly they heard the fire alarm followed a few moments later by the group of men spilling out of the main church doors. Intent on the action across the road, they failed to notice the approach of two large men, baseball bats hanging from ham-sized fists. Movement of the air startled Johnathan, who began to turn just as a baseball bat connected with the side of his head. Cyndy heard the ugly, hollow sound of the bat hitting Johnathan's head. She started to move in response and was just in time to see Johnathan crumple to the ground. This was her last sight as a second bat caught her at the base of her skull. She, too, crumpled with Johnathan's name stillborn on her lips.

The two looked at their handiwork and smiled at each other.

"Maaiken promised a month's wages to whoever got these two. Guess we're in luck."

The other man stepped closer to Johnathan.

"What about the giant. He went down pretty hard."

He knelt and put his finger on Johnathan's throat

"I don't think this guy's going to make any more trouble. I think he's dead."

He stood up.

"How's the girl?"

The other man knelt down and peeled back one of Cyndy's eyelids. Then he put his head down over her chest.

"Yeah, she's OK. Just knocked out. Guess I didn't hit her as hard as you did the big guy. Just as well. I think Maaiken wants her alive. Gimme a hand."

Together they hoisted Cyndy's slack body and walked across the road to where Rory and the other members of the gang were starting to run toward the back of the church.

"Hey Rory, this what you guys're looking for?

Rory stopped and spun around.

"Great going guys. Where'd you find her? Where's her big friend?"

"Not going to have to worry about him any more. What's left of him is lying across the road in the bushes."

"He's dead? Nice going guys. Let's get this broad into the church and give her to Maaiken. Jake, go back and make sure the big guy is really dead. Pop him again if you have to."

Rory and the rest carried Cyndy's unresisting body into the church while Jake went back across the road. When he got to where he'd left Johnathan he stopped, puzzled. Johnathan's big body had disappeared. Alarmed, Jake raced back across the road and into the church. By the time he caught up with the others they were already crowded into Maaiken's study. Cyndy had been dumped onto a settee that ran under one of the big windows. Her hands were now tied and the rope securely looped around the settee's back spindles. Maaiken was standing over her, his rage still evident on his face.

"Boys, the big guy's disappeared. When I went back across the road his body wasn't there."

Maaiken looked furious.

"Rory, take this rag taggle bunch of misfits and find that man. This time make sure he really is dead."

Rory looked at his boss and then started pushing the men out of the door as he headed back out to find Johnathan.

Left alone in his study, Maaiken watched a moment as Cyndy's chest rose and fell then checked her pulse, listened to her breathing and went back to his desk where he pulled out the little box that held the crystal vial of mysterious liquid that had killed Jeremy Slokem. He smiled. Then he carried the vial over to where Cyndy's unconscious body lay.

"This'll be an easy way to get you out of the way you little bitch of a witch. I don't know what you did to George but I'm not taking any more chances with you. My anointing oil will take care of you. It sure killed Jeremy in hurry. No reason it shouldn't do the same to you."

Maaiken took the little crystal vial out of its ornate box and held it momentarily in his hand, letting the power race up his arm and through his body. He began to shake. He took a deep breath and steadied his arm. He reached out to take Cyndy's nerveless hand to place the vial in it when she began to stir. He pulled back a moment, waiting, a mad look in his eye.

Cyndy took a deeper breath, then another. Her eyes flicked open. For a moment she just lay there while Maaiken hovered over her, holding the fatal vial but keeping it away from her body.

Cyndy, beginning to breath more easily, looked around, trying to orient herself, still feeling the pain where the bat had struck her head. But even as she became aware of the pain she also became aware that the pain was diminishing as her own great spiritual strength took hold of the damaged cells in her body and restored them to their genetic blueprint.

She became aware of Maaiken standing just above her and saw the vial of glowing liquid in his hand. She also realized she couldn't move her hands and saw how they had been bound.

With Maaiken standing so close to her, she could feel the radiation from the liquid and let it wash over her, relishing the feeling she always received from the liquid. She remembering that feeling as she had often felt it in the church and now lifted her head and looked up at Maaiken. She even tried to smile at him but failed as she felt the lack of strength in her body. Fear grew as she recognized her new powers were gone maybe never to return. How would she fight Maaiken without her special powers?

Then questions leapt to her mind. She saw again the image of Johnathan falling to the ground, heard the ugly sound the bat had made as it cracked against his skull. She began to sob.

"Maaiken, what are you trying to do to me? Why am I tied up? Where's my friend John? Where's Lady? Maaiken, if you've harmed John I'll..."

"You'll do what you stupid witch? I've got you now and I'm going to get rid of you. The boys have gone back right now to make sure they finish off that big man. And who the hell is he anyway? And what did you do to George? How could you have stopped him dying? Even I can't stop someone from dying when they're as far gone as George was and out of the church."

He leaned closer.

"Tell me what you did. Was it some of your grandmother's herbs or something? I want to know. It might be helpful for me in the future."

He smiled a mad little smile at her.

"Maybe I won't be so rough on you if you tell me what you did. How you did it. People were watching, they say they didn't see you do anything but hold his hand. But it had to be something else. Come on, tell me before I beat it out of you."

Cyndy, worried about Johnathan and Lady, was paying little attention to the mad man just feet away. She could feel Maaiken's power but she was so dizzy it was like feeling a soft breeze, not the hurricane he had seemed in the past.

Just then Rory came back into the room.

"I talked to Jake, he's the one who thought he'd killed that big guy. He says he even felt for his pulse and couldn't find one. But when he went back, the big guy was gone. He'd just disappeared and Jake don't know how that could be. What have you found out from the witch here? Has the big man come looking for her or anything?"

Maaiken looked displeased with the interruption.

"I've just been asking some questions before I dispose of her."

Maaiken paused and looked at Rory, an insane look in his eye.

"But you've given me a thought, Rory. Maybe I should use her for bait and get that big man to come for her. If he's still able to get around with a cracked head then maybe we can get him to come to us."

He laughed at this idea. Rory decided it would be best if he laughed too.

"Rory, have you sent the boys out to find the big man?"

"Yeah boss, you said to do it but it's getting so damned foggy out there they can't see but a foot or two in front of their faces."

"Well, tell them to belay it and get back in here. I've got the perfect plan to dispose of this witch and get the big guy to come after her at the same time."

He began to laugh again and Rory looked at him in some alarm. Even Cyndy, sick as she was with pain, felt the fear knowing that Maaiken was completely insane and knowing that she was still too weak to fight against him.

The room seemed to spin as she looked at the rope that bound her hands and struggled to free herself but without success. She tried to reach Johnathan with her mind but there was just a jangled blur in her head. Her powers and her strength were gone. She began to weep. The world continued to spin faster and faster and she finally just went with it as she fainted with mad Maaiken's laugh ringing in her ears.

Chapter Twenty-One

Still stunned, Johnathan heard the men leave carrying Cyndy's unconscious body. Barely conscious himself, he had had just enough strength to stop his heart and respiration when the man checked him out. Now he let his heart and lungs begin their usual rhythm. For those few moments he had applied an old Indian fakir practice to control his heartbeat and breathing. He could appear dead for hours if he needed to. Fortunately, this time it was only a few minutes by the time the man had felt for his pulse and the two of them had hefted Cyndy up and moved across the street.

Johnathan lay there for a few more moments, struggling to stay conscious. He realized the surprise blow to his head had come dangerously close to killing him. A sharper angle might very well have shattered his skull and that would have finished his physical life. He was no superman. He could be killed. He lifted a hand to his head where the bat had hit him. He could feel the fine, hairline fracture and willed his body to start to repair the damage.

The world was spinning, but he realized that he couldn't stay where he was. Whoever had almost ended his life might return to make sure. Weakened as he was there was no way he could defend himself. Even as the world threatened to black out he struggled and managed to get to his feet and begin to stagger back away from the road. He continued, weaving, grabbing at trees to stop from falling, stumbling against anything that lay on the ground. Finally, his legs just let go and he fell forward into a small ditch. Blackness finally ended his fight to flee.

It was just a short time later when Jake, still carrying the baseball bat, returned to the now-empty area where Johnathan had been hit. He stopped, looked around to make sure he was in the right place then, confused, searched a small part of the area before quickly sprinting back across the road and into the church.

The night was dark, and crickets sang love songs to each other. The fog that had threatened all afternoon was finally arriving and, with it, a smothering quietness.

Still Johnathan lay as one dead, only a slight motion of his chest indicating any life at all.

A rustling of the brush failed to disturb him. Then a cold, damp muzzle pushed at his cheek. A rough tongue licked at his face. Johnathan's breathing became stronger and his head rolled away from the persistent tongue. Finally he eyes opened and he looked up into Lady's concerned and loving eyes.

"Hello dog, who're you?

Johnathan's eyes were blank, devoid of understanding. Lady barked at him and Johnathan laughed.

"That's OK sport. Don't need to bark at me. Just tell me your name."

Again Johnathan laughed, this time at the idea of telling a dog to say its name. He laughed then groaned as the laughter brought a dizzying pain response from his head.

"Ouch! Damn, what's the matter with my head."

Carefully he felt his head and found a sticky wetness near the left temple.

"What's this sport, I seem to have messed up my head."

Johnathan lifted his head from where he was lying flat out on his stomach.

"Man it's dark. Wonder where I am?"

He sniffed the air.

"Smells like fog, old dear."

Lady responded with another bark and tried to lick his face again. Johnathan rolled his face to one side, put out a hand to stop the licking, then tried to sit up but had to put his head down again as the world spun out of control.

"I don't know Lady, what's the matter with me."

Johnathan stopped at that and wondered out loud.

"Is that your name? Is your name Lady?"

Lady gave a short happy bark.

The fog in Johnathan's mind began to lift even if the outside fog remained thick and concealing.

"Yes, of course, you're Cyndy's Lady and..."

He paused and tried to concentrate around the thundering pain in his head.

"Yeah, I'm... Johnathan or is it David? Oh my God, what'm I doing here with my head broken and filled with more pain than I can ever remember? Where's Cyndy? Oh dog, can't you do anything but bark? I need to know what's happened to Cyndy. Oh yeah, I remember someone coming up behind me and slugging me with a baseball bat. Yeah, that's right, now I remember, two guys with baseball bats and one got me a good shot. I must have been able to get myself away, though damned if I can remember how."

Just then the fog took on a different but familiar scent, faintly but positively of apples. Johnathan remembered that delicious odor. He looked around but the fog covered the whole world in a gray veil.

"Grandmother, you must be there, your ever present apple blossoms say so anyway."

"Oh Johnathan, you poor dear. You've got a broken head and our Cyndy's in mortal danger and I don't have enough power left to even light you a lamp. I used all my available ectoplasm energy when I took Lady over to the church and set off the fire alarm. Guess it wasn't a great idea after all. Look what's happened to you and Cyndy. I feel it's all my fault.

Johnathan groaned and pushed himself up enough to roll over on his back. He looked into the fog but saw nothing.

"Stop it right there, grandmother, not your fault. If anyone's to blame it's me, being sloppy and not setting up a rear guard. For a while there I didn't even know who I was. Lucky that guy didn't kill me outright with that bat of his. Came bloody close, too close if you ask me."

Johnathan stopped and willed the pain to diminish in his head. A little of his strength had returned and he was able to get a response to this thought. Then he tried to sit up again and was successful this time, although for a moment the world took a small lurch. Fortunately it didn't tip right over as it had before and his balance gradually returned.

Now he put one hand on the ground, pried his body into a kneeling position then, grunting, into actually standing up. He took a deep breath, staggered and waited for the pain to diminish again. He looked around but the fog prevented him from seeing more than a foot or two in any direction.

"Which way do we have to go, grandmother?"

"Sorry Johnathan, but I can't be much help to you for the moment. Best you sit down here and try to get your body to heal. When the fog lifts, then we'll see what's what. In the mean time I'll make sure that Lady's all right. No matter what you have to do, someone or somethin's going to have to look after Cyndy's dog."

"Boss, the boys are all back in the church. What'd you want them to do?"

Maaiken looked at Cyndy's pale face. He listened to her breathing.

"I don't want her to die on me, I mean to send her off myself. I've got work to do. Take her out and put her on the couch in the secretary's office. Keep her tied up. Don't you dare lose her on me or it'll be your scalp I'll take. Either you or one of the guys keeps watch on her at all times. I'll call you when I'm ready."

Maaiken waited and watched as Rory and the man, Jake, cut Cyndy loose from the spindle back of the study settee and hefted her body out of the office. Closing and locking his door, he checked the amulet under his shirt, then went to the bookcase, pressed the knot under the mantel and entered the doorway to the cellars below.

He felt along the wall to the light switch. Stepping carefully he continued down the steep staircase. From there he went on to open the door to the inner sanctum. He paused in the doorway and looked into the darkened room. There, on the table, a faint glow was visible. Even at this distance the amulet began to feel warm against his skin.

Slowly, as if pushing against a wind, Maaiken entered the darkened room. He pushed another switch and a dim light revealed the ancient leather case sitting in the middle of the antique table. The table had been the repository for the case since it was first brought into the church back in 1732. Both table and leather case seemed singularly untouched by time. The cellars had withstood the great fire in 1846 and preserved the artifact. These cellars had remained hidden from those who cleaned up the area and rebuilt the church. His grandfather had reconstructed the entrance after the other workers had left the site.

The object, even cloaked as it was by its case, was having a powerful effect on him. His rate of breathing increased as he pushed his way into the room. His heart began to pound and he paused again, still some feet from the case. He took deep breaths, trying to urge his heart to slow its rapid beat. His stomach ached and threatened to disgorge his latest meal. He spoke his thanks to the original Templars who had brought the case to Nantucket and given his great, great grandfather the amulet and prayers that kept one safe from the deadly powers of the object within.

As he looked at the leather and its intricate decoration he recalled his first encounter and the healing that had transpired. It was one of the peculiarities of the hidden object that it had healed him when he was ill or injured but it could make him feel like shit if he was well. And the strange force it exerted in the room, it was a force he had to struggle against to even approach it. He knew anyone else exposed to the force of this ancient object would be killed. He was safe by virtue of the amulet and because he, alone, knew the ritual that would preserve anyone who used it.

At last he forced his way to where he could reach and begin to open the leather case. It had been some time since he had had to actually use the hidden object. He only ever opened the case when he needed to create more of his anointing oil, the blessed oil that was the secret to the extraordinary healing he performed each week within the church. He came here as infrequently as possible, the affect being so uncomfortable even to him, the only one who was inured and safe from its powers.

His old fingers fumbled with the intricate clasp then he had the lid open and was gazing into the interior, where, nestled in the fitted interior, glowed a small, polished cup of curiously carved stone. He gazed in utter fascination, thinking of the furor this cup would create if the world ever learned of its existence. Forcing his hand forward, he carefully and gently clasped his fingers about it and drew it out holding it up to his eyes, watching as the engraved symbols seemed to move with a life of their own.

The energy of the cup throbbed in his arm. Then, holding the cup reverently, he knelt where he was and began to pray. Slowly, as his words came forth, the light of the cup began to change and the energy became less painful. He continued praying; he would continue for at least an hour. He had much to say to God and the prayer, as always, affected the power of the cup. It had always been thus as his father had shown him, as his father's father had before that, all the way back to 1732.

Reginald St. James walked along Vestry Street to where it met Main, moving slowly along the fog-shrouded road. His purpose was to reach the Sheriff's office. He'd just been down to the docks and had been told that the ferry wasn't running due to the fog. He'd thought that strange, for these boats were equipped for foul weather navigation. And the businesses he had passed were all closed. So it was for several hours that he had felt something was terribly wrong.

He had decided to risk meeting with the Sheriff in his persona of St. James, archaeologist, so unlike the way they had first met when he was Luke the drunk.

Main Street was eerily deserted; he had never seen it with absolutely no traffic. It had to be more than just the fog, thick as it was. People here had been dealing with fog for hundreds of years and never stopped their activities, just went a bit more slowly.

When he finally reached the Sheriff's building, all he could see was a truck parked in front, not a Sheriff's department vehicle. Carefully, he approached the window beside the door. Through the window he could see a man he didn't recognize sitting with his feet up on Clem's desk. The man wasn't in the uniform of a Sheriff's deputy but he had a large handgun sitting on the desk beside his legs. The man was also asleep, his head angled against the chair back, his mouth open, probably snoring, but with the window closed St. James couldn't tell. Upstairs the windows were dark.

It was apparent to St. James that something or someone had taken over the Sheriff's office. That meant the Sheriff and his deputies must be out of action some way, or perhaps a party to whatever was going on. Whatever was going on worried him. The deserted streets and now this stranger holding down the Sheriff's office made him back off for a moment. Finally he went around the side of the building and down the alley that ran to a back laneway. Here was where the holding cell windows looked out.

From his new perspective, St. James could see several barred windows. Lights shone dimly through the fog. He could hear voices and realized the windows were open. He listened for a moment trying to hear what was being said but distance and fog blurred the voices. St. James pondered the situation. With the Sheriff and his officers out of action it could be a golden opportunity for some prospecting out at the church. Even if he set off an alarm, who would respond? He chuckled and walked back down the alley and set off for the church and what he might find there.

Johnathan looked up to where the sky should be, but the fog seemed destined to remain forever a shroud over his head. Lady whined and looked uncomfortable. There was now no sign of the grandmother; the scent of apples was no longer in the air. He had never felt so lost or cut off from the world. He groaned in frustration and sat on the ground burying his aching head in his arms.

Lady came over and sat beside him, turning occasionally to whine and lick what little of his face was still exposed. There was no other sound, the fog covered and muffled everything. The world was an amorphous gray mass with no shape or form.

Rory looked at the limp figure of Cyndy now lying on the secretary's couch, tied hand and foot. Even disheveled by all that had happened to her, she still looked pretty good, he thought. He could see making other use of her but then thought better of it. Maaiken was acting weird enough to worry him without pissing him off even further. He turned away and walked to the door to look out into the corridor. The building was in silence except for voices coming down the hall from the church where his men were waiting for some action. He wondered where and what Maaiken was up to. He had heard the door being locked behind him when he and Jake had walked out with Cyndy.

St. James turned into the path that led to the service door. The fog made the going slow, but he'd been here before and remembered the lay of the land. The door appeared through the swirling mists of fog and he listened. Walking through the church parking lot he had been aware that there were several cars and trucks parked there. Warned of possible danger, he moved with extreme caution.

The light was dim in the hallway but it was much clearer than the fog-bound exterior of the church. He slid through the door then paused again, listening. Now he could hear male voices reverberating down the hallway. Across from Maaiken's closed study door he could see the half open door to the secretary's office. Even as he watched the door swung open and a man he didn't recognize stepped out, looked back in, then closed the door and walked toward the voices in the main body of the church.

Intrigued by what the man had checked on before leaving the room, St. James waited until the man had disappeared from sight then eased his way along to the closed door. He paused to listen with his ear pressed to the door but heard nothing. Still he waited, nervously, unsure, then scowling, turned the knob and slowly opened the door. It took him a moment to bring the room into perspective before he realized he was looking at the bound figure of a woman. He slid into the room and closed the door, stepping quickly to the couch for a better look. It was then he recognized the victim as none other than the cute little astronomer, the wife of the man in the hospital recovering from a motorcycle crash.

"What the hell?"

The figure on the couch stirred restlessly, then fluttered open her eyes.

Cyndy's first view of the room revealed a man standing over her. It took a moment but then she recognized the man as a recent arrival on Nantucket, the one purported to be a famous archaeologist.

She shook her head, trying to clear away the fog that held her brain captive. The side of her head still hurt but the pain was easing. She tried centering herself to escape but her mind still refused to cooperate. Finally she just closed her eyes again, darkness returning to entrap her thoughts.

St. James thought rapidly. He mustn't stay long in this room; he had no idea when the previous occupant might return. First, before leaving, he rapidly loosened Cyndy's bound hands and feet. Then he draped the ropes to look as if they were still tied. Satisfied he had done all he could do for the moment he re-opened the door and slid quietly out into the corridor and then out the service door. There were too many men about to risk going as far as the study.

St. James had just exited from the secretary's office and out the service door when Rory came back from the church, laughing at a joke that Jake had made about his looking after the astronomer. He checked Maaiken's door but it remained closed and silent. He opened the secretary's office door and re-entered, seeing Cyndy still lying with her eyes closed.

He listened to her breathing and was satisfied that she was in no immediate trouble. He went back out into the corridor, walked restlessly to the service door and looked out at the fog, which seemed as heavy as ever. Then he walked back to Maaiken's door and pressed an ear to the heavy pine panel but there was no sound to be heard. Damn the man, what was he doing in there?

Rory walked back to talk to the others, bored with his own company.

Cyndy regained consciousness again. She looked about the room but the man she had seen previously was now nowhere to be seen. She wondered if she had dreamed the whole thing. She shifted her body and stretched her arms. As she moved, the ropes fell off her hands. She gasped and tried to sit up, swinging her legs off the side of the couch. As with her hands, the ropes now fell off her ankles. She was free to move. She paused for a moment to let the room settle down.

Her head felt much better now, though there was still a dull ache where the bat had hit her. She could feel some of her normal strength returning to her body. Swaying slightly, she stood and moved to the door, cautiously opening it and, seeing no one but hearing voices echoing down the corridor, turned and walked to the service door and out into the fog.

Her intention was to get as far from the church as possible. Then the picture of Johnathan falling like a log after being hit by the baseball bat came frighteningly to her mind and she stopped, turned and tried to sense where he might be.

Johnathan lifted his head; he could feel Cyndy's mind in his own. It was then that he realized that some of his old strength and power had returned. He put his hand to his head and felt for the shattered bone but all seemed normal once again. He took a deep breath and called to Cyndy, feeling her answer deep within his being. He felt her joy at finding him and then her concern for her own safety. Now that she had located him, she turned and began to walk slowly through the fog to where she could sense him to be. She found the edge of the road and carefully crossed to the other side.

Back at the church, Rory went once more to check on his charge, leaving the guys laughing at one of his jokes. He swung open the door and stopped dead seeing the couch empty and the discarded ropes on the floor.

"Shit, Maaiken will have a bird. How'd that bitch get free?"

He ran into the church shouting.

"Jake, get the guys and check around inside and outside the church. That bitch's gone and got away. We've got to find her before Maaiken comes out of his study or he'll go crazy."

The men, bored with inactivity, leaped up from where they were sprawled in various pews, some smoking and a couple playing cards. In a moment the church had emptied and the men were running through the corridors of the building. Jake and two others went out the main doors to check the parking lot, only to stop as they hit the wall of fog.

Through the fog, Cyndy heard the noise and recognized the danger if they should find her. Due to the fog and her weakness from the baseball bat strike to her head, she had made very slow progress and was only just off the road across from the church. The fog both helped and hindered her. The headache only hindered, she felt weak and faint again. The searchers couldn't see her but she couldn't see to hurry. Then the noise confused her, causing her to lose contact with Johnathan, and for the moment she was lost.

Jake and the others, stumbling and cursing at the fog, felt their way to where the parking lot met the road then started across. Cyndy, hearing the approach of feet and the constant ugly sound of cursing voices, felt icy chills of fear and sank down behind a small clump of bayberry bushes. She was lost again. She couldn't find Johnathan, she couldn't concentrate, her head hurt and her heart pounded with fear.

Johnathan still sat in the ditch where he had awakened listening for Cyndy but realized couldn't hear her voice any more. He called with his mind but the effort made him wince, and still there was just silence. What had happened? He feared the worst and staggered to his feet to try to go back towards the church. Then he stopped. He had no idea which direction to go. The fog still pressed like a gray blanket, preventing him from seeing more than a few feet in front of him. Lady pressed up against his leg and he kneeled to hold her neck and rub her ears. There was nothing else for him to do.

Hidden by the fog, St. James listened to the noise made by angry, frustrated men as they lunged about trying to find their way. Although he couldn't see the action, he could see the glare of light spilling from the front of the church, lighting up the fog bank.

Whatever, he figured the astronomer had made good her escape. He waited to see if he would get another opportunity to enter the church. He was still anxious to explore, for he was sure the missing artifact was hidden somewhere within the white wooden building. It was then that he felt the warmth against his chest. When he lifted the carved amulet from within his shirt he could also see that it was now giving off a soft reddish glow.

"Well, well, what have we here? The damned thing works after all. Maaiken must have unleashed his prize from wherever he hides it and it has awakened my amulet. Now I know I have to get back into the church."

He realized he was talking to the fog and stopped as he sat down, clearing away several small rocks and leaning his back against a convenient tree. He would see how all this played out and he intended to be a player. First he had to be sure that he could do so unobserved. There was definite danger here and he had to play it safe.

Maaiken finally rose from his prayerful position, legs aching, old joints protesting, and stood quietly for a moment, catching his breath, before turning and slowly exiting the hidden room. Leaving the wall opening as it was, he headed straight for the steep steps up to his study. These he climbed slowly, holding the softly glowing cup before him. This was the first time he had ever brought the cup up out of the cellars. His eyes shone with a mad delight as he held the cup with great care. He had a plan to remove the witch forever more and the time was now.

As he came out from the bookshelves he blinked in the stronger lights of his study. Without pausing he went to the door, turned the latch and stepped out into the hallway. It was then that he heard the men calling to each other as they searched every possible hiding place for Cyndy. He caught sight of Rory.

"Rory, Rory, what the hell's going on here?"

Rory stopped his desperate searching and swore.

"Damn and blast, it's the witch, boss, she's gone and got herself out of the ropes and disappeared. I checked those ropes, they were snug and the knots impossible to undo. I think she really is a witch."

Maaiken began to tremble, his breath came in short gasps, his nostrils flared and his eyes were awful to see. When at last he could speak he shouted with rage.

"You worthless incompetent! I told you to keep a strict watch over her. Now you've let her get away. I should give you a dose of what I'm going to give her."

Here he made a threatening gesture with the cup and Rory jerked back in pain.

"Shit boss, that hurts like hell, what're you doing? Ahhh! Stop it! Stop it!"

Rory lunged at Maaiken, coming within about two feet before he suddenly collapsed at Maaiken's feet. His eyes began to bulge, his heart was racing and he couldn't breathe. Soon his muscles took on a life of their own, twitching and shuddering.

Maaiken had watched impassively before stepping back, taking the cup out of dangerous range of Rory. The effect on Rory was immediate: his lungs began to fill with air once more and his heart began to slow to a normal beat. The muscles that had been dancing their way to hell stopped their shuddering; his eyes sank back to normal. He lay gasping like a fish suddenly lifted from its element. He stayed there for several more moments, weak and unable to lift his head, before he felt strong enough to finally pull himself up and again face Maaiken.

"Geeze boss, I'm sorry, I never meant you any harm. It's just that I was getting jolts like lightning when you waved that thing at me. I forgot myself, that's all. I didn't mean you any harm, believe me, boss."

"Oh shut up your mewling and tell me what you've done to find the witch. And don't come any closer to me or you'll get another dose of energy from this cup and this time you might just die."

Maaiken made a little wave of the cup at Rory and he jumped back with another curse.

"Shit, stop hitting me with that thing, whatever it is, boss. It hurts like hell every time you aim that thing at me."

Maaiken smiled.

"Just remember what I told you. Now what's going on? How are you planning to find the girl? Where's her dog by the way? I saw that dog just before all this shit started. Now it's disappeared, too. And what about the fire alarm? Was there any fire?"

"Naw, boss, something or someone pulled one of the fire alarm switches. There never was any fire. I've got some of the boys looking through the church. Jake and the others are outside but the fog's thicker than a wool blanket out there. So far I haven't heard from them. I was just going outside when you called me."

"Well, get out there and find out what's happening. I'll be in my study if you find her."

With that, Maaiken turned and re-entered his study, leaving the door ajar. He saw he'd left the bookshelf door open and went quickly to close it. Then he began to pace the floor, muttering and gesticulating. He looked at his hand as if seeing it for the first time and went to his desk to place the cup safely in the center.

Outside, Rory listened and could hear Jake's rough voice calling out in the fog. The men were on the opposite side of the road. Rory cautiously found his way to where they were standing.

"What's happening Jake? You got any idea where she's gone?"

"Well, 'less she's a damned cat and able to see through this shit she can't have gone far, Rory. Me and the boys're going to spread out about five or ten feet apart and walk in from the road. I think we'll find her stretched out behind some bush or other. Come on you bastards, let's find the bitch."

With that Jake and Rory and the two others stretched themselves out into a line spaced so they could just see each other and then started to walk into the scrubland that bordered the road.

Cyndy, sprawled out behind the bayberry bushes, could hear everything that was said and was terrified. What could she do? They'd find her and take her back. She began to cry, sobbing softly, trying not to make any noise, tears streaking through the dirt on her face.

Johnathan suddenly heard her distress. Could suddenly see through her eyes.

"Cyndy," he whispered to her, "Cyndy, can you hear me?"

Cyndy gave a small gasp. Johnathan's voice was in her mind once more. She sent her thoughts out to where she could now feel his presence.

"Oh, Johnathan, where are you? I need you. I'm in danger. I escaped from the church but those men who hit us are just a few feet away and they are starting to come toward where I'm hiding."

"Listen to me Cyndy, my darling. If you can hear me you can start to move toward me. You'll know which way to go. Just crawl away from those men and come in my direction."

Cyndy realized that Johnathan was right. She could feel exactly where he was as if she had a compass and he was the North Pole.

Immediately she moved, hearing the men fumbling and stumbling but getting closer to her hiding place. She turned to face Johnathan, then began to crawl, quietly as possible, slowly, trying to see what was in front of her face. As she struggled to see, her healing mind reached out ahead of her and she realized that she could now see in her mind exactly what was ahead. Every bush, tree and bit of scrub stood out clearly as if she were wearing night vision glasses and the night was not shrouded in fog.

She was able to move quickly now. But still she moved with caution, striving to make little or no noise. Gradually the sounds of the men behind became less and less as she distanced herself from them and the fog ate all sound and left emptiness behind.

St. James listened to the men as they went across the road and stopped to argue about what to do next. This, he thought, might just be his only opportunity, if ever there was going to be one.

He walked quietly back to the service door and listened then stopped. He could hear voices, one shouting in pain, and the other snarling commands. The commands were in a voice he recognized, Maaiken. The voices were coming from the open study door. He was intrigued that something that Maaiken was holding was hurting the other. From what was said it couldn't be something ordinary like a whip or club. Then he heard the sound of a body falling and other sounds of pain, gasping for air.

He listened for a moment longer, heard the man speaking weakly, apologetically, heard Maaiken's answer. Soon the man came out of Maaiken's office, staggering slightly, and headed away from him to the main door into the church.

St. James listened but heard only a muttering and the sound of feet pacing. Cautiously, he walked up the corridor, the carpet swallowing any sound his feet might have made, until he was able to see past the doorframe and catch a glimpse of Maaiken's desk and the window behind. His eye was almost immediately drawn to the small object that sat in the middle of the desk. At the same time he was aware of the heat from his amulet, now almost painful.

That's it, he thought. That's the cup. It's real after all. And Maaiken's taken it out of its hiding place for some reason.

He drew back a bit as Maaiken came into view, still pacing and swearing beneath his breath. Then Maaiken turned towards the door and started to walk forward. Alarmed, St. James almost ran as he retreated to the back of the service door and, peering around, watched Maaiken come out of his study and walk up the corridor out into the church itself.

Instantly, St. James ran back up the corridor and into Maaiken's study. As he approached the desk he stopped suddenly, hit by a wall of pain. The amulet burned into his chest. Struggling, he backed away from the desk. As his distance from the desk increased the pain lessened, stopping completely just inside the door. St. James stared at the object of his quest, unable to think what to do. He had very little time. There was no telling when Maaiken would return.

In the fog, Cyndy now stood up and began to run though the woods, guided by Johnathan and her clear insight. Finally she broke into the little wooded glen where Johnathan sat, his back to a scraggly white pine, his head cradled in his arms, Lady still sitting and nuzzling him from time to time. He looked pale and Cyndy's heart nearly broke. She ran to him and kneeled beside him, putting her arms around him and pulling him to her. Lady barked and scrambled to her feet lunging at Cyndy, almost pushing her to the ground.

"Johnathan, dear Johnathan. Lady, stop it. I'm glad to see you, too."

Then she gave in and sobbed, pulling herself closer to the large man.

"Oh Johnathan, at first I thought you might be dead. I was desperate. I had no strength, no power. I couldn't fight them. I didn't know what to do. I passed out in Maaiken's study and the first time I was conscious again I was all tied up on the couch in Maaiken's secretary's office and there was some man, oh yes, it was that archaeologist, St. James. Anyway I passed out again. When I came to the ropes were loose on my wrists and legs. I don't know, maybe St. James untied me, I just don't know but I got up and ran out of the church. Oh Johnathan, are you all right?"

Johnathan gave her a weak grin, put his arm around her shoulder and pulled her even closer to him than she already was.

"Well, you're the healing witch, Cyndy, what's your diagnosis? If you want my opinion, I'm healing and healing fast. My mind began to clear when I could hear you. My skull has already healed where the bat fractured it. Now I have you in my arms, even my heart's healing."

He grinned again, more strongly and with a new look in his eye. Cyndy pulled her head back and stared at him.

"You sound much better. And you're right. I have my ways and I was forgetting. I do have the power to heal, even stop death. Just let me collect my thoughts."

With that Cyndy now closed her eyes and put her hands, palms out, in front of Johnathan. She smiled, opened her eyes and hugged him.

"Dear Johnathan, you are amazing. I see into you and I see this white mist, shining white mist, and I see you are one with the mist. What am I seeing? It's something I've never seen before, even when I was working on George and could see inside him and was pulling him back from the light. There wasn't any white mist, just a sort of brightness that I knew was George's spiritual self. What is it? Why are you different?"

Before he could answer, Cyndy stopped and gently pressed her lips to Johnathan's, then grinned at him.

"I could see something else, John. Somehow I could see love. Now don't ask me what love looks like but I can see it and know it. And I see it in you. You love me, John. Me, a married woman and you love me. What am I going to do with you?"

She smiled.

"I may have to make an honest man of you yet. In the meantime, we need to make a plan to get out of here before we're discovered.

Those men were walking very slowly but look, the fog is beginning to lift. Soon they'll see well enough to make good time. Come on, my big invalid. Can you get up? We have to be going."

Even as she spoke they could hear twigs snapping and male voices arguing. Cyndy began to pull up on Johnathan's arm. Slowly he raised his giant frame and stood a moment to let the world stop spinning. Cyndy reached a hand to his brow and his mind cleared almost immediately. Slowly, they walked away from the sounds of the approaching men.

Soon the sounds were well behind them as they continued, Cyndy leading the way with her returned vision. Before long the fog had indeed lifted, suddenly, as these things happen near the ocean. The land was once more clear around them.

Cyndy had led the two of them into the town and was approaching her observatory when she caught at Johnathan's arm and stopped him. Parked before the door into the building was an ominous black truck with a man slumped behind the wheel, cigarette dangling from his lips. He appeared to be singing along to his radio but from their observation point all they could see were his lips moving, splashing ash from his cigarette.

Even as they watched, another man came out of the building pushing Cyndy's graduate student in front of him. Her hair was tousled and her eyes red from crying. The man gave her a final push and she collapsed on the sidewalk beside the truck.

"How long we gonna wait here, Ripper? If I have to put up with this mewling little girl I may just have to give her something to cry about."

His stubbled face broke into a leer as he leaned down and pulled the girl upright.

"Yeah, maybe I just give you something to remember me by, little girl."

The street was deserted except for the men and the terrified girl. The cigarette smoker leaned out of his truck, then climbed down to the sidewalk.

"Let's take her inside and have us some fun, Jocko. Toss you for who has her first. Loser holds her down. Winner gets first go."

He laughed.

"We might's well have a little sport. That fuck-up Maaiken has had us holed up here since last night. No sign of the witch so let's stretch our legs. She ain't gonna come here now. Maybe they already caught up with her. Come on."

He grabbed one of the girl's arms and pulled her back toward the observatory door, the stubbled one now following behind, running his hand down the back of the young woman's jeans and reaching for his own belt. The woman found her voice and began to scream. Ripper reached his large hand around her mouth and stopped the noise.

"Be good now, little lady. Don't you go screaming. Nobody gonna hear you anyway. They's all holed up in their houses, 'fraid Maaiken may come and do them in with his magic. No way anyone's gonna try and stop us. So relax little lady. It won't hurt. You might just enjoy it."

Here they both laughed and pushed their captive in through the door.

"Oh God, John, they're going to rape her. We have to do something."

Johnathan just grabbed her hand and rushed the two of them across the street. Slowing down, he eased in through the door, Cyndy following closely behind him. It wasn't difficult to find the men. They were in Cyndy's office, arguing violently as to which would get to have first go at the girl. The intended victim was crouched in one corner of the room sobbing.

The stubbled man suddenly swung a fist at the other, striking him a violent blow to his face and sending him stumbling back, tripping and falling backwards into the fireplace. There was an ominous hollow thud as his head hit the fire irons and he lay completely still. The other man suddenly lost interest in the girl and went to the man, pulling him clear of the fireplace and laying him out on the rug.

"Hey Ripper. You OK Ripper? Come on boy. I just gave you a little love tap there. Come on Ripper."

Here he slapped Ripper's face but Ripper never moved and his open eyes never closed.

Slowly the stubbled man backed away from Ripper's body and just stood, lust forgotten, confused by the speed with which this tragedy had occurred.

It was then that Johnathan and Cyndy entered the room, Johnathan going to the man while Cyndy went to the crying girl.

The man turned, startled, and tried to hit Johnathan but missed as Johnathan easily sidestepped and then swung the smaller man up by his shoulders.

"If you want to get hurt, just keep it up buddy. Otherwise keep silent."

Johnathan gave the man a push, causing him to stagger and then bounce against a wall before collapsing onto the floor. He lay watching them, then looked over to where his friend lay so still.

Johnathan went to him and pulled the man's belt from his pants. Then, rolling him over, he pulled the thug's arms roughly behind his back and used the belt to secure them. With the man's arms well-trussed Johnathan picked him up and carried him to a couch. Putting him roughly back on the floor, Johnathan tipped the couch over so it firmly pinned him, making any movement beyond breathing impossible. The man started to swear at Johnathan but stopped when Johnathan pushed a pillow into his face.

"You want to go on breathing, buddy, button up. If not I'll feed you this pillow bit by bit."

The man made gagging sounds and Jonathan pulled the pillow back, allowing the man to breathe again.

"You going to be good now?"

The man scowled but said nothing, just nodded in reply.

"OK, now if you just shut up and stay put for a while I'll decide what to do with you."

Next Johnathan checked the body that now lay so still on the floor. No doubt about it, the man was dead, his head broken open when he hit the metal in the fireplace. Johnathan doubted that even Cyndy and all her healing powers could put this man's spirit back into his body. He looked over to where Cyndy and her student were huddled, Cyndy stroking her hair and holding her close in her arms.

"You're all right now, Rose, just cry as much as you want. Nothing's going to hurt you now; you're all right. Those men can't hurt you with us around. There, it's OK."

Rose slowly stopped her sobbing and looked frightened at Johnathan towering over the two women.

"Don't mind him, Rose, he's one of the good guys. Now you go back to your room and get cleaned up. Johnathan and I have work to do."

She stood up, helping Rose to her feet. As Rose left the room, sobs still struggling from her small frame, Cyndy turned and went to the body so still on her rug. She knelt and felt for the man's pulse, then put her hands onto his chest.

"It's too late, John, this man's already gone. I'll just make sure he goes on to where he can get proper guidance. Guess he'll be surprised when he does his life review."

She continued to kneel and was silent, her spirit going out to make sure even this wretch found his way back to the spiritual reality. Johnathan listened in with his mind and followed her spirit as it went to where the dead man's spirit still hovered confused above the body. He watched as she quietly held him in her spirit arms, then followed as she carried him up a white tunnel of light that suddenly appeared before them. They arrived in a vast white space filled with figures. As they stood together, a man appeared before them. He smiled at Cyndy.

"Dear lady, thank you for helping my brother get here safely. He might not have made it without your help. But I can take him now."

With these few words he took the spirit body from Cyndy's arms and led him away. Cyndy followed them with her spirit eyes until they just seemed to disappear. She turned then, noticing Johnathan standing beside her, and together they followed the tunnel back to physical reality. Standing physically together in her own room she gave him a hug, tucking her arms around his waist.

"Johnathan, that's the first time I've ever done that. But it just seemed right. Have you been there before?"

"Yes, my darling. You've just been to the point we all go to when we die. It's a gathering place to meet guides and friends who will help take us to the next stage, a lovely place that looks to our eyes like a beautiful park. It's very lovely. We must go there together when we aren't dodging Maaiken and his uglies. All Shaman learn this journey. It forms an important part of their work, making sure the recently deceased are safely off to their spiritual rest. With your abilities, I can show you all these wonders now."

They stood quietly together for a moment enjoying the physical world and the sensations of their own physical bodies.

Chapter Twenty-Two

St. James had only a moment to worry about Maaiken's return when he heard footsteps approaching. With very little cover in which to hide, St. James slid behind the open door just as Maaiken strode back into the study. Not pausing, he went to his desk, picked up the sacred object and carried it to the bookshelves, where, activating the door mechanism, he immediately went down the stairs, the book shelf door closing silently behind him.

St. James watched in some amazement. A secret door. Now he knew where the hiding place was. He couldn't see all that well when Maaiken did something at the fireplace to cause the door to open, but he thought he might be able to find it now he knew the location of the opening mechanism.

St. James walked quickly to where he'd seen Maaiken stand while causing the bookcase to open. His view had been obstructed somewhat. Still he looked to where Maaiken had apparently placed his hand and quickly detected the discolored, raised knot. Tentatively, he pressed on the knot and was rewarded with a slight clicking as the shelf swung toward him.

With due caution he slipped into the opening, trying not to create a squeak or other noise. Suddenly the door swung shut behind him, tripped by a hidden lever. The blackness stopped him from going farther. Then, as his eyes became adapted to the darkness, he realized that there was a faint light coming from below, enough to show him the steps that led down into the cellars. He listened but heard nothing from below.

Slowly St.James began to descend the dimly lit steps, again trying not to make a sound. His heartbeat quickening, he stopped for a moment to get his breathing under control. Finally he started down the steps again and soon came to the beginning of a tunnel. Small lamps set into the walls provided enough light to see ahead. He crept slowly along, feeling the warmth of his amulet beginning to grow again. A voice from somewhere ahead brought him to a halt and sent his pulse racing again. He crept forward, slowly, one foot at a time, then pausing, waiting, listening.

The tunnel began to swell out into a large cavern. Here he could see an opening of some sort ahead of him. Also he could hear the voice more clearly and thought it must be Maaiken. The words sounded like a prayer. He inched forward until he could see through the opening. He saw Maaiken at last, on his knees, pouring oil from a silver goblet into the ancient cup. At the same time he was reciting what must have been a prayer as the thin stream flowed from the one container to the other. From his perspective above Maaiken, he could see that the priest wore an amulet similar to his own, suspended from the same intricate chain.

He watched in awe, almost without breathing, as he watched the liquid take on an unearthly, blue-violet glow when it reached the cup. The glow pulsed in a rhythm that echoed the glow emanating from the amulet hanging loosely on the front of Maaiken's gown.

Finally, Maaiken carefully tipped the cup, allowing the glowing oil to flow into a crystal container. As he watched Maaiken replaced the golden stopper, St. James thought it must be the same crystal vial he had seen Maaiken use in the church for Shirley's healing. He realized with a thrill that he was watching the preparation of the healing oil.

St. James' amulet was uncomfortably hot and he absent-mindedly reached inside his shirt to pull it out. As he did the motion caught Maaiken's eye. He looked up in surprise.

St. James' amulet had begun to glow earlier in the day as it sensed the nearby location of the cup, but now its light was bright enough to cast a shadow. As he pulled it free from his shirt he saw the cup in Maaiken's hand also begin to glow as if answering some call.

Maaiken was at a disadvantage, kneeling and holding the cup in one hand and the crystal vial in the other. He looked startled, then confused as he realized he couldn't move without putting at least one of the vessels down.

"Who the hell are you? What's that you're holding? What's happening here? I've never seen the cup glow like this before. Who the devil are you, maybe you're the devil himself?"

Still on his knees while trying to twist around Maaiken suddenly started to lose his balance. He twisted back, trying to save himself and the two precious objects.

St. James had felt the power of the cup earlier, and was wary of approaching any closer, but became nervous that Maaiken might drop it. Nothing must happen to that important relic.

He darted forward, reaching to steady Maaiken, but only succeeded in further startling the priest who, shouting in anger, tried to ward him off only to pitch forward, struggling all the while to save the cup and the crystal container.

St. James, reacting without thinking, reached his left hand out to take the cup only to freeze in pain as his hand enclosed the sacred relic. Maaiken, in the mean time, continued to pitch forward, until he crashed to the floor face first.

As the power of the cup began to wreak its terrible effects on his body, the amulet St. James still held in his right hand suddenly gave forth a burst of white light enclosing both the man and the cup. In unison the cup flashed an intense flare of blue light that met and blended with the white rays from the amulet. There was an intense but silent explosion of energy, then both cup and amulet darkened.

By this time both Maaiken and St. James lay silent, unmoving, on the stone floor of the secret room. Whatever the condition of the humans, cup, amulet and crystal vial were still intact and undamaged, St. James holding the cup and amulet, Maaiken still clutching the crystal container. The room was eerily still, no sounds, until a gasping gurgle and uneven breathing broke the silence.

Cyndy pulled away from Johnathan, her eyes still glowing with unusual intensity. She took a deep breath and smiled as she spoke.

"I've done all that I can do here, John. Whoever he was he's well on his way with his guide. What are we going to do now?"

Johnathan looked at her then turned his head in thought before facing her again.

"I think we should try and find out where the Sheriff and his deputies are and why they aren't responding to what they must know is a crisis and illegal. If they're party to all this then we have little chance to do anything but try to get off the island. We can't fight Maaiken with his powers and his thugs. It only works if we can get them one or two at a time. We may not be so lucky next time. Go see that Rose is OK. Give her something to make her sleep if necessary, then let's get down to the Sheriff's office, see if we can find out what's going on."

Cyndy disappeared to find Rose, while Johnathan went out briefly to check the street. The sun had set and a clear sky was beginning to show Jupiter and Venus, bright enough to be seen even though the sky wasn't fully dark. There was no one on the street; the truck was still parked where the men had left it. Walking to it and pulling open the door of the cab, Johnathan saw that the key was still in the ignition.

The door to the observatory opened and Cyndy came out, walking briskly, showing none of her recent trauma. She had taken time to wash her face and the coolness of the water had brought some color back to her cheeks.

Johnathan pulled himself up into the driver's seat while Cyndy entered the cab from the other side and sat, twisted around, her legs pulled up under her, facing toward Johnathan. Johnathan turned the key and the truck's engine roared into life.

The eerie emptiness of the streets continued. All the doors they passed were shut; windows too, were shut with drapes or blinds drawn.

Finally, parking a block from the Sheriff's building, Johnathan and Cyndy walked carefully along the street to the point where they could see into the front of the building.

Clem's desk was empty; they couldn't see into the Sheriff's office but the door leading to the holding cells was open and a man lounged in the doorway, smoking and seemingly talking to someone. A large handgun sat on the top of Clem's desk.

They pulled back and looked at each other. Cyndy pointed to one side.

"John, here's the alley that leads back to where the holding cells are located. The garages for their cars are back there, too. I think there's a door that leads from the garage to the office, maybe it's unlocked."

Johnathan nodded and together they slipped into the alley, walking swiftly until they came in sight of the holding cell windows. Johnathan stopped and held Cyndy's hand.

"Stay a moment, I want to see what's going on up there."

With that, Johnathan stilled his mind, centered himself and let his consciousness float up into the holding cell area. Immediately he could see the Sheriff and all the deputies crowded together in the three cells. The man they'd seen from the street still lounged in the door, goading the law enforcement personnel. He was laughing and enjoying the obvious discomfort of his prisoners.

"If you need to pee just go right ahead, boys and girls. That's what your prisoners have to put up with, no privacy. We're all big boys and girls and the girls all know what your dicks look like."

This struck him as hilarious as he laughed hard enough to begin to choke. Then he swore at the men and women in the cells.

"I can't do nothin' for you until I hear from Maaiken, see. So just shut up your bellyachin'. It's all gonna be over soon. Maaiken gets his hands on that witch from the observatory, he'll be lettin' you bunch out."

He paused, smiling then snarling out the next words.

"'Course, you'll all have to be good boys and girls or he'll fry you and your families. You know he can do it so just shut up."

With this parting remark, he threw the cigarette down on the floor, twisting his boot on it, before turning and going back into the front office.

Johnathan sensed Cyndy beside his spirit body and sent her his thoughts.

"Glad to know this bunch at least had to be restrained. Maaiken may have them frightened but he had to put them behind their own bars. Come on Cyndy, let's get rid of the guard and get these guys free. Maybe then we can work with them to help get Maaiken."

With that they returned once more to their physical bodies. As Johnathan lead the way, they walked cautiously to the garage area, then through a door. Although they had seen no other guards, they still moved quietly worried that somehow they might have missed something. The garage smelled of oil and gasoline and was filled with white cars, bars of blue lights on their roofs.

At the back of the garage, a door led to stairs. Slowly, Johnathan and Cyndy crept up to a landing that led to several other doors. They listened and heard the complaining voices of the Sheriff and his deputies. Johnathan tried this door only to find it locked.

"Time for one of my magic tricks, Cyndy. Watch this."

Johnathan once more let his mind center and soon the tumblers of the lock became clear. Using the force of his mind he aligned the tumblers, then used his hand to turn the knob. The door opened without any trouble and they walked carefully into the squad room, its desks empty, the computers dark. Seeing the way clear, they opened the door to the stairs that led to the lower floor. Johnathan held Cyndy's hand and stopped to let his mind go ahead. Soon he could see the guard, sitting at his desk, his back to the door at the bottom of the stairs.

"OK Cyndy, stay here 'til I take care of this thug."

Johnathan began to sneak down the stairs. As he did so he was aware that he was being followed and stopped to turn. Cyndy's eyes laughed into his own. She whispered into his mind.

"I'm not your average timid girl anymore, John, I'm going in with you whether you like it or not."

Johnathan hesitated then turned and began to descend the stairs again with Cyndy following closely behind.

Johnathan stopped at the bottom of the steps to look through the door. He could see the guard still sitting with his back to the door. The doorknob turned silently in Johnathan's hand and he eased the door open until it would allow his large frame room to pass through.

Now he could see with his physical eyes. The man was busy reading some files he had pulled from the Sheriff's filing cabinet. He was laughing at whatever lay before him on the cluttered desk. The gun still occupied space on the desktop, the black handle not more than six inches from his hand. The gun was a large, heavy, six-shot pistol. It looked ugly and dangerous.

Johnathan took a deep breath and focused on the gun, fixing it in his mind until he could feel the smoothness of the metal. Slowly exerting his full psychic power, he managed to pull on the trigger until the hammer was fully cocked.

The click that it made caused the man to look over sharply just as the gun exploded and shot off the desk, propelled by the force of the bullet leaving the barrel. The lamp on the table by the wall splintered as the bullet smashed its way through the shade and the bulb. The gun itself came to rest against the far wall.

The man flung himself back as the gun went off, tipping the chair backwards, tumbling onto his back and hitting his head sharply against the old pine boards of the floor, stunning himself for a moment.

Johnathan took advantage of that moment to step quickly over to him and, pulling him clear of the chair, slammed him back down on the floor where he undid the guard's belt and pulled it clear of the pant loops. Then, with equal vigor, Johnathan flipped the man over face down and quickly trussed him securely with the belt.

When he straightened up Cyndy had picked up the gun and was looking at him.

"My, you are a warrior, John."

She placed the pistol gently on the desk and turned to the door into the holding cells where shouts were now echoing, brought on by the sound of the shot. Cyndy turned back and in a moment had found the cell keys under one of the file folders that littered the desk. Quickly she and Johnathan went to the door and into the holding cell area. The Sheriff was the first to shout at them in confusion.

"What's going on? What the hell, Cyndy? Johnathan? What was that shot? Can you open these doors?"

"Hold your horses, Sheriff, we just took care of the guy with the gun out front and here, we have the keys. We'll get you out of those cells."

With that Johnathan took the keys from Cyndy and moved from cell door to cell door, unlocking each as he went, each cell erupting with shouts of pleasure. Shirley ran to hug Cyndy as soon as the door to the cell that held her was opened.

"Cyndy, honey, how'd you get here and what the hell's going on? We were all taken at gunpoint by a bunch of men. Those of us who were in the building got stuffed in the cells first and then each of the others as they came in. We never had a chance to resist. Oh, thank God you got us out of there. I need to pee so bad and I didn't want to use the facilities in the cell. 'Scuse me, I'll be right back."

With these hurried words she shot out the door and up the stairs to the washroom. The Sheriff came up to Johnathan and pounded him on the back.

"I don't know how the hell you came here or how you took down that bastard in the front office, but thank God for little mercies. Come on boys and girls, it's time we took Nantucket back from the bad guys. Johnathan, you know where those thugs are right now?"

"Some are back at the church with Maaiken, some are out at Cyndy's beach house and a few are looking for us in the brush across from the church or were the last time I saw them. They knocked us out with baseball bats earlier. They left thinking I was dead or the nearest thing to it. I was able to crawl away before losing consciousness entirely. When I woke up I could hear them looking for me in the fog so I beat it."

He nodded his head in Cyndy's direction.

"Cyndy, they took into the church and tied up. When she woke up somehow the ropes had come loose so she was able to get away from Maaiken and his gang and finally found me."

The Sheriff looked confused and angry.

"Well, can you tell me what's really going on? Has Maaiken gone mad? I know he is the power around here but I'm damned if I'm going to put up with his telling this town what to do anymore. When I find him I'm arresting him for inciting civil disobedience and any other ordinance I can find. I don't care if he can heal the world. And if he threatens me again with that Holy Oil of his, I'll shoot him."

Johnathan gave the Sheriff the briefest account he could of how Maaiken had decided to eliminate Cyndy because he thought she was threatening his authority. No way the Sheriff would understand what Maaiken was really up to.

The Sheriff began to issue orders to his officers. As soon as he was finished he turned again to Johnathan and Cyndy.

"You two better come to the church with me and the deputies. I'll want to keep an eye on you and maybe you can help me when I confront Maaiken."

He turned and laid his hand on Cyndy's arm.

"I know how you seem to have helped your husband get better at the hospital when it looked like he was dying. I don't pretend to know what that's all about either but it sure set off that madman Maaiken. This is the last time I let him take the law into his own hands, damned if I will."

With the deputies organized, Taylor, Cyndy and Johnathan piled into the lead car and led the heavily armed posse toward the church.

Soon the cars were at the bottom of the street leading to the white church perched at the top of the small hill.

"OK, everybody, we go from here on foot. Fred, you and Shirley peel off and see if you can find anyone in the brush across from the church. The rest follow me, and be careful, I don't want any casualties."

Fred and Shirley disappeared into the brush and began to work their way up the side of the hill. The Sheriff and his four other deputies plus Johnathan and Cyndy walked carefully up the macadam of the road, keeping lookout for any guards.

Two shots, fired from where Fred and Shirley had gone, stopped the party with Taylor looking anxiously into the brush. Soon four men came trooping out followed by Fred and Shirley, guns drawn and at the ready.

"Found this bunch camped out a ways back having a smoke. They tried to put up a fight but a couple of shots and they calmed right down."

"Yeah, well cuff them and attach them to something they can't move."

Fred, Shirley and the other deputies soon had the four firmly secured, hands daisy-chain cuffed, one to the other, and the two ends of the chain cuffed to the bumpers of one of the cars.

With that bit of business taken care of, the group again turned their attention to the church. As they walked up the hill and into the parking lot, Taylor detailed two to cover the front and took the rest back to the service door.

"Quietly now."

He waved Cyndy and Johnathan back.

"You two, keep to the back."

Cyndy and Johnathan stood still as the others advanced up the corridor to the doorway to Maaiken's study. The door stood open and they were quick to see that the study was empty.

Taylor waved to Johnathan and Cyndy to join him.

"What do you think? No sign here of Maaiken, although the desk looks like he's been here recently. Think he heard us coming and just vamoosed?"

"Not too likely, Sheriff. More likely he'd challenge you being here on his own home ground. Maybe he's in the main part of the church."

The Sheriff nodded and waved his hand toward the door into the church. With his deputies at his back he disappeared through the doorway.

This left Johnathan and Cyndy staring, confused, at one another. Johnathan motioned to Cyndy to follow him and went to the fireplace.

"I know that there's a hidden entrance here somewhere. I don't know where it goes but I think there are stairs to an underground cellar."

He looked under the fireplace mantel and immediately saw the discolored area. He experimentally put his finger on the spot and pushed, feeling the wood sink under his touch. As he did, they heard a click and watched as a section of the bookcase swung forward revealing a dark space.

"Well, what have we here?"

He poked his head into the space.

"Sort of dark. What we need is a light. What can you do for us Cyndy?"

Cyndy looked thoughtful and then put her hand out. Within a moment a softly glowing ball of light appeared and floated gently just above her palm.

"There John, that should do the trick. Neat isn't it? Let me go first and I'll just float it ahead of us."

"Can you float it ahead of me? I'd rather go first if it's all the same to you."

"Stop protecting me, John. Oh, well, you go first. We can argue about it some other time."

The ball of light floated freely from Cyndy's hand and hung soundlessly in the dark opening, showing the steps leading to the cellars. With Cyndy following closely behind him, Johnathan stepped into the opening. They were both startled when the door closed behind them. Johnathan stepped back to see why and noticed that the boards just at the beginning of the steps depressed when walked on, a hidden lever for closing the door behind whomever entered.

As Cyndy floated the light just in front of him he examined the wall and was relieved to see that another panel, discolored from years of use, was visible beside the door. When he pressed it the door again clicked open. It closed again as he went to the steps and began to descend, following the light as it obeyed Cyndy's unspoken commands.

Behind the two, now hidden by the closed portal, the Sheriff and Shirley entered the study. The Sheriff looked around, confusion showing on his face.

"Funny, I thought those two were still in here. Wonder where they disappeared to?"

With that they again left the study.

Reaching the bottom of the stairs Johnathan stopped with Cyndy pressed up hard against him. Together they listened but heard nothing in the gloom. Slowly they stepped out into the tunnel and then into the larger cavern. Still silence. As they proceeded through the larger cavern, Johnathan could see yet another room, this one with a door that stood open but from which very little light issued. Cyndy pulled at his arm.

"Johnathan, I feel the power of Maaiken's anointing oil, but there's something else, something much more powerful."

Johnathan nodded at her.

"I'm sensing the same thing, Cyndy, something powerful and yet something more, something...I don't know how to express it."

Together, now holding each other by the hand, they walked toward the opening. Cyndy gasped and stopped.

"Yes, it's the anointing oil I feel. It has a power that repels or hurts most others, except Maaiken and those he's healing. Strangely, I've always felt drawn to it. George says it makes him nauseous whenever he helps Maaiken out at the Church healing services. But what is the other power I feel? It's the same but it's different."

She looked at Johnathan then started forward again, now walking as if against a stiff wind. Johnathan followed and put his arm around her shoulders. Together they finally reached the open door and could see within.

"Dear God, Johnathan, look, it's Maaiken and another man. I think it's that archaeologist, St. James."

Johnathan looked at the scene. Maaiken was pitched forward on his face, his hand holding a glowing vial of oil. To his side was the man he recognized as St. James, face contorted, more on his back than his side, stiff arms cradling a strangely carved cup in one hand and an equally unusual pendant in the other, the chain still looped about his neck. Both men were still, but one was breathing in ragged gasps.

Johnathan now could sense a power he had felt only once, when with the Masters. He paused and pulled back.

"Don't go in there, Cyndy. I'm not sure but I think it might be dangerous for us to touch those things. The power is mighty but I feel it's also sacred, something of God. I feel like going to my knees and praying. But which of them is still breathing?"

He struggled to see in the gloom then, remembering, stretched out his mind.

"It's Maaiken. He's still alive. But I don't think you or I can go in there. I know I can't. That force, it's too much for me."

"Let me try, John. I don't feel repelled by the force. Strange but I feel as if this is a cathedral and Jesus himself is here."

Johnathan suddenly smiled and pulled Cyndy back and out of the room.

"Oh Cyndy, you bright child, of course, how could I miss it."

"Miss what?"

"That cup, I've heard so much about that cup but no one seemed to know what had happened to it. No wonder the oil that Maaiken uses in the church has healing power. That cup, it's the Grail, Cyndy, the Holy Grail, the cup that Christ passed from disciple to disciple at their last meal together before he was taken and, ultimately, crucified."

His voice was filled with awe and wonder.

"How did that cup ever end up here, on Nantucket? And more to the point, how did Maaiken ever get his hands on it? Anyway, now I know what I should do."

Cyndy pulled back from Johnathan and took a tentative step toward the open door.

"But shouldn't I try to see if Maaiken's OK? We can't just leave him lying in there, even if he did want to kill me and you."

She stopped moving, waiting for his answer.

Johnathan regarded her with grave eyes and didn't reply.

Instead he lifted his face, closed his eyes and began to center. Cyndy, wondering, also centered and was able to follow Johnathan as his spirit sent out a call, a call she had never experienced before but which felt natural to her.

In an instant she felt another presence in the room with them, and, quickly returning to physical reality, saw a quiet, white-robed man who had suddenly appeared in the cavern. Even as she watched him he reached to Johnathan and they embraced.

"I heard your call, David, and came at once knowing you only call under the most extreme of circumstances."

"Thank you Master. First, here's someone you must meet."

Johnathan pulled back then turned to Cyndy who was standing, confused by what she was witnessing. Who was this man? How had he just appeared like that, and what did he mean calling Johnathan, David?

The man looked as if he should be ages old but had a youthful radiance about him. He turned to smile at Cyndy and she felt as if she had been lit up by a searchlight.

"Well, yes David. This is someone I should meet. I can feel she is a most unusual young woman. David, don't keep me waiting for an introduction. She has the power. I feel it. But, why does she have the power? What has happened here, anyway?"

Cyndy was waiting for John to speak. She wanted to speak herself. She wanted some answers herself, among which why was this man calling Johnathan, David?

"Master, she's one of the chosen all right, one who reached her maturity more quickly than might have been the case except for an accident. It was during an accident, where she experienced Near Death, that Jesus came to her and took her in his arms, comforted and blessed her and directed her back to her body to begin a journey of healing."

He stared at his mentor.

"She's been a changed person ever since. Problem is she doesn't yet have any idea of her own strength. Yes, she's indeed an unusual young woman. In all my years I've never met her like. But first I have urgent need of your help and advice."

He paused, thinking how to explain the enormity of what had happened in such a short time. The gentle, white-robed man waited, a questioning look in his eyes.

"Master, since I arrived on Nantucket, I've encountered a rash of strange happenings. First we have a man, the rector of a church, Maaiken Starbroke, who has been healing the un-healable. Well, he seems to have gone mad and tried to have us both killed. In fact it looks as if he, himself, has almost been killed, may even be dying as we speak. He's in the room back there in the company of another of whom I know little. And, the most magical thing of all Master, I've just found that he was using the Grail, itself, to gain his unusual healing powers."

"Ah, the Grail. It disappeared when the Templars took it away to keep it from the Muslims during the end of the Crusades. We have often wondered where it had gone. Even we have been unable to locate it in all this time. We thought it lost forever, perhaps at sea in some shipwreck."

He sighed then nodded at the man he called David. Cyndy bit her tongue to stop from breaking in with her own questions.

"I know now why you called me, my son. This most important cup must be preserved. I may have to refer to the council for advice. In the meantime, I think you will have to be the one to take care of it. Yes, I feel the power within this place. Come, show me what you have found. But first, come here girl, let me give you a greeting."

He drew Cyndy into his arms and Cyndy felt such a glorious power flowing from him to her that she almost fainted. Releasing her, the Master smiled into her face and kissed her on the forehead.

"You have so much to offer this world young lady. It is such an honor to meet you. You, blessed by The Master Himself, and you don't yet know what you have become. Well, we'll see to that little oversight. When this is all over, you will come and spend some time with us while you complete your learning."

He turned to the man called David.

"Come, David, show me this wondrous cup. But first, let me give you both protection from the powers that radiate from the Sacred Vessel. Although a blessed relic, its power is now too much for a mere mortal to withstand without sacred protection. Not that I think you two are mere mortals."

Here he laughed gently, then drew Cyndy and her Johnathan, who now seemed to be David, together and raised his hands above them, palms upturned. Almost immediately two intricately carved pendants appeared in his palms, each complete with what appeared to be an equally curiously carved gold chain. To Cyndy it seemed as if a shower of stars passed over her head and down into her body. She heard Johnathan, David, take a deep breath and knew he was feeling as she did.

"Good, put these amulets around your necks and you will be safe. God's own protection is with you. What God protects let no man or woman try to interfere with. Lead me David, show me the cup and the man who has had its custody all this time."

Johnathan went to the dark door. Cyndy's ball of light floated out ahead of him and into the room, filling it with light for the first time. The Master followed and peered into the room, head cocked to one side, studying the tableau. Cyndy edged around his robe and took another look, the radiation from the Grail and oil now reduced to a barely noticed sensation. The amulet around her neck gave off its own feeling of comforting warmth.

As they looked Maaiken gave a cough and began to move. First he looked at his hand with the vial of glowing oil. Then he looked at his other hand, jerking his head up as he saw that it was empty. He groaned, set the crystal vial down and, unsteadily, began to push himself up, getting to his feet and swaying, breathing in heavy gasps like a man who has been running and, finally, looked about.

As his eyes caught sight of St. James, deadly still, with the Grail clenched in his hand, he stopped and started to turn. As he did he looked up at the door and the trio who were silently observing him. Maaiken stopped, still swaying, trying to make sense of what he saw.

More quickly than his condition would seem to warrant, he stooped to snatch away the Cup from St. James's dead hand. In the same moment he also picked up the crystal vial and then retreated towards the other end of the room, stepping around the table that still supported the leather box that housed the Grail.

The group in the doorway was held motionless by their surprise and only began to advance on him by the time he had reached the far wall. Here he jerked down a peg that protruded from the wall and, in that instant, a heavy stone slab thundered down just in front of the table, hiding him from Johnathan, Cyndy and their strange visitor. Dust billowed up from the ground.

"What the devil… sorry Master, what has that crafty old man done now?"

Even as he spoke there was a crash outside the room that shook the ground under their feet. Johnathan turned and raced out to find that a pile of boulders and stones now blocked the corridor from the stairs that led up to the study. Dust made seeing difficult. They were trapped with no apparent exit. Except for Cyndy's ball of light, the cavern was in complete darkness. There was no sound except for some small stones still falling from the roof. Cyndy had grabbed at his left arm and was standing, staring at the scene. He turned to the Master.

"What can we do, Master? We're trapped here unless there's another exit. I never learned how to pass my physical body through solid matter."

He looked at Cyndy.

"Don't know about Cyndy, though. With her powers, maybe it would be possible for her."

"You are right, David, that is not an easy process. No, you weren't ready for that my son; your learning path is still too low. And I am not here in my physical body but merely a spiritual manifestation. I can go back to my body but I'm afraid for you two. And my time here is just about finished anyway. I am called back to my body. I can't stop myself from leaving you. Please my dear spirits, I will come back as soon as I can but the two of you must try to stop that man and retrieve the precious Grail."

He turned his luminous eyes on to Cyndy. She gasped at the love she could feel.

"My dear Cyndy, you have great powers. My son David here has some remarkable powers himself, but neither of you can pass through solid matter. Try to find a way out. I will come back as soon as I can."

With these words his voice became fainter as his image faded from sight. When the image had gone they could hear him no more. Cyndy looked at Johnathan, alarm making her face grow pale.

"What has happened John, David or whoever you are? This isn't the time or I'd want a full explanation of why you told me your name was Johnathan and it turns out to be David."

She pulled away from him, now hurt and frightened by all the strange happenings.

"Steady my darling, that can come later. Let's explore this place. There may yet be another opening."

They both heard the sound at the same time. It sounded like some one filling a bathtub only louder. Along with the sound water began to wet the floor.

"My God, Johnathan, the place is beginning to fill with water. Please, what are we going to do?"

Johnathan/David looked around trying to find the source of the water. He went to the room where Maaiken had been working, the water already beginning to float the body of St. James. Then he saw it, an opening at the top of the wall of the inner room, unnoticed before due to a grating that covered the front of it. Now a fast flowing flood of water cascaded through the opening, a miniature waterfall.

Already it was ankle deep in the room and rising rapidly.

"You know Cyndy, water can't fill a container unless there is a way for the air to get out. Otherwise air pressure will eventually stop the flow by balancing off its pressure. I can feel the air flowing away from us. It has to be going through some exit somewhere. Come on."

He grabbed at Cyndy's arm and dragged her out of the small room and back into the corridor, forcing the door closed as he went. The immediate effect was to stop the rapid rise of the water in the tunnel.

Quickly, he went to the rubble blocking the stairs but could see no opening for air. He paused to look around. As he did the door to the smaller room gave way and a small wall of water gushed into the corridor. Sloshing through water that was beginning to reach to Cyndy's knees, he went along the corridor away from the original stair's entrance and past the room that had held the cup, water once more flowing freely into the corridor.

Cyndy followed dumbly in his wake, then stopped, startled, as St. James' body floated out of the door and into her path. With a feeling of revulsion she pushed it aside and chased after John/David. Water was beginning to reach to the tops of her legs and her groin. The cold began to penetrate her lower body. It had further to go on John/Dave or whoever he was before he would feel it. Their only source of light still floated but was hanging near the ceiling at the entrance to the room where they had found Maaiken.

"Cyndy, control the light ball, please. We need it if we're going to see a way out of this mess."

Cyndy pulled back sharply and shook her head.

"Sorry John or David, I'm letting you down by being frightened."

With that she turned to look back at the light ball and it immediately floated along until it was ahead of Johnathan.

With the light now casting illumination ahead they could see that the corridor went only a few more paces ending in a blank wall. Water was now reaching the top of Johnathan's legs, putting it about waist level on Cyndy.

"Damn it John, Dave this is getting serious. If we don't find a way out here or a way of stopping the water, we'll drown in a few minutes.

"Cyn, darling, you're a genius. I need to go back into the cup room. Come on, and bring that light ball."

He turned and strode back in the rising water. Cyndy, trying to control the light and follow her large friend, felt she could do better by swimming, the water now reaching to her mid-chest. She was getting very frightened now, her heart pounding, her breathing rapid but shallow.

Reaching the room behind John/Dave she stopped swimming, put her feet on the floor and watched as he stopped. She could feel him centering but was too cold and wet to try to follow him. Instead she watched in amazement as a large boulder suddenly appeared in the mouth of the opening, rolled forward a few inches, then became wedged. The torrent immediately slowed with just small jets of water still spurting from the reduced opening.

Cyndy looked in amazement and gasped.

"What did you do? What magic trick is that?"

"Not really magic, though it looks like it. Called manifesting. Jesus could do it, did it with the loaves and the fishes. Sai Babba does it all the time, makes small keepsakes for his visitors, but his critics claim he's palming the items. We all have the power, but most of us haven't the knowledge. The Masters taught me. It was all I could think of, manifest a boulder big enough to jam in that opening. Don't know how long it'll hold though. There's a lot of water pressure there. Right now we need to try and find some way out of here before that boulder gives way and the water really starts to pour in here again."

Cyndy swayed in the water, her body beginning to feel chilled. Johnathan/David caught her and held her to him for a moment then turned and went back out of the door into the corridor.

"Come on Cyndy, use your powers, help me find a way out of here. Start scanning for another door or exit. I can't believe that the way we came in is the only way. Look at Maaiken. He had another escape route. Well maybe there's still another somewhere."

The water swirled around his waist as he moved. Cyndy resorted to swimming again as her feet slipped on the floor under the water. She concentrated on the globe of light. Of course, she thought, that's what I've done to make that light but I never gave it a name. I manifest the light; guess I can manifest other things too. Then she noticed that the water was beginning to recede slowly, it was only at her waist now. She walked and paddled after her strange friend and began to concentrate on the walls around them.

"Oh shit, Cyn, I don't see anything but solid rock around us. And I can't imagine being able to move all that rock that's sitting between us and the stairs to Maaiken's study."

He slumped. Cyndy reached and pulled herself up, using his arm as a lever. Finally she had herself looking directly into Johnathan's eyes

"What do I call you, Johnathan or David? At least tell me that much. If my days are going to end here I would like to know your real name."

She sounded sad but defiant. He reached his other arm around her and hugged her close to him.

"My real name is David. That's the name my mother and father gave me. Never mind why I go by Johnathan. We ever get out of here we can go into all that. Right now I'm stumped. You and I, we have great spiritual powers and I'm stumped about how to deal with the physical reality."

As he spoke, Cyndy, in looking up at David, looked above him at the tunnel roof. She realized that she could sense an openness.

"David, look up. Have you tried to see through the roof? I think there is some kind of opening. That's where the air was going when the water was coming in so fast. Look around above us. The walls are solid except for the stairs and the tunnel where Maaiken escaped."

David looked up then sent his spiritual eyes to scan above them. Immediately he could see the opening even though it was hidden by a grating and some rock-colored cloth.

"Of course, Cyn, it's an air inlet. Must have been dug a long time ago. It's big enough to get a body through, well a body your size. Don't know if I'll fit. We have to move quickly. The boulder in the water inlet won't hold forever. I'm going to lift you up on my shoulders. I think you can reach it then."

Quickly David hoisted Cyndy up until she could get her feet on his shoulders. He steadied her, water streaming from her jeans until he had to turn his head away to keep the water from his eyes. She pulled at her light ball until it was positioned to illuminate the ceiling just above her head, then straightened up to find her head just below the rough rocky roof.

Now she could see how the grating had been hidden by cloth. She reached up with her hands, finding a good grip and pulled, releasing a cloud of dust and small rocks. She coughed, temporarily blinded. When her vision cleared she could see crude, hand-forged bars of iron. Her spirits sank. How would they be able to dislodge this obstacle? She pulled at her ball of light and it came, obediently, to hover just to one side. Now she could see clearly. She gave a whoop.

"John... I mean David, the opening is blocked by an iron grate but it's hinged and I can see how it's latched. I'm going to try to get it to swing down."

The iron bars were held by a frame of wood and the whole hinged to bolts driven up into the rocky roof. At the far side from the hinges a great iron padlock looped between iron circles fastened into the body of the grating and the rock itself. She reached up and pulled on it but the metal was rusted and she couldn't even move the lock in the iron loops.

"There's a great padlock, David, And it's all rusted. Can you open it? I mean like you opened the lock in the door at the Sheriff's office."

David was starting to shiver from the water still reaching up to his waist.

"I can't, Cyndy, I'm getting too cold. I can't control my thoughts."

Johnathan began to shiver even more and Cyndy was afraid she might slip.

"Can't you do something to warm up David? What about all those things I read about Tibetan monks sitting out in the freezing cold?"

"It's not what the Masters taught me, that kind of control over my body. I don't have that kind of power. Sorry, Cyndy, it's all I can do just to keep you up on my shoulders."

Cyndy realized that everything depended on her now. If they were to escape it would be through her efforts. She looked at the barred grill above her head. She couldn't move the padlock. What could she do? She shivered with fear. Her breathing became labored. Beneath her feet she could feel David shivering from the cold. She could feel his great strength beginning to wane.

Then the calm, measured voice began to speak in her head.

"Chosen one. You have powers yet unknown to you. Greater powers than David has ever had. You have the power over materials. You can make metal melt."

Cyndy almost screamed.

"But how? How do I make metal melt? I don't know this?

"What are you saying, Cyndy? Are you talking to me?"

"No David, someone's talking to me. Someone's saying I can make metal melt and I don't know what he's talking about."

The fear and desperation made her voice break and she was close to tears.

The calm voice began again.

"Cyndy, you possess great powers. Be calm. There isn't much time. You must listen to me and do what I tell you."

Suddenly Cyndy felt a warmth and peace descend over her and could see rather than hear. She watched as her hands reaches out to the iron loops that held the padlock to the grating and to the rock of the tunnel roof. Her hands were reaching out without conscious volition, her mind trying to understand. The voice continued.

"That's right Cyndy, put your hands on the iron loops and concentrate on intense heat, your hands will not be harmed but you can make those iron loops melt. But warn David to move to one side when the metal begins to melt. It could burn him if it hits him."

Cyndy's hands were now grasping each loop of iron and she could see that each was beginning to turn bright red, then white and under her hands she could feel the metal beginning to form drops.

"Look out David, the iron is melting. Don't let it drop on you."

David looked up startled then pulled to one side, Cyndy trying not to lose her balance. Within seconds molten iron began to cascade down to drop sizzling into the water beside David's shoulders. The cascade of incandescent metal continued to pour from where Cyndy's hands were holding the iron loops, yet she felt only a mild warmth. Suddenly the massive padlock dropped into the water and the grate began, slowly, to swing down, creaking in protest until it had swung clear of the airshaft above. Cyndy ducked her head, just clearing the massive iron bars as they swung past.

Now the way was clear. Cyndy nudged her ball of light so it floated up the shaft. She could see iron steps set into the rock. The bars of the grill made a sort of ladder for her to pull herself up and into the shaft.

Cleared of her weight, David looked up and saw her legs disappearing above him. With the last of his strength he reached up to the iron grill, now hanging just above his head, and pulled his body up to where he could get some purchase for his legs. He paused, exhausted, breathing heavily. From her perch above his head Cyndy watched with concern.

"Are you OK, David?"

"I think so Cyn. I've just got to get some strength back. I'll be all right. I don't know what you did to get that grill open but tell me some other time."

Just then there was a large splash followed by the sound of a waterfall.

"That boulder I manifested in the opening has just been dislodged, Cyndy. We need to get out of here."

With that David pulled himself up from the grating to the beginning of the iron steps set in the tunnel rock face. He climbed further up into the tunnel to where he could see Cyndy's legs disappearing above him. He climbed up after her with a grunt of exertion.

"Where does it go Cyndy? Can you see?"

"I've just come to a ledge, it's the edge of a tunnel that goes off from this shaft. Are you OK? Can you follow me?"

"Yeah, yeah, I'm OK, I'm starting to feel much better. The feeling's back in my legs and I'm not shivering."

Below him he could see the water still rising.

"Get going Cyndy, I'm right behind you. Don't know how far that water can rise but it's still coming up."

Cyndy cast one last look down at him then disappeared into the tunnel she had found. David pulled his bulky body up behind her, grazing his shoulders on the sides of the tunnel.

Finally he arrived at the opening to the offset tunnel and went forward on his hands and knees, keeping his head low to avoid hitting it on the roof. The tunnel was just barely big enough for him to slowly make his way forward.

He cast a cautious eye ahead, trying to see Cyndy, but all he could see was a faint glow of light. As he closed the distance to the light it seemed to brighten. It was only when he had actually reached the point where the light seemed to originate that he realized it only marked a turn in the tunnel, just a reflection off the wall. He tried to see around the curve but the length of the turn prevented him from seeing anything but more tunnel.

"Cyndy, where are you? Where does this interminable tunnel go to anyway?

"Just a few more steps, my darling; come, see what I've found."

Cyndy sounded happier than he had heard in days. The curve of the tunnel almost defeated him; he had to turn so he was sliding on his side in order to get his body to follow the bend. Finally the path ahead straightened out and he could see that the narrow confines were broadening all around him. Still ahead was light. Above him the roof dropped away and he could stand. With a sigh of relief he picked his way carefully to where the light beckoned.

Just at that moment Cyndy's ball of light floated out from a hidden turn in the rock, followed by Cyndy herself.

"Oh John... I mean David, come quickly, it's amazing."

Her excited voice echoed in the tunnel.

Chapter Twenty-Three

The Sheriff and Shirley left the study and joined the group of deputies now lounging in the church waiting for further instructions.

"Anybody seen Cyndy or that big guy she's with?"

Several shook their head or grunted in the negative.

"Yeah, well I left her and Johnathan in the study. When I went back they had just disappeared. Damn! Wish they wouldn't do that. They know more about what's been going on than anybody. Now they're gone again. Damn!"

He looked at Shirley who squinted back at him.

"You're her buddy. You got any ideas?"

"Sorry Taylor, I want to talk to her myself. I thought she was in the study. We were only gone for a few minutes. They're better at disappearing than David Copperfield."

"Yeah, well guys, no one's doing anything here. Why don't two of you go see if you can find them. The rest of you get back to the station. Jeff, get the duty roster and organize the shifts. And get those thugs behind bars and start writing them up. Shirley, come with me. We're going to see if Cyndy headed back to the observatory."

With those words the various deputies took their handcuffed prisoners and soon only the Sheriff and Shirley were left to take one last look around. It was then they heard the rumble under their feet and a low thudding sound. They could feel a physical shock and the building trembled slightly.

"Christ, Shirley, what's that? We having an earthquake or something?"

In a moment the noise had stopped and the building once more quiet under their feet.

The two of them turned and cautiously re-entered the back of the church, looking for some explanation for the noise and vibration. When they reached Maaiken's study they looked in then stopped and stared at the bookshelves beside the fireplace. The once-solid facing of bookshelves now gaped open. The violence of the vibration had sprung the latch and the hidden door was open, exposing a passage shrouded in darkness.

"What the hell?"

The Sheriff quickly walked to the gaping entrance. Shirley followed and pushed around his side to enter, pulling back abruptly almost at once.

"I can just make out some steps leading down. It's pitch black, we need a light."

She looked around and spotted the dented Coleman light on the shelf. Pulling it down she shook it experimentally.

"Too bad it's empty, mantle's broken too. Wonder why Maaiken keeps it up there? Lucky I've got my full kit."

She reached down and unhooked a flashlight from her equipment belt.

"Here, Taylor, you want to take the point?"

Taylor took the flashlight and clicked its beam into the dark space, then followed the light past the open door and into the area leading to the steps. He shone the light down.

"Shit, the steps seem to end at a pile of rocks. Must of been what we heard, a rock slide. Hope no one was down there when that fell. He shone the light at his feet. On the floor was a handkerchief. Shirley reached down and picked it up. It was an old fashioned handkerchief, delicately embroidered. Shirley stared at it then lifted it to where the Sheriff could see it in the beam of the flashlight.

"I've seen this before or one like it. Cyndy has a drawer full of them. She found them in her grandmother's stuff after the old woman died. She likes to use them, mostly for nostalgic reasons I guess."

The Sheriff looked thoughtfully at the small square of cloth.

"Yeah, well I sure hope it doesn't mean Cyndy went down those steps, but it seems a good bet that's how she and her friend disappeared so fast after we left them. Somehow they knew about that secret door--maybe they saw old Maaiken use it. Whatever. We can't follow them. I hope there's another way of getting to wherever these steps lead. Might be a back entrance somewhere. Let's radio to get Henry's bloodhounds up here; see if there's any scent to pick up around the building. Then we we're going up to the manse. Maybe old Maaiken's holed up there."

Together they left the study and went out the service door to where the Sheriff had parked his 4x4.

David reached for Cyndy and held her for a moment,

"What is it Cyndy? What's so amazing?"

Cyndy replied by grabbing him by the hand and pulling him into the opening from where she had just come. The obedient floating ball of light went just ahead of them, illuminating a large chamber outfitted with crude furniture and sporting another opening on the opposite wall. As David peered about he couldn't believe his eyes.

"God in heaven. The Cup, it's here."

Indeed what they both stood and beheld was the ancient carved stone cup they had last seen when Maaiken dashed away from them and the wall had fallen to prevent them from following. They were then aware of their pendants glowing softly against their chests. The strange amulets were obviously working to protect them from the damaging energy given off by the Grail, the same radiation that had ended St. James's life, energy that had apparently driven Maaiken mad instead of ending his life.

Slowly, David approached the table.

"So, what's this place? How did the Grail get here? Wonder where Maaiken has gone, why he's left the Cup here, unprotected?"

"Unprotected from what, David? As far as he knows, we're both dead down in the lower cave. He undoubtedly started the water flowing. He thought we were trapped to drown and that would leave only himself with knowledge of the Grail and its great secret."

"So, where's he gone, then?"

Together they turned and looked at steps cut out of the rock, leading up from the cave. Cyndy waved at her light and it floated over to the steps. David and Cyndy cautiously crept to peer up the staircase.

"Far as I can make out these steps go straight up but I can't see where they end. Float that light up the stairs, let's see what's at the top."

Obedient as always, the light drifted up the steps with David and Cyndy following. The ball of light stopped at a seemingly dead end. They were looking at what appeared to be a rock wall.

David scratched at his head. Cyndy giggled.

"I can't believe you just did that."

"Believe I did what, Cyn?"

"You just scratched your head. I thought that was just a saying. Didn't know people really scratch their heads when they're puzzled."

"Give me a break, darling. Sorry if I disappoint you. Guess all primates have to scratch their heads from time to time. But this can't be the end. Just a minute, I'm going to try and project into that rock. There must be something I can't see with my physical eyes."

David slowed his breathing and centered himself, releasing his consciousness to probe forward. Within moments he found himself looking into the darkness of an open space. Then a ball of light appeared and he could see it was an ordinary basement of a house, ordinary except he didn't know houses on Nantucket had basements. He turned slowly, realizing Cyndy had followed him into the non-physical world.

"So who's watching our backs if you're here too?"

"I thought you might need a light, dear. So, what's the secret, John, I mean David? Darn, I'm never going to get your name straight. How do the stairs end on the other side of this wall?"

"Must be like the entrance in Maaiken's study, Cyn. Must be a secret door of some kind."

David slowly rotated his point of view until he was looking back at the wall. With his sharpened vision he could see where the stone foundation of the house had an unusual line that jigged and jagged around the rough stones. He looked for some lever and saw where one of the stones seemed darker than the others.

"Come on Cyndy, let's get back into our bodies. I know what to look for now."

Within moments they were looking at each other with their physical eyes once more. David went to the rock face and began to go over it. He quickly found one rock that appeared darker than the rest. Cautiously he put his hand on it and pushed. He felt it yield then heard a click as some latch released. A ragged door moved inward then swung on hidden hinges. Once more they were looking at the basement.

Cyndy's light ball, which had followed them back when they returned to physical reality, now had followed them through the opening in the wall and was lighting the underground space. David looked at it tentatively then looked around the basement.

It was small for a basement, just a single room with a wooden stairs leading up to a door. Some plumbing was visible with a small sink in one corner. A single light bulb hung down from the ceiling, dark now. David experimentally pulled on the string that hung down from the socket. The light came to life, spreading brightness around the small space. Cyndy reached out to touch her own light globe and it disappeared.

"I think I know where we are, Cyndy. I think we're below the manse. It makes sense, a way into the caves from both the church and Maaiken's house. That's where he's gone and that's why he left the Grail hidden in the upper chamber. As far as he knows we must be dead by now. He doesn't want to risk exposing the Cup to discovery should he get picked up by the Sheriff. The Sheriff had better be careful. Maaiken still has the anointing oil. It's can be a vicious weapon in his hands."

With that assessment, David walked to where the stairs angled upward. He could see the wooden door in more detail now. He tried the first stair, then cautiously climbed until he was standing before the door itself.

"I think it prudent if we explore before we commit our physical bodies. What say Cyndy?"

"Lead the way boss, I'm right behind you."

Together, they quieted their minds, centering and then projecting their spiritual selves, emerging through the wooden door almost together. Once on the other side they halted, moving their consciousness around, slowly, to view the room. It was the kitchen, darkened but with light spilling in through the windows. Looking back they saw nothing but a large open hutch behind them.

"Darn but the man likes to hide his entrances and exits. I'm surprised to find that it's daylight. I've lost touch with time completely. How many hours have we been moving, anyway?"

"I don't rightly know but it's been many hours. I think it was yesterday when we started." "No wonder my physical body's beginning to feel like lead. We're going to have to rest soon or we won't be good for anything."

"You're right, but I'm too excited and nervous to rest at the moment. I think Maaiken isn't far away. He may still be in this house somewhere. We've got to find him and see what he's up to. Any delay could be fatal to someone. I'd hate for the Sheriff or one of his deputies to tangle with him."

"I agree, darling, let's find him and figure how we can neutralize his power. Between the two of us we should be able to think of something."

Even as Cyndy spoke these words, the sound of the doorbell pealed loudly throughout the house. David and Cyndy both moved to the window looking out on Garden Street. They could see the Sheriff's car at the curb, two large bloodhounds leaning out of the back window.

"Oh my God, David, it's Shirley and John. Do you think that Maaiken will answer the door?"

"I still don't hear anything inside the house, Cyndy."

The doorbell sounded once more and they could hear Taylor shouting outside.

"We can't do anything like this. Come on let's get back to our bodies. Then we'll be able to answer the door."

With those words he quickly return to the cellar and his own body. Looking around he found Cyndy also back in the physical form.

"Common, Cyn, Let's get back to the front door. I'm going to open it. Be a big surprise for Taylor and Shirley but we've got to get our act together and find out where Maaiken has hidden himself. The Sheriff can help."

They found the latch that moved the hutch to one side and re-entered the kitchen where they opened a door leading into the hall and the big, old, oak front door. The doorbell was pealing again. The door itself was securely bolted and chained. As David worked to undo these barriers, he could see the Sheriff staring at him through a small window set in the middle of the door. There was astonishment in his eyes. He turned and spoke to Shirley and pointed at the man they knew as Johnathan behind the small window.

At last David got the door open. Taylor grabbed at his arm.

"John, how on earth...?"

"Sorry Sheriff, no time for explanations, we've got to find Maaiken. I think he's gone mad or something and he's got some of that anointing oil. Long as he has that he's deadly dangerous. Better remember he's as armed and dangerous as you and Shirley or any of the deputies for that matter. I think you should get a rifle so you don't have to get very close."

The Sheriff eyed the big man for a moment.

"OK you two, later then. You've got a lot to explain but you're right, we got to find that crazy wizard before he does any further damage. Any idea where he might be hiding out?"

David looked around at the big old manse and thought out loud.

"This old building's already shown us one hidden surprise. Bet there are others. Ever hear of priest holes? They were popular in England when Oliver Cromwell was looking for priests who were against Henry. Priest holes were built into houses in a way that made them difficult to find. This old house goes back almost to those times and traditions. Might be it has a hidey hole or two around here."

"So how do we go about finding a hidey hole, John? You got any ideas?"

"Well Sheriff, a priest hole might as well be on the grounds as in the house. Why don't you and Shirl go over the grounds; see if there is any sign of recent activity in the hedges and look in that old bit of a barn in the back. Cyndy and I'll go over the house."

Taylor looked over to where Cyndy and Shirley were still hanging on to each other, trying to talk and each crying with the joy of finding each other. He looked back to David.

"OK, but I'm putting in a call for reinforcements before any of us goes anywhere. You and Cyndy'd do better to stay out here 'til we get some help. Know what I mean? You're not law enforcement and I don't want you taking chances. Shirl and I'll start on the back. That barn looks a tempting place to hide out. But wait here."

With that Taylor ran back to his unit and pulled a mike out through the open window. He spoke urgently for a few moments then hurried back.

"Don't know what's going on, can't get anyone on the blower. We'd better get back but let's suss out this place first. OK Shirl my girl let's get at that barn."

As Shirley and the Sheriff disappeared around the side of the house, David turned to Cyndy.

"Come on Cyn, I've got an idea. We need to be out of sight of the law so we can get out of our bodies and do some proper searching."

The stepped back into the house together and David closed the door.

"I just seem to smell that man. I'm sure he's hiding right around here somewhere."

"Speaking of smelling something, do you smell an apple scent, David?"

"I wondered when you'd notice me Cyndy dear. I've been tryin' to get your attention but your mind is too busy."

"Grandmother, where are you? Why can't I see you?"

"Because I'm not corporeal, dear."

There was a sound like a pair of old pants ripping down the back, and the slight figure of the grandmother appeared, sitting in an elderly Captain's chair set against the wall of the front hall.

"That better, dear?"

"Oh grandmother, I do love it when you show up. I don't think I'm ever going to get over you not being here all the time for me."

The slightly transparent grandmother smiled lovingly at her granddaughter.

"Oh I don't know, Cyndy, I think I've been here for you quite a bit lately."

"But what are you doing here now, grandmother? Not that I don't love it that you are but you only seem to turn up when I need help, desperately."

"You always were a bright girl, dear. And you do need my help, desperately. If somethin' isn't done and done fast about that demented minister, your friends stand to get badly hurt, maybe even killed and we wouldn't want that now, would we?"

"What do you mean grandmother? Why're Shirl and Taylor in danger?"

"I'm not referrin' to just the Sheriff and Shirley, dear. Maaiken's men left the property and went to the jail to get his men free. When they do it you will be on your own again and look what happened the last time. Remember he's armed with his dangerous oil and he won't hesitate to use it. Just the presence of that dangerous substance can kill as you've seen and if he were to throw it on anyone, you can be sure death won't be far behind. And those brutes of his will be armed with guns from the Sheriff's office. Can't let that happen, can we?"

David took Cyndy's arm.

"Come on Cyn, let's get down there. Remember he said he couldn't get any response on the radio. Maybe something bad has already happened. And we have no way to tell the Sheriff how we know that Maaiken's left the property. Let's go. We'll just have to help ourselves to Taylor's car. Only way we can get down to the jail in time. Have to explain later, if there is a later."

Cyndy and David left the grandmother gradually fading from sight as they raced out the door and down to where the shiny blue and white car sat at the curb. David tried the door but it was locked.

"Easy pickin's here, Cyndy."

David quickly had his energy focused on the tumblers of the door lock and the door opened.

"You've got to show me how you do that, David. It's a neat trick."

"Don't want you to get in trouble stealing cars, Cyndy. Maybe I shouldn't show you."

He laughed as he performed the same magic on the ignition lock and had the engine going by the time Cyndy had made her way around the car and into the passenger seat. Her door barely closed before he jammed his foot against the accelerator and the car squealed its wheels as it raced down the quiet, tree-lined street.

David dodged a small blue truck delivering bottled water. The traffic was getting back to normal. People were out of their houses, the streets filling as they neared the center of town. Finally they were at the station. David turned the next corner onto Macy and skidded the car to a stop in front of a No Parking sign. Both he and

Cyndy had their doors open and were out of the car the moment it stopped. Quickly they ran back toward the Sheriff station.

"The door, Cyndy, look, it's open."

Cautiously now they approached the open door and peered inside. The first sight was Fred lying sprawled out on the floor. Cyndy ran to him. David followed looking around for possible danger.

"Oh my God, David, his neck has been broken."

"Is he still alive, Cyndy?"

"He's breathing but his pulse is so faint I can hardly find it. I've got to work on him right now or he'll die."

Cyndy sat for a moment in complete silence then put her left hand on Fred's chest over the heart chakra and with her right she began to gently stroke the neck area. It seemed to David as he watched her that he could actually see energy swirling about her, blurring the light. Listening, he wondered if he was hearing a radio as sweet music played in his head. Looking nervously at the closed door to the holding cells he moved closer to the door and tried the knob. It was locked.

He turned to see that Cyndy had now put both hands under Fred's shoulders and was lifting him up so she could put her arms around his body. She held him, her lips moving silently. Then she laid him back on the floor and stood up. Fred lay quietly but his breathing seemed stronger. Cyndy took a deep breath then looked around for the first time to see where he was. She smiled.

"I caught him just in time, David. He was beginning to float out of his body; his body was so damaged it would have been only moments before he was on his way home. But I was able to call him back and now he is going to be OK, I feel it and I feel God's presence. Fred's going to be OK."

Suddenly she slumped and took another deep breath.

"Oh David, I've got to get more used to doing this healing work. It pulls at my spirit so."

David came to her and gently pulled her up to her feet. But he didn't stop there. He pulled her close to him and brushed her lips with his own.

"You're a wonder Cyn, a wonder. Your powers are so strong and you're still just learning. Only God knows where this is going to lead you."

"Well I hope it leads me back to my telescope. That's where I really want to be. Let me cover Fred with that coat hanging on the coat rack. I don't want to move him yet and I want to keep him warm."

David released her and went back to the locked cell door. He centered and released his consciousness to slowly pass through the thick wooden boards. He was aware that Cyndy was also in non-ordinary reality with him so it was together that they viewed the bodies thrown into cells. It appeared all of the deputies had been in the station when something, whatever, had surprised them. Only Shirley and Taylor seemed to be missing from the devastation.

"Oh David, are they all dead?"

But even as she spoke it was became apparent that at least some were still alive. As they listened and watched they were aware now of groans and several of the deputies were moving although none was yet standing up.

"Quickly, Cyn, back into our bodies, I've got to get this door open so we can help them properly."

In a moment they were both back standing in front of the locked door. David did his lock tumbler trick and swung the door open. Together they began to check out the injured. All appeared to have been brutally beaten about the head and body. Two had broken arms and were in great pain. All bore bruises on their faces. Almost all were bleeding from head wounds.

Cyndy went from one to the other, placing her hands on their heart chakras then moving them to the various areas of injury. As quickly as she touched them they relaxed and lay limply, color coming back into their cheeks, groaning replaced by sighs of contentment.

As David watched he felt again a flow of energy surrounding Cyndy. In his head he again thought he could hear music playing. So spectacular was Cyndy's healing that it was only moments before most of them became fully conscious and soon were standing. Only the two with broken arms were slower to get to their feet but even they eventually joined the crowd around Cyndy and David, shouting questions at their saviors.

David and Cyndy learned that some of Maaiken's men had appeared with guns, threatening Fred working at the front office desk. Fred had backed away from the confrontation allowing them to make him open the cells and release the rest of Maaiken's band of ugly thugs. Jake, himself, had then taken delight in beating Fred up, breaking his neck in the process, before they took the guns out of the gun rack and raced up the stairs to round up the remaining deputies. The thugs took turns beating each the deputies senseless before slinging them into the cells they had so recently occupied.

No one had any idea where the gang had gone. David began to look for some clue when the phone rang. One of the deputies answered. It was an angry Sheriff demanding to know why the phones and radio had been unmanned when he first called to report his unit stolen by David and Cyndy.

They could all hear his swearing as he shouted into the phone and chewed out his deputy. Then he became quiet as the deputy began to tell how they had been surprised and taken prisoner by Maaiken's men, the gang released, and only now had they been rescued by the very same David and Cyndy. He gave orders for one of them to pick him up at the manse and the others to organize a search for the missing villains.

Fred, still lying on the floor, sat up and looked at the deputies milling about. His voice croaked at first but became stronger almost immediately.

"What happened? Why'm I lying on the floor? Shit I feel strange, like someone tried to break my neck or something. Give me a hand."

Several of the deputies crowded around, pulling him to his feet.

Standing off to one side, David and Cyndy looked on with growing alarm. None of the deputies now showed any sign of their previous injuries.

"Maybe we should get out here, Cyndy, these guys are going to start wondering just how come they look so good when they were beat up so bad just a couple of hours ago. I don't think we want to answer questions. What we need to do right now is to find Maaiken. Long's he's free we're all in danger. I'm wondering. Where would he be going now with his gang of toughs? He thinks he has the law and order under control. What's his next move?"

Together they strolled to the open door and slipped out unnoticed in the ongoing confusion. Once on Main Street they hurried to get away from the Sheriff's station. They had barely turned the corner onto Macy when they heard voices calling their names.

"It's a strange situation. Maaiken's free, he has his gang but what can he be thinking? Is he going to try to turn Nantucket into a fortress? Does he think he can run the whole world from here? No, not even Maaiken with his huge ego can think that... unless there's something we don't know about that Cup still hidden in the tunnel. I wonder? Come on, let's go back and retrieve the Cup."

Quickly, they opened the doors of the Sheriff's blue and white and turned back towards the church, just visible above the trees. David made a sharp turn onto a side street and then into a driveway. In a moment a Sheriff's car went by with John and Shirl. They had just been picked up by one of the Deputies.

As soon as the way was clear they continued towards the church. At the foot of Church Street they stopped. The manse wasn't visible from this angle but they could see the path that ran between the church and the manse. A rough looking man in torn jeans and a Boston baseball cap turned backwards was leaning against one of the trees. David killed the engine and opened the door.

"That's one of Maaiken's men. I recognize him. He's the one had the baseball bat when I got slugged."

David and Cyndy got out of the car. As they watched another man appeared holding a leash. Lady was tugging and pulling at the end of the leash until the man kicked her hard in the ribs. Lady gave a squeal of pain and quit struggling.

David turned to Cyndy and was stopped by the look of fury on her face. Even as he watched her hand came up and blue fire seemed to sprout from her fingertips. The man who had kicked Lady was suddenly thrown backwards into the trees, where he collapsed in a still heap.

The first man turned to see what had happened to his buddy. He looked back and, seeing Cyndy and David, started to run towards them, pulling a handgun from his pocket. More blue fire and he, too, was picked up and smashed into the same tree where his friend now lay. Now the two bodies lay heaped on one another, not moving. Lady, feeling the freedom of the leash dragging on the ground, began to run but quickly stopped, whining.

"Lady, here. Come on girl."

Lady stopped, turned and suddenly yelped in pleasure as she saw Cyndy at the foot of the street. Her honey-colored legs staggered as she hobbled down the hill and into Cyndy's arms. As Cyndy hugged her she gave a howl of pain.

"Oh girl, what did they do to you?"

She felt along Lady's chest.

"Damn them, David, that brute has broken her ribs. Here baby, let your momma fix your pain."

She carefully placed her hand under Lady's chest and with the other pulled the great head towards her until it was buried in her neck. David again had the sense of a whirl of energy enveloping Cyndy and again thought he could hear singing.

Lady whined and tried to pull away for a moment then began to relax. Cyndy held her firmly for several seconds then released her so she could lie on the ground. David and Cyndy watched her as Lady lifted her head, then put out an unsteady leg, then another until she had support under her and stood, finally, on all four feet. Now she took a tentative step then another then began to jump up onto Cyndy. Her pain was obviously gone. Cyndy gave her a hug and laughed.

Mark up another miraculous cure, David thought. Maybe Cyndy had a future as a vet, he laughed to himself.

"Cyndy, put Lady in the car. We need to find Maaiken. His men seem to be here, so he's probably here, too."

Cyndy opened the car door and pushed Lady up into the front seat, making sure the windows were all open to allow air to circulate, then turned to David.

"I want to check out those men I pushed into the tree. I was so angry. I shouldn't have reacted so violently."

"How'd you do that exactly, Cyn? I've never seen you throw a force before. I don't even know how to do that. Where're you learning this stuff?"

"Don't know, David. I just felt angry and it was there."

"Well, remind me not to get you angry at me. Are you sure you're OK?"

Cyndy looked at him, her eyes dark shadows.

"Except for being out on my feet from lack of sleep, I'm fine. Let's get on with it. What's your plan?"

"We've got to get back into the cellar at the manse. Let's see if there are any more of Maaiken's minions around."

David took Cyndy's hand and they walked over to where the two men lay crumpled on the ground. Cyndy pulled the one man over while David leaned over Jake.

"How's your guy, Cyndy? This one isn't going to be hitting anyone on the head again. That's a mean power bolt you throw."

Cyndy looked serious for a moment.

"This one's dead, too. What have I done?"

David reached down and pulled her to her feet.

"These were bad men, Cyndy, don't waste your sympathy on them."

"But David, I'm not supposed to kill, I'm supposed to heal. I don't think I can go on."

Cyndy crumpled to the ground with her head cradled in her arms. David leaned over her with his hand on her head.

"Hush, Cyndy, you're just exhausted. I'm going to teach you how to renew your energy when you have been deprived of sleep. It will take both of us twenty minutes but without it neither of us is going to be able to catch up to Maaiken."

He pulled her slowly to her feet.

"I feel like dropping. Come back to the car. We need to close our eyes for the next twenty minutes while I direct the universal energy into our bodies. I wish I could do it faster but it does take real time."

Putting his arm around her slight frame, David led her back to the Sheriff's car. Lady watched all this with her tail wagging.

Opening the door, David shooed Lady into the back seat while he put Cyndy into the front passenger seat. Then he walked around and slid into the driver's seat. He started the car and backed it into a small lane where he parked in a shady spot under an ancient oak tree, adjusted the windows to allow some breeze to enter the car, locked the doors and leaned his head back against the seat head rest. Lady licked at his right ear.

"Cyndy, tell Lady to lie down, would you? I can't concentrate with her licking at me."

There was no response. He looked over at Cyndy, her eyes closed, her chest rising and falling. She was already fast asleep.

Feeling exhaustion beginning to slow his thinking, David again took the time to center, reaching out to Lady's doggie brain and putting the idea of lying down into her cortex.

Lady whined then dropped off David's seat back and stretched out on the back seat. David sighed, again centered and reached out to the energy field, directing it to both himself and to Cyndy. He smiled as he looked down on her from outside his body. Then he re-entered his own body and settled down to let the energy flow into his system. His breathing became regular and soon he slept, too.

The quiet was soon broken by the sound of feet, walking down the lane. What David had not noticed in his need for rest was the fact that this lane ended in a small path that led up to the back of the Manse. The feet belonged to Maaiken. Only the dog responded, lifting her head.

Chapter Twenty-Four

Maaiken hesitated for a few more moments until he was sure the Sheriff and deputy were well out of the house. He and the two others had scurried to the priest hole with the dog when he saw the Sheriff's car first drive up to the house.

He didn't feel it was time to take on the Sheriff, even with his anointing oil. He had just come from the tunnel and joined the two others who had the astronomer's dog. The dog was just a last minute choice. He knew Cyndy should be dead in the tunnel under the church but, ever since she had escaped from the secretary's office, he wasn't sure. And that bloody giant, he just made him feel nervous even with the anointing oil in his hand. There was something unusual; he could feel some force he couldn't identify.

Maaiken needed time to make sure his men had secured the airport first. When he had finally decided that he had to leave Nantucket for his new Church of the Healing Christ, he needed to have his route clear and unencumbered.

He had known his days of controlling Nantucket were dwindling. The Government was starting to take a closer look at the miracles. Both the FDA and the IRS were beginning to make noises. If he stayed here much longer the great weight of the Government would finally take him down, his secret revealed, his ownership of the Christian icon revealed for the whole world to know. That's why he had worked for the past few years finding the ideal location for a new center for his healing.

Another important factor was that the islanders had always been difficult to keep under control. Now resentment had built up to the point he was surprised he was still able to get everyone off the streets when he had so ordered. Oh they were still terrified of his powers, and they all remembered their sisters, mothers, sons and daughters healed, but more and more they were questioning his right to order them around.

He had finally decided to relocate. He would continue to do God's work in healing but he would also make it God's work to put a proper price on such a priceless commodity, healing the truly unhealable.

His new church was located in much more secure territory, not a part of the United States. His net worth would increase to the point where he could afford to build a true healing Mecca for the world's ill.

He would be in charge. His fame would surpass all the Binns and other TV healers. His healing would be attested to by doctors and proper medical work-up. There would be none of the tent show, TV hustle.

In his mind, the line began to blur between Christ healing the lame, halt and blind and his, Maaiken's healing, which would be just as spectacular, maybe even more if he would allow TV cameras to follow his procedure and to interview the medical people who would be his witnesses.

He looked up at the small carriage clock that sat on the little table in his hiding place. More time than he thought had passed. He couldn't hear any sounds in the house now.

He pulled himself upright with a grunt, aged bones and joints protesting. Maybe he could heal himself of age-related disease. Funny it had never occurred to him. Later, now he had to put the rest of his escape plans into effect. Jake and the other man watched him with respect. Lady whined at him.

"You two, get out of here and take that dog with you. Jake, make sure that we're alone here.

The two men pushed their way through the small opening dragging Lady on her leash.

Maaiken followed. First he had to go back to the church to pick up some of the historical archives relating to the arrival of the Cup on the island. Later he would go into the tunnel and retrieve the sacred relic. But he would do that only when he was absolutely sure it was safe.

He decided to exit the manse through the back entrance and make his way down the lane that led to the end of Church street. As he came out of the manse he paused but could hear nothing alarming. The other two were out of sight.

He entered the top of the lane and began to walk down its length. It was just as he was approaching the end of the lane when he paused, startled to see a Sheriff's car parked under the old oak. Were they still watching his house?

Then he saw a dog's head lift up and look out the back window, right at where he was standing. He pulled back, then waited, but there was no activity from the car. The dog's head disappeared. Where were Jake and Al? How could the dog be in the car?

He pulled out his vial of anointing oil and cautiously walked forward. Still he could see no signs of activity. Finally he was in a position to see into the car's interior. His lip curled and his heart beat with fury.

Those two again. He thought they had perished in the tunnel below the church when he released the rockslide and the water gate. Yet here they were, the two of them, and, for some reason, both sound asleep. The dog's head appeared again

He stood uncertain what to do. The dog just shouldn't be here.

The last time he'd seen her she was with Jake and his buddy. Where were they?

Then he opened the vial of anointing oil he was carrying and made a move forward, raising the vial so he could throw its contents into the car. As he did so the dog recognized the enemy and began to bark fiercely through the partially opened window. The sudden noise startled Maaiken and he stopped and jerked his hand back from the window. The reflex motion was fast and deadly, the glimmering oil gushing out of its container and splashing him full in the face.

Maaiken gave a convulsive shout, dropped the crystal vial and covered his face with his hands. Some of the oil had actually entered his mouth and both eyes had received drops. He dropped to his knees, struggling for breath, his mouth contorted, his fingers continuing to dig at his face and eyes, his skin turning pale, his whole body convulsing. He swayed for a few more moments then dropped face forward onto the ground.

His protection had been from casual contact with the oil. His protection had been at a distance. He'd never experienced its direct effects on his body. Now he did, with deadly consequences.

During Maaiken's encounter with his anointing oil Lady continued to bark. Inside the car the noise was deafening. It finally woke both David and Cyndy from their energizing sleep.

"Lady, what's the matter, why're you barking so? David, are you awake, Lady is making such a racket it woke me up. David?"

"Yes, Cyn, I'm awake, but I feel groggy. Why's Lady upset?"

David pulled himself up from the seat and turned to look at Lady, still barking and growling and baring her teeth out the opening in the window. As he turned Maaiken's thrashing body caught his eye. He was so surprised he couldn't move for a moment.

"Cyndy, Maaiken's outside the car but he appears to be having a convulsion or something, he's lying on the ground. That's what Lady's barking at."

David pulled up the door latch, pushed the door open and pulled his large frame from behind the wheel. Now standing up he stepped closer to Maaiken, and knelt down to check on him. Maaiken's body had stopped its thrashing and was quiet. David reached to put his hand down to feel the carotid artery but pulled back suddenly as he felt the force of the anointing oil.

He stood up and quickly backed away, studying the scene before him. Cyndy had her door open by this time and was pushing Lady to keep her in the car. Finally she was able to get her door closed and walked around the back of the car to where David stood gazing down at the silent figure of Maaiken.

"Careful, Cyndy, don't touch him. There's anointing oil all over his head and on the ground."

"Is he dead, David? I can't sense any life force in him."

"Yeah, I think he is, but I'm not sure what happened. Best guess I can make is that he was coming down this lane when he saw the car. We were both completely out of it, but I could hear Lady barking. She must have seen him coming and she sure had no love for him or his gang. But why he's got his own anointing oil all over his face is more than I can imagine."

"Then let me fill you in with the details, my children."

Apple scent swept over them.

"Grandmother, where are you?"

"I don't have the energy to materialize, my dear Cyndy, but I was here, waitin' for you to regain your own energy when I was witness to that old scalawag, Maaiken, coming down the lane from the manse. I was worried because I couldn't materialize and I had no way to wake you. But that blessed Lady did it for me. Did more than that. Startled that beast before he had a chance to harm you; startled him so bad he went and did himself in. Oh, there'll be a special place in heaven for you Lady when you're ready."

Lady perked up her ears and whined. The gentle voice continued as the grandmother related the bizarre events that had led to Maaiken taking his own life just as he was about to threaten their own.

"I think this ugly story has come to an end, children. Without Maaiken, his gang won't be much further trouble to the Sheriff. Incidentally, they're mostly out at the airport, waitin' for Maaiken so they can fly away to his new lair. Now he has flown away without them. I think it's time I flew away too, Cyndy, I don't have much more time to be with you anyway. You have found the true you now. My job is over. David there's got a bit of explainin' to do but I'm sure you'll both be fine now.

Tears began to moisten Cyndy's eyes. Then a small stream of tears ran down both cheeks. She couldn't help herself; a sob tore from her throat. She struggled to speak.

"Oh please, grandmother, I can't stand to be here alone without you."

Then her sobbing prevented further words.

"What, you don't listen to your old grandmother, child. Stop your sobbin' and straighten up those shoulders. I just told you, you aren't alone anymore. You know who you are now and you've got this big lunk or so it seems. I don't think you're alone at all. I was only here to help you realize your new powers. You are unique here on earth, Cyndy, darlin' and you didn't have anyone to learn from. Even big David here is small potatoes compared to you and your gift from God. Now all you have to do is decide how to spend this gift. I can't help you there. So I'm bein' called back home. Time for me to get on with my between-life. I've done what had to be done.

The voice became fainter, the scent of apples less apparent.

"Oh, and yes, you're goin' to have to decide what to do with that George of yours. My, you've got a lot on your plate, young lady.

Another pause, then fainter then ever, more like a whisper of the wind in the trees.

"And don't ever forget me, my little darlin'. I love you."

Then there was no sign of the grandmother. Even her apple scent had vanished. She had truly gone.

Cyndy looked around, eyes filled with tears. She took a ragged breath. Finally she looked at David who was standing looking concerned. She smiled.

"Don't look so worried, David, I'm OK. We need to do something about Maaiken, though. Can't leave him just lying there."

"Your right as usual, Cyn. But I'm not sure just how to handle him. He's as hot and dangerous as a nuclear bomb right now. Anybody else finds him is apt to join him."

Finally, he took the amulet from his neck. It was glowing faintly even in the brightness of the day. He swung it experimentally, closer to the inert body. As he did so it brightened.

"I wonder, Cyndy. Give me your amulet."

She pulled the chain over her head, threading her hair through it and handed it over to David's outstretched hand.

First he swung it experimentally, close to Maaiken's head, as he had with his own. It too brightened. He repeated the action with his own. He looked carefully at each of them, wrinkling his brow then, bringing them close to his eyes, he examined the detail of each. Finally he held each one separately, his in his right hand and Cyndy's in his left and closed his fingers around them. He became quiet, his attention on the sensations he was feeling. He finally looked at Cyndy.

"They're not the same, you know. They are Yin and Yang, female and male, opposites. I think they may be made to operate as a pair and not just as we have been using them for personal protection. I feel they have unusual energies. When I hold them together, they begin to almost vibrate.

Here, take yours and hold it to one side of Maaiken's head. I'll stand on the other side with mine. Approach him slowly; try to keep it the same distance from his head as I keep mine. Let's see if something happens."

Doing as told, Cyndy now walked around Maaiken's body and stood with her amulet dangling from her hand. David took a position opposite her and at the same distance.

"OK, now slowly bring your amulet closer to his head as I do the same on this side. Slowly now, slowly."

As the two amulets eased towards each other and Maaiken's head, both began to take on a growing brightness.

"Very slow now, Cyndy."

Each gently eased their amulet closer and, inch-by-inch, the amulets responded by increasing their brilliance. When they were about twelve inches from each side of Maaiken, a streak of light, like a bolt of colored lightening, emanated from each amulet, meeting and encompassing the grizzled old man. Cyndy cried out in alarm. David flinched but kept his amulet in position.

"Keep still Cyndy, don't drop your amulet."

At first David couldn't see, his eyes dazzled by the flash. As his vision cleared everything looked the same. The amulet still swung at the end of its chain. It looked quite normal. He noticed that it no longer glowed. Checking Cyndy's amulet he noticed that it, too, appeared to be unremarkably normal now.

Looking at Maaiken's head, David thought he looked different somehow. Then he realized the oily sheen caused by the anointing oil seemed missing. Maaiken's face was pale but the luster he'd noticed before was gone.

"Move back and come over to this side, Cyndy. Tell me what you see or feel."

Cyndy stepped carefully around the body and stood beside David.

"I don't feel the force of the anointing oil now. It was so strong before; I could hardly approach it. Somehow those amulets neutralized it. Brilliant, David. How'd you guess?"

"That's just it, it was a guess. I could see the amulets were opposite energies and that they reacted somewhat differently when each was close to the anointing oil. Somehow… maybe my Master was whispering in my ear… but it seemed that they might be able to work together. And they did."

"So now what?"

David didn't answer but reached over into the Sheriff's car and clicked a switch. Immediately the air filled with sound of the dispatcher at the Sheriff's department. He listened for a moment; traffic was busy as she called commands to various units. There was an action in progress, something about armed and dangerous men, the airport, wait for State Police for backup.

David waited for a pause, then depressed the mike button.

"This is Sheriff's unit 702, on Church Street just below the church manse. Maaiken Starbroke is dead or unconscious. Please have someone respond."

He put the mike back and switched off the radio.

"Sounds like they're busy but I sorta think someone'll be here pretty soon. We'd better get out of here. We'll have to walk; I'm leaving the Sheriff's car here. Let's go to the observatory."

Together, hand in hand they walked away from Maaiken's body. Soon they were out of sight of the church and the manse. Then Cyndy pulled David to a dead stop.

"The cup, David, the cup. What'll we do about the Cup? It's still down in that tunnel."

"And that's where it's going to stay 'til I get some instructions as to what to do with it and how to handle it safely. Come on, let's get you back to the observatory. Things are going to be a little confused around here for a while but it'll all be sorted out soon enough, I imagine. You and I have much to talk about and plans to make. Oh yes, you also have to decide what to do about George and Shirley. Then you have to decide how you want to handle the rest of your life. We've got a lot of talking to do."

They continued on their way swinging their arms, hands still clasped together.

Chapter Twenty-Five

Cyndy settled back against the seat cushion and braced her body against the acceleration of the wide-bodied jet as it raced down the Boston Airport runway. Soon the engines had powered the massive plane into the air and the buildings began to shrink below.

As the plane reached its cruising altitude and cabin attendants began to circulate, Cyndy sighed and unclasped the hand of the large man sitting next to her.

"Really David, I feel I've left so much unfinished on Nantucket."

"You've done fine, darling. Just relax. In a few hours we will be with the Masters, where you will meet your teachers. There you will begin to understand and fine-tune your incredible gifts so you can use them for the benefit of the world."

"Yes, yes, I know, you keep telling me... but I'll miss Lady. She looked so sad when I said good-bye."

"She's fine. Shirley will look after as her well as you would. And, I'm just guessing, but I think she will be spending lots of time at your house. Shirl and George are a declared item. With you gone they're bound to be together. Of course they'll have to move in little while. George said he would proceed with the divorce; when you get back it'll all be over. And you will be another person by then anyway."

"What do you mean, 'another person'? You keep saying things like that and I don't really know what you mean. Different in what way, for goodness sake? Will I have two heads? Will I be able to fly on a broomstick?"

Although joking, Cyndy's voice became somewhat tremulous, as if near tears. David reclaimed her hand.

"Hush, don't worry, don't feel frightened. The world you are going to enter is truly magical and you are its first new citizen in almost a century. When I entered it, it was due to the kindness of the Masters; they had been friends to old Mr. Spalding and his dad. I didn't have any real calling to be a member of this group but look what they've been able to teach me. With your unusual powers I can't even imagine what heights you'll reach."

She squeezed his hand, sensing the spiritual being that lived within that great body. She felt his true love. She sighed.

"I told them I would be back in a year, David. Do you think I'll ever return?"

The Nantucket Inquirer and Mirror

Head of Church Suffers Mysterious Death
Gun Battle Rages At Airport

The Sheriff's office announced today that the well-known head of The Poor Soldiers of Christ Church, the Reverend Maaiken Starbroke, has been found dead near the manse of his church.

Sheriff's deputies on routine patrol found his body lying in a lane that leads up to the manse from Church Street. Some mystery surrounds the discovery and subsequent disposition of the body. Officials are not revealing the cause of death, nor why the emergency task force was called in to sweep the area. The Sheriff's department issued a statement that said the death was being treated as suspect.

One source, who insisted his name not be revealed, confirmed rumors that Reverend Starbroke had been the subject of an island-wide search prior to the discovery of his body. Further reports are expected soon. The church has been closed and will not reopen until another Rector can be found and the Board of Selectmen have had an opportunity to completely review events of recent months.

Shortly before the Sheriff's deputies found Reverend Maaiken's body, reports were received that there had been a short but fierce exchange of gunfire out at Nantucket airport. Witnesses say an armed gang of thugs had taken over control of the airport and were in the process of preparing a private jet for flight. Sheriff's deputies and State Police combined forces to overcome the armed gang. No further information has been released.

Our Astronomer Goes Off Island

While we wait to learn more about Reverend Maaiken's untimely death and the gun fight out at the airport, we learned today that our popular young astronomer, Cyndy Vorester, has announced she is taking a sabbatical and leaving Nantucket to visit India. Cyndy says that her plans are indefinite for the moment and that the University will be filling her position at the Observatory on a temporary basis.

Cyndy's popular and highly successful husband, George Vorester, is remaining on Nantucket. Friends will be pleased to know that George has fully recovered from his severe motorcycle accident and is back running his cyber business.

The End

Printed in the United States
39701LVS00003B/127-147